WHEN THE ONLY LIGHT IS THE MOON

RITA WILSON

an imprint of Sunbury Press, Inc.
Mechanicsburg, PA USA

an imprint of Sunbury Press, Inc.
Mechanicsburg, PA USA

For information about special discounts for bulk purchases, please contact Sunbury Press Orders Dept. at (855) 338-8359 or orders@sunburypress.com.

To request one of our authors for speaking engagements or book signings, please contact Sunbury Press Publicity Dept. at publicity@sunburypress.com.

FIRST MILFORD HOUSE PRESS EDITION: May 2024

Set in Adobe Garamond Pro | Interior design by Crystal Devine | Cover design by Lawrence Knorr | Cover art by Rita Wilson | Edited by Kendall Taylor.

Publisher's Cataloging-in-Publication Data
Names: Wilson, Rita, author.
Title: Where the only light is the moon / Rita Wilson.
Description: First trade paperback edition. | Mechanicsburg, PA : Milford House Press, 2024.
Summary: Reeling from a recent breakup, Demi decides to clear her head by joining her mother, aunt, and cousin on a trip to Greece. A chance encounter with a charming villager wreaks emotional turmoil while Demi's mother, aunt, and cousin examine their own fears, hopes, and dreams, aided by a witty British author who endears himself to them with his amusing counsel and sage advice.
Identifiers: ISBN : 979-8-88819-216-0 (softcover).
Subjects: FICTION / Women | FICTION / Romance / International | FICTION / Family Life / Siblings.

Designed in the USA
0 1 1 2 3 5 8 13 21 34 55

For the Love of Books!

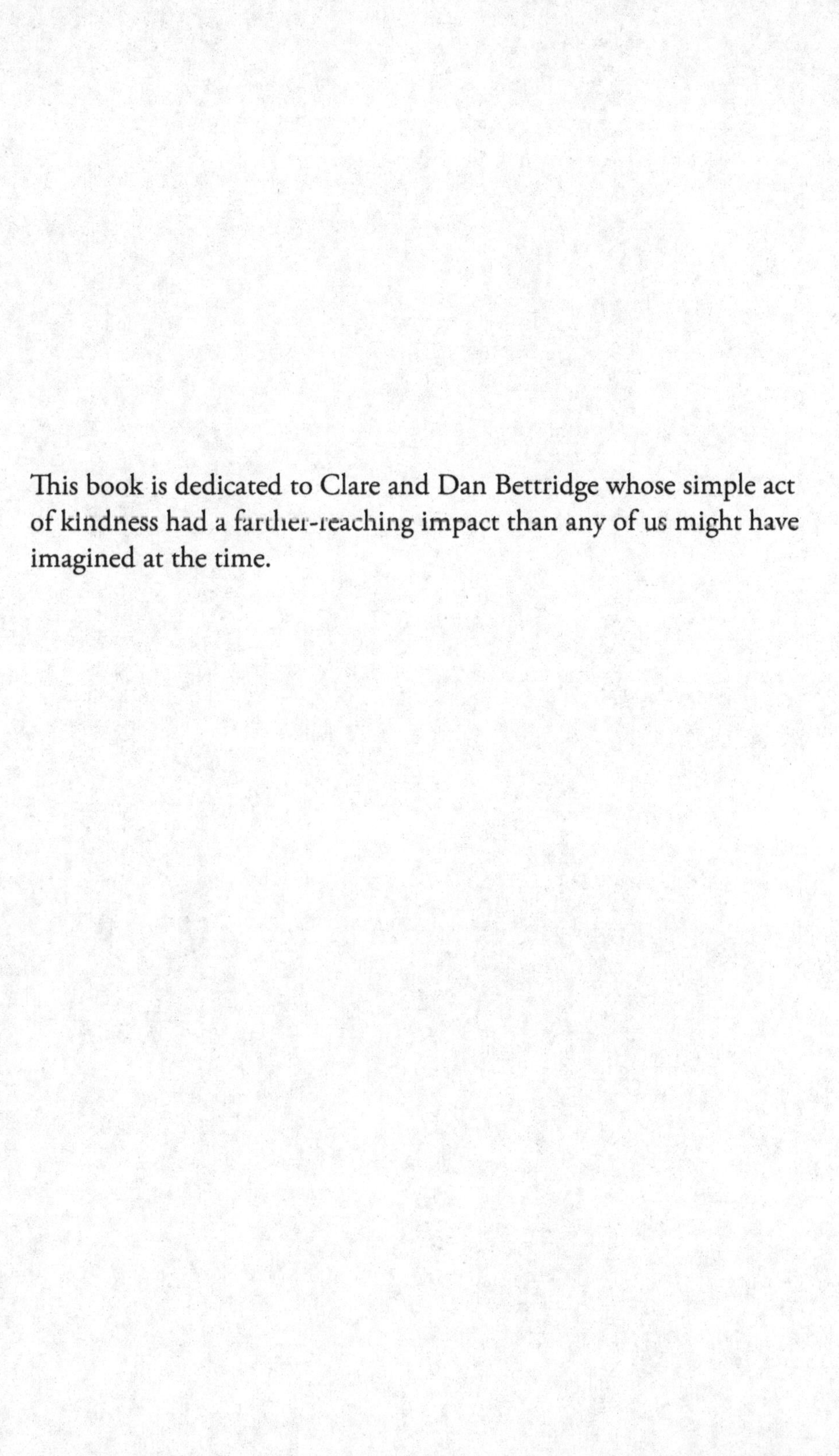

This book is dedicated to Clare and Dan Bettridge whose simple act of kindness had a farther-reaching impact than any of us might have imagined at the time.

PART I

CHAPTER 1

"Mom, I seriously have to pee! Isn't there anywhere we can stop?"

"Demi, do you see anywhere to stop?" Georgia glanced at her daughter in the rearview mirror, then back at the road ahead. "Because all I see are trees, bushes, and dirt."

Zoe turned around from the passenger side to face her niece. "Why didn't you go before we left the museum?"

"I did go before we left," Demi said, squirming in her seat. "I drank a lot of coffee."

"Mom, you don't have to make her feel bad about it,' Sophie said. "If she has to go, she has to go . . . I'm just glad *I* don't have to pee."

Demi clenched her teeth, partly from irritation by her cousin's comment and partly from her growing need for a bathroom. She had come on the trip to Greece to clear her head after a breakup with her longtime boyfriend, and for the most part, the vacation had gone smoothly. She repressed the urge to shoot Sophie a reproachful look and turned back to her mother. "Mom, why are you driving so slow?" The rental car was chugging like a slow-moving train approaching its next stop.

"I'm not doing it on purpose, Demi. Something is wrong with the car."

"Oh my God, that's just what we need," Demi said. She leaned back, folded her arms, and crossed her legs.

"Georgia, maybe you should pull over," said Zoe.

"Really? Where do you suggest I do that?"

"There's a sign over there. A village, maybe?" Zoe pointed to the right, where a sign listed several words in large Greek block letters.

Georgia turned the sluggish Hyundai onto the narrow two-lane road. The car crept past groves of silvery olive trees, following the curve of the road as it wound away from the highway. Ahead to the right, a small white stucco house with a red tile roof sat back from the two-lane road.

"Are you pressing the gas, Georgia?" asked Zoe.

"All the way down. I'm literally going seventeen miles an hour."

"I really think you should stop."

Georgia downshifted the car and maneuvered to a stop in front of the house, slightly off the road and onto the dirt, where sparse tufts of grass broke through the dusty soil and gravel. In the yard, two orange trees with small green fruits suspended from their branches grew on either side of a stone path that led to the front door. A short metal chain link fence encircled the property.

"Now what?" Demi asked.

"I guess I better call the rental car company," Georgia said, reaching into the canvas backpack she had tucked between herself and the door.

"I still have to pee," Demi whispered to Sophie.

"Why don't we walk up that way?" said Sophie, pointing towards the windshield. "There's got to be something up there—a restaurant or maybe a store?"

"Fine, let's go," Demi said, pushing the car door open.

"Wow, it's hot out," Sophie said. She wrapped the blue ponytail holder from her wrist around her thick dark hair, pulling her hair up into a loose bun on top of her head.

"I don't know why you weren't wearing your hair up to begin with," Demi said. "It's got to be ninety degrees out."

Sophie ran her fingers through the loose hairs at the top of her neck. "I hate having all these short hairs sticking out." She pulled them for emphasis.

"At least you've got thick hair," Demi said, pushing her shoulder-length wavy brown hair away from her face.

"Yeah," Sophie said. "On my head, on my arms, on my legs . . ."

Demi looked down at her own tan arms, whose hair had faded to a light blonde in the sun, matching the highlights in her hair. "Come on, let's go."

"Be careful!" Zoe called after them.

"Seriously, Aunt Zo," Demi muttered under her breath. "What do you think is going to happen to us in broad daylight?"

Georgia put her phone back in her bag and turned to Zoe. "They're sending someone to look at the car."

"How soon?"

"They didn't actually commit. They said *amesos.*"

"Wait, that means right away. That's good!"

"Right," said Georgia. "But who knows what 'right away' means in Greek time."

The girls disappeared down the road, and Georgia and Zoe got out of the car. "Mmm, it smells good here," Georgia said. "There's a fragrance in the air. I wonder what it is. Sage, maybe? It smells so fresh." A chorus of cicadas hummed in unison to break the silence of the afternoon. "It's so peaceful."

"And hot," Zoe said, feeling the waves of heat radiating from the sun's reflection on the car hood. "Maybe it's siesta time?"

"Oh, no. You might be right. In that case, we're never going to get the rental company here. And I have to be in Gytheio by seven."

Zoe glanced at her watch. "It's only two forty-five now. You have plenty of time."

Up ahead, they saw the bright yellow of Demi's long, knit sundress and Sophie's tall, thin silhouette coming towards them, backlit by the sun. The figures approached them. "Did you find a place already?" Zoe asked.

"No," Demi said. "I didn't want to go too far. There's nothing up that way, just a couple more houses. And I still need a bathroom. And some water. I'm thirsty."

Georgia glanced left and right. "I don't see any bushes around. I could hold the car door open and hide you." She walked towards the rear passenger door. Demi looked around, shrugged, and followed, and Georgia opened the door.

"*Kalimera*!" A voice startled the group. They turned to see a woman wearing a pale blue cotton dress with a tiny floral print covered by a faded muslin apron at the doorway of the house. Her white hair was pulled back into a small bun at the nape of her neck. Her face was wrinkled, but she wore no glasses, and her eyes were bright. She looked curiously at the group. "*Hriaseste voithia*?" she asked. "You need help?"

"Our car broke down," Georgia said. "We're waiting for the rental car company."

The woman surveyed the group, looking from one to the other, and took a few steps forward. "Very hot today. You wait inside? Not so hot."

Georgia nodded towards Demi. "She needs to use the toilet."

"Oh, *tst tst tst*! *Elate*, come!" She waved them in.

Georgia lifted the gate latch, and the group entered the yard. They walked single file down the short stone path and into the house. The woman pointed Demi down the hallway and turned to Georgia. "You are Greek?" she asked.

"Yes," Georgia said. "My mother's family is from this region. Our mother's," she said, pointing to Zoe.

"You come to see your relatives?" the woman asked.

"Well, no. They've all moved to Athens. We visited them last week. I'm here to speak at a Literary Festival in Gytheio."

The woman looked at her blankly.

"A literary festival," Georgia repeated. "With writers. And books."

"Festival?" the woman said. "You came to sing?" she asked.

Georgia returned the blank stare. "No, no, I'm going to read from my book."

"You came to a festival to read a book?" The woman lifted her eyebrows.

Zoe laughed. "It's not actually a festival—it's a celebration of books. Several writers will read from their books."

"Ah," she smiled at Georgia. "You are a writer."

The girls returned, and the woman addressed them. "What are your names, *despinides*?"

"I'm Sophie."

"I'm Demi. Thank you so much for letting us use your bathroom."

"You are Greek, and your name is *Demi*?"

"Well, actually, it's Dimitra." Demi's father, Jimmy, had been pleased when Georgia suggested that they give her the female version of his name as her first name, breaking with the tradition of making that her middle name.

"Nice to meet you, Dimitra." The woman extended her hand to Demi, and she shook it. The tops of her hands were soft, but Demi felt callouses on her palms.

Georgia and Zoe introduced themselves.

"Nice to meet you," she smiled at the group. "I am *Kiria* Eleni Stavropoulou. Come in." She nodded towards the kitchen. "I make coffee."

"Please don't go to any trouble," Georgia said.

"No trouble. *Elate*, come."

They followed her down the hall, where an old fan in the corner stirred the warm air in the small kitchen. The floors were covered in a mosaic tile pattern of dark blue and white, and the ceramic tile behind the sink echoed the blue color. Below the sink hung a curtain that hid whatever *Kiria* Stavropoulou had stored behind it.

"You like Greek coffee or American coffee?"

For a moment, no one answered. *Kiria* Stavropoulou pressed her lips together, then nodded to herself. She turned to the refrigerator and opened it, bringing out an old-fashioned glass bottle of Coke. "You like Coca-Cola?" she asked the girls. Without waiting for an answer, she set the bottle down and pulled two small juice glasses out of the cupboard. She opened the bottle with a bottle opener and poured the fizzing Coke into the glasses, the foam filling half of each glass. "*Kathiste*, sit!" she said, pointing to two chairs at the small wood table. She nodded towards the front of the house and turned to Georgia and Zoe. "Please, you go there. I make coffee."

Zoe eyed the *briki* and recalled her father making thick Greek coffee in a similar small copper pot, which always left a viscous residue at the bottom of the coffee cup. "Oh, no, thank you," Zoe said. "I don't drink coffee."

Kiria Stavropoulou raised her eyebrows. "You want I make you some tea?" she asked.

"Oh, no thank you. I'm fine."

Kiria Stavropoulou shrugged, then opened the refrigerator and took out a small bottle of *lemonada*. "Go, go," she shooed Georgia and Zoe into the front room. She turned toward the girls as she worked in the kitchen. "How old you girls?"

"I'm 29," Demi said, "and Sophie's 24."

Kiria Stavropoulou struck a match and held it to the burner as she turned on the gas to light the stove. She took a small metal pot with a long handle from the shelf above. "You are the age of my grandchildren," she said. "My *eggoni,* Veatriki, she is 24. And my Stavros, he is 30. Veatriki, she go to school in Athens. And Stavros, he work here. Kiria Stavropoulou waved her hand to indicate somewhere beyond the walls of the house. She poured water into the *briki* and measured two small spoons of finely ground coffee from the metal can next to the stove. She added a spoonful of sugar and set it on the burner to boil.

The phone on the counter rang, and *Kiria* Stavropoulou picked it up. "*Embros*?" She smiled. "*Nai. Nai. . . . Yia ti ohi? . . . Oraia.*" She finished her conversation and placed the lemonade and coffee on the tray, then turned to the girls. "Okay, you stay here. I think maybe not too hot." She walked into the front room and handed Zoe the small bottle of *lemonada* and a glass of ice, then placed the tray, with a small demitasse cup of thick Greek coffee and an equally small sugar bowl with tiny cubes of sugar, on the table next to Georgia, along with a glass of water, and some Greek shortbread cookies.

"Thank you so much," Georgia said, taking a cookie from the plate. "*I love kourabiedes*!" She bit into the cookie, and the buttery sweetness seemed to melt in her mouth. "These are delicious!" she said, brushing powdered sugar from her lap. She stirred a cube of sugar into the coffee and took a sip. The coffee was strong and bitter, and she was thankful for the water.

"How long you stay in Greece?" *Kiria* Stavropoulou asked.

"We're here for two weeks," Georgia answered. "We have five days left."

"Two weeks is not so long to come to Greece."

"I know," Georgia said. "We wanted to stay longer, but we all work back in the States."

"Where you from?" *Kiria* Stavropoulou asked. "New York?"

"Pittsburgh," Georgia and Zoe both replied.

"Ahh, Peetsborg. I know Peetsborg. "My cousin, he live in Peetsborg. They have restaurant—'Kostas.'"

"We've been there!" Zoe said.

"Yes," Georgia said. "I know your cousin—he was a chef on Jackie O's yacht! I remember he said he used to make her a special cake."

Kiria Stavropoulou smiled broadly. "*Nai, nai*!" She paused, then frowned. "His wife *pethane,* she die last year. Hard for Kostas. He need help. His mother, she too old to cook, but she still work at the restaurant."

Georgia and Zoe exchanged glances, each trying to figure out how old the mother was. *Kiria* Stavropoulou appeared to be in her seventies. It was likely that her cousin Kostas was of similar age. Which would make his mother . . .

"*Yiayia*!" A male voice entered the house, followed by a tall young man with shoulder-length, dark curly hair. He wore a tight white tee shirt and blue jeans despite the midday heat.

"Stavro!" *Kiria* Stavropoulou said and began to rise.

"*Ohi, Yiayia, kathise.* You sit." He leaned over and kissed his grandmother on both cheeks, then turned to Georgia and Zoe. "Hello," he said. "You are abandoned, yes?"

"Abandoned?" Zoe said.

Stavros looked at his grandmother, then back at Zoe. "Yes, my *yiayia* say to me on the telephone that your car is not work. And you are abandoned."

Georgia smiled. "Yes, we are abandoned. We're waiting for the rental car company."

Stavros glanced at his phone and raised his eyebrows. "It is siesta time. They will not come for another hour, I think."

Georgia closed her eyes and rubbed her temples with her fingertips. She sighed and looked at Zoe.

"No, no, you are okay," *Kiria* Stavropoulou said to Georgia. "The company, he come. You will get to your *yiorti*." She turned towards Stavros and began to push herself up from the chair. "I get you something to drink."

He waved her back towards the chair. "No, no, *Yiayia*. I can get myself something. You stay with your *parea*."

Stavros walked down the short hallway towards the kitchen. The girls sat next to each other at the table, with the empty bottle of Coke in the middle and the glasses of Coke in their hands. Sophie's arm was outstretched as she held the phone away from them, and they smiled into the phone camera.

Stavros burst out laughing. The girls turned, open-mouthed, to face him. "You are American, I see!" he chuckled. His height filled the doorway, his head almost touching the door frame. He stepped into the kitchen, still laughing.

"Why are we obviously American?" Demi snapped. "Because we're taking a selfie?"

"No," Stavros replied. "Because you are beautiful!"

Demi laughed despite her irritation. Sophie felt her face blush.

"You are too hot in the kitchen," Stavros said. "Come outside. Under the *platania* is shade." He led them out the back door. Two wooden chairs sat under a large plane tree next to a small table covered with a red and white checkered plastic tablecloth. The tree's branches reached out towards the chain link fence that continued around the back of the yard. "I will go inside to see my *Yiayia*, but I will come back." He winked and walked back into the house.

"What a player," said Demi, shaking her head.

"But he's so cute!" said Sophie. "Did you see his green eyes? And those long lashes? He's so handsome."

"I guess," said Demi, adding, "I think they're hazel."

* * *

Georgia sipped the thick Greek coffee as she and Zoe chatted with *Kiria* Stavropoulou and Stavros in the front room. Almost an hour had passed, and there was still no sign of the rental car company.

"Let me see the papers," Stavros said. Georgia handed him the paperwork from the rental company. Stavros placed a call and began to speak in rapid Greek. "Okay," he said, "they come now. You will be okay."

Ten minutes later, they heard tires skid to a halt on the gravel. By the time they walked outside, the man from the rental car company was looking under the hood.

"*Kalimera*," Georgia said.

"*Kalimera, Kiria*," the man said. He released the hood latch and let the hood fall with a bang. "This, I cannot fix. I believe it is, mmm . . . *elektrikos*. In any event, we will have to tow it."

"It is electrical," Stavros explained.

Georgia's shoulders rose and fell with her heavy sigh. "Now what?" She glanced at her watch. "I have a presentation in Gytheio at seven. I haven't even checked in to the hotel yet." She turned to the man from the rental agency. "How soon can you have a replacement car here?"

"Hmm. We do not have another car in Sparta for you. Maybe we find one in Kalamata."

"Kalamata!" Georgia said. "That's over an hour away!"

"It's no problem," Stavros said to Georgia. He patted his chest with his fingertips. "*I* will take you to Gytheio." He nodded towards a motorcycle, which was partially obscured by the other man's truck. The metallic black paint of the Vespa glistened from the sunlight hitting the rear fender.

"Oh!" Georgia said. "Thank you so much. That's very nice of you." She considered his offer. "Unfortunately, I need my box of books with me. Isn't there a taxi that we could take?"

"Yes, I can call you one, but maybe they are having coffee. Maybe 15 minutes. I will call," Stavros said and scrolled through his contacts.

"Shit," Georgia whispered, "Shit, shit, shit, shit, shit."

Zoe put her hand on Georgia's arm. "It's okay. You'll get there in time."

"I hope so."

Stavros spoke rapidly on the phone, then put it in his pocket. "He is on his way," he said.

"*Ti yinete*?" his grandmother asked. Stavros explained the situation.

The ladies pulled their suitcases and backpacks out of the rental car and piled them on the side of the road. Georgia looked at the four carry-ons, the four backpacks, and the box of books for the book talk, and a knot of anxiety formed in her chest.

"What's wrong, Mom?" Demi asked.

"I don't think this is all going to fit in the taxi along with all of us."

Her thoughts were confirmed when the taxi pulled up ten minutes later. A stocky middle-aged man with dark brown eyes and thick black hair got out of the car and looked over the pile of suitcases. "*Po po po po*," he said, shaking his head. "You want I take you or your suitcases to Gytheio?" He looked at Georgia and Zoe. Georgia's blond hair was short and curly; Zoe's dark hair was long and wavy. Their slim figures and smooth skin belied their ages. "*Protimo na sas paro*," he said, smiling.

"I understand Greek," Georgia said, retrieving her teacher voice.

The driver shrugged. "I do not lie."

"What did he say?" Zoe asked.

"He said he prefers to take *us.*"

Zoe giggled.

"Let's see if we can all fit," Georgia said, looking at the taxi. "Is there room in your trunk?" The driver opened his trunk to reveal two fishing rods, a tackle box, and a cardboard box full of rusty cans and old towels. "We fit one bag in here—maybe two." He picked up two of the carry-ons and wedged them in beside the cardboard box.

Georgia set the box of books on the passenger side floor, then straddled it and sat down in the front seat. Zoe and Sophie slid into the back seat while the driver piled the other two carry-ons next to them. "I guess you could sit on my lap?" Georgia said to Demi. "Or maybe you guys can squeeze closer together?" She looked behind her at Zoe and Sophie, who were scrunched together, their backpacks on their laps.

"It is not a problem," Stavros said and nodded toward his motorcycle. He winked at Demi. "You will come with me."

Demi rolled her eyes, but she grinned at the thought of a motorcycle ride in Greece.

"Alright," Georgia said. "Please wear a helmet."

"Of course," Stavros said. He lifted the brown leather seat to reveal a shiny black helmet.

Georgia started to buckle her seatbelt and realized she had not thanked *Kiria* Stavropoulou. She climbed out of the taxi and went over to her. "*Efharisto poli*, thank you so much for your kindness."

Kiria Stavropoulou clasped Georgia's hands and kissed her on each cheek. "*Tipota, Kiria*. It is nothing. Enjoy your *yiorti*." She bent down to wave at the others in the taxi.

"*Efharisto*!" they called out the window. Georgia got into the taxi.

"*Pou pas, Kiria*?" asked the taxi driver.

"Gytheio. Hotel Aktaion."

"Which one? There are two."

"Oh no, um, I don't know." Georgia sighed in frustration.

"The resort or the other?"

"Oh," Georgia laughed, "it's not the resort."

"*Endaksi*," the driver said, "Okay." He put the car in gear and pulled onto the road. "I am Yiorgos," he said, looking at Georgia as he turned the taxi around in the middle of the road. "Nice to meet you."

Stavros straddled the bike. "Get on," he said to Demi. She lifted the hem of her sundress and bunched the excess material between her legs. Stavros glanced down at her tanned legs and the brown leather sandals on her feet. "Hmm," he said. "This is not good clothes to wear on a Vespa. You must hold on to me. We do not want to make angry *Kiria* Georgia."

"*Prosexe*!" *Kiria* Stavropoulou called out. "Be careful!"

"*Vevaios,* of course, *Yiayia*," Stavros said.

Stavros reached into his back jeans pocket and pulled out his cell phone. With his left hand on the handlebars, he balanced the bike with his legs and extended the phone outward with his right hand.

"What are you doing?" Demi said.

"It's for you," Stavros laughed. "It's a selfie!"

CHAPTER 2

The taxi approached the outskirts of Gytheio, emerging from a terrain of gnarled olive trees and tall, dry grasses. The gentle curves gave way to a sharper curve as they appeared to be driving straight into a cemetery. The taxi took a sudden left turn, and now the cemetery loomed on their right, like an elusive moon on a nighttime stroll. A low stone wall bordered the cemetery. Thousands of bright white monuments and headstones topped with vases of pink flowers or large white crosses were packed together like beach towels at the shore in July. A small church stood nestled among the headstones.

"Excuse me," Sophie asked over the headrest. "Why are the headstones so close together?"

"What do you mean?" Yiorgos said.

"There's no room for the coffins," she said. "Are they all urns?"

"Oorns?" Yiorgos said. "What is oorns?"

"For the ashes," Sophie explained.

"*Panayeia mou*!" the driver exclaimed, "This is an Orthodox cemetery. There are no ashes, only *kokkala*, bones."

"Bones?" Sophie said, her eyes opening wide.

"Yes," Yiorgos said. "When you are Greek and you die, you are buried. You stay in the ground until your, hmmm, your *sarka* is rotten. Three years, maybe more. Then, they wash the *kokkala* in wine, and put them in a box."

Sophie stared at the driver, her mouth agape.

"Why do they do this?" Zoe asked.

"Why?" Yiorgos asked. "It is what they do." He turned to Georgia. "You know this?"

"Yes," Georgia said, turning around in her seat to face Sophie. "They don't have enough room in the cemeteries for all of the deceased, so once the bones are removed to an ossuary, they will re-use the gravesite." She pointed to the church. "I'm guessing that contains the ossuary for the cemetery." Sophie drew in her breath but said nothing.

"You are Greek but do not know about the *kokkala*?" Yiorgos asked Sophie over his shoulder.

"I guess we do things a little differently in the states," Georgia said.

They approached a fork in the road, and Yiorgos veered left onto a two-way street divided by a narrow strip of cement planters filled with bright pink and red geraniums. He navigated the street easily, swerving confidently around parked cars and delivery trucks. As they passed bakeries, seafood markets, pharmacies, and tourist shops, the sweet aroma of baked goods mingled with the fishy smell of the day's catch. On both sides of the street, ouzerias, coffee shops, and fruit markets occupied the bottom floors of three-story apartment buildings, while awning-covered balconies decked the top two floors. Ahead of them, the Ionian Sea glistened. Yiorgos made a right turn to parallel the sea on the left, passing several seaside restaurants, which were empty except for a few couples having drinks on wicker couches. The deep bong of a distant church bell reverberated, followed by five more slow, steady notes.

A minute later, Yiorgos pulled up to the front of a faded yellow three-story building, weathered from decades of salt air blowing in from the Gulf. The hotel sat on the main road, directly across from the sea. Across the top two floors, the doors resembled a line of soldiers watching over the gulf at attention, caged by their wrought iron balconies. "The Aktaion," Yiorgos announced, turning off the engine. He got out of the car to open the trunk and take out the bags.

Zoe and Sophie slid out of the back seat, and Sophie grabbed her backpack and sprinted across the street to the stone walkway along the water. "Sophie, be careful!" Zoe called.

"I know, Mom." She wasn't sure whether her mother was concerned about her getting hit by a car or falling into the sea.

"*Efharisto*," Georgia said, handing Yiorgos his fare along with a tip.

"*Parakalo*," Yiorgos said, handing her a card.

"What's this?"

"This is my number," Yiorgos said. "In the event you should require my services."

Georgia raised her eyebrows, both at his suggestion and the sudden improvement of his English. "I think we'll be alright." She smiled and turned towards the hotel.

"Goodbye," Zoe said, "thank you."

"Thank you!" Sophie called from across the street. She aimed her phone at the group in front of the hotel and snapped a photo, then waved and turned back to the water.

Georgia and Zoe pulled their suitcases into the lobby of the boutique hotel. A lanky, curly-haired bellman brought in the box of books and set it on the white tile floor. The lobby was an eclectic mixture of leafy potted plants, Victorian-style red tufted chairs, and a modern wood check-in desk. "*Kalispera sas*," the desk clerk said. "Good evening."

"*Kalispera*," Georgia replied. "Two rooms under Karras."

The clerk began to type on his computer. "I see your room is covered," he said, glancing up at Georgia over his reading glasses. "May I have your passport and a card for the amenities?" Georgia handed him her American Express card and her passport. He flipped the passport open with one hand, taking a long look at her photo, then raised his eyes to look at Georgia. He cast his eyes down at the photo again, then back up at her. "This is not you," he said. "Maybe it is your sister."

"*This* is my sister," she said, pointing at Zoe. "*That* is definitely me."

The clerk reexamined the passport photo of a brunette woman with straight hair and a pale face. The woman before him had curly blonde hair, more pronounced cheekbones, and rosy color in her face.

"That's an old photo," Georgia said, taking out her driver's license and pointing to the photo. "This is me. That is my passport."

The clerk glanced once more at the passport, shrugged, then snapped it shut and returned it to Georgia. "*Signomi*, my apologies."

Georgia bristled at the clerk's brusque manner. "I have to get to the Cultural Center as soon as possible," she said. "I'd like to leave these in the lobby while I get ready."

"Yes, *vevaios*, of course," the clerk replied. He had yet to crack a smile.

"And can you get me a taxi in about fifteen minutes? I'm already late."

"You will not need a taxi," the clerk said. "The *kendro* is a very short walk from here."

"Yes, but I have my books," Georgia said, pointing to the large box.

"It is not a problem," said the clerk. "Dinos can take them for you." The clerk nodded at the skinny bellman, who was distracted by the sight of Sophie walking in. Long strands of her hair had blown loose, and her cheeks were flushed. "Dino," the clerk called. "*Ela*, come here." Dinos's large brown eyes followed Sophie across the lobby. "Dino!"

"Yes, yes," he said, running up to the desk. "I am here."

"Take these bags up to rooms 14 and 15," the desk clerk said. "And then you will take this box to . . ."

"No," Georgia said, "but thank you. Please have a taxi here in 15 minutes."

"*Vevaios*," the clerk shrugged. "As you wish."

"Should we wait for Demi?" Sophie asked.

"Oh!" Georgia gasped upon realizing that she had forgotten her daughter. She turned to Zoe and Sophie. "Would you mind waiting for her?"

"Of course not," Zoe said.

Georgia turned to Dinos. "Could you bring this one up for me right away?"

"Yes, *Kiria*, of course," he said. He picked up Georgia's suitcase, his eyes still on Sophie.

"Dino!" the desk clerk said, "*Amesos!*"

"Yes, yes, I take now!" said Dinos, a blush forming on his cheeks. Sophie smiled to herself.

Georgia turned to the desk clerk. "My daughter will be here soon. Please give her the other key to my room."

The clerk nodded. "*Vevaios, Kiria*."

* * *

Georgia quickly looked in the mirror as she applied her lipstick, a plum shade that complemented her green eyes and sun-kissed skin. She heard the key in the lock. "Oh, wow!" Demi said, looking straight ahead. The door to the balcony was open, letting in the rumble of motorcycle engines and an occasional car horn. The evening breeze ruffled the translucent white curtains, revealing the sparkle of the sun on the gulf. Demi went straight out to the balcony, ignoring the twin beds with their crisp white sheets, red-striped covers, and wrought iron headboards.

"I hope we're going to be able to keep the window open tonight," Georgia called, "but I think it might be too loud. And I'm not sure about mosquitoes. How was your ride?"

"It was okay," Demi said as she walked back into the room.

"Just okay?" Georgia asked.

Demi's face was still flushed from the motorcycle ride. "Wow, Mom. You look nice!" she said. Georgia had changed into a short sleeveless blue and white print dress and white low-heeled sandals. She had applied a little mousse to her hair to tame the curls that had blown around during the taxi ride.

"Do you think it's dressy enough?" Georgia asked, looking down at her dress.

"Why don't you wear the jewelry you bought in Athens?"

"Good idea." Georgia went over to the open suitcase on the bed closest to her. Rumpled clothes and two pairs of shoes lay strewn beside it.

"Geeze, mom," Demi said. "It looks like your suitcase threw up!"

Georgia laughed. "Yours is over there," she said, pointing at the foot of the other bed. She reached under the clothes still in her case and pulled out a small white box. She took out two earrings, which dangled delicate beads of various shades of blue on thin silver wires.

"Perfect!" said Demi as she watched her mother put on the earrings.

"Okay, I'm going to go over to the Cultural Center. Aunt Zoe and Sophie are waiting for you to get ready. Can you meet them in the lobby in about fifteen minutes?"

Demi laughed. "Aunt Zoe is waiting for me? Are you sure *I'm* not waiting for Aunt Zoe?"

Georgia laughed. "I'm guessing it's a toss-up. Anyway, please try not to be late. It's almost six-thirty now. The festival starts at seven, and I'm not sure how far the Cultural Center is from here."

"Okay," Demi reached over and hugged her mother. "Good luck, Mom."

* * *

Georgia's heels echoed in the marble stairwell which led to the lobby. "Your taxi is here," the desk clerk said, nodding towards the door.

"*Efharisto*," said Georgia.

The same taxi that had brought them to Gytheio was parked outside the hotel. Yiorgos, the driver, was leaning on the passenger side door, legs crossed at the ankle, smoking a cigarette with one hand and scrolling through his cell phone with the other. He glanced up when Georgia came through the door. "*Kalispera, Kiria*," he said, tossing his cigarette onto the ground and putting the cell phone into his front shirt pocket. He opened the door and bowed slightly, waving Georgia into the front seat of the taxi. The box of books was already in the back seat. "You are going to the Cultural Center, yes?"

"Yes," said Georgia, "but why are you still here? Aren't you from Xirokambi?"

"Eh, I have nothing better to do," Yiorgos shrugged. He pulled away from the hotel and made a U-turn. "*Eise poli oraia*," he said, "You look nice."

"*Efharisto*."

"I think you are *diasimotita*?"

"I am what?"

"You are *diasimi*?"

Georgia raised her palms upward and shook her head. "I'm sorry, I don't know what you're asking."

"People follow you. You write your name for them. You are *diasimi*."

"Famous?"

"Yes, yes, you are famous!"

"Oh, my goodness," Georgia said. "No, I'm not famous." The idea made her smile. "I just won a writing contest. I'm speaking at a literary festival tonight."

"Festival?" Yiorgos said. "There is no festival tonight in Gytheio."

"No, it's not . . ."

Yiorgos stopped and announced, "We are here."

"Already?" Georgia asked. She looked over at a large pale pink building whose doors and windows were framed in marble. A large stone-tiled terrace led from the road to the building. A bubble of excitement formed in her chest.

Yiorgos ran over to the passenger side and opened the door, ushering her out with a sweep of his arm. She reached inside her purse. "No, no, no. It is only two minutes." He opened the back door of the taxi and took out the box of books. Georgia looked again at the sprawling terrace. Aside from a man walking into the front door, she saw no one else. *So much for famous,* she thought, wondering how she was going to manage the books. She had not realized she would have to carry them across a long walkway. Georgia heard footsteps and looked behind her to find Dinos running up to the taxi.

"I am here, *Kiria*!" Dinos said, his breath coming in short huffs.

"I guess I could have walked," Georgia laughed.

"Yes, *vevaios*," Yiorgos said. "But I am glad you did not." He handed the box of books to Dinos, then turned back to Georgia, extending his hand to shake hers. "Well, *kali tihi*, good luck, *Kiria*."

"Georgia," she said. "Thank you, Yiorgo." She held her hand out to Yiorgos, who took it in his, raised it to his lips, and kissed it. "I am at your service, Georgia."

Georgia burst out laughing and shook her head. She turned to follow Dinos, who was already carrying the books across the empty terrace.

CHAPTER 3

Georgia walked up the short marble staircase and leaned into one of the tall red double doors, juggling the box of books as the leather strap of her canvas bag fell off her shoulder. She balanced the box and the bag, which now hung from the crook of her elbow, while she pushed the door open with her weight.

"*Kiria* Karras, Georgia! *Kalos ilthate*, welcome!" Georgia looked over the box to see a short, plump, smiling woman in front of her. "So nice to meet you," said the woman.

Georgia set the box down on a nearby table, recognizing the middle-aged brunette director of the conference from her photo on the website. "*Kalispera*, Popi," she said. "It's nice to meet you."

"We were worried when you did not arrive," Popi said.

"I had car trouble in Xirokambi . . ."

Popi interrupted. "Let me show you where you will be talking. We will be starting soon." She pointed to the box of books. "Why you did not ship these?"

Georgia sighed. "It would have been much easier to ship them than to carry them around Greece with me, but I could have bought another airplane ticket for what UPS wanted."

Popi led Georgia to a short stage at the far end of the room. She pointed to a chair at the end of the table that was covered by a large white tablecloth. "You will be sitting here," she said. Next to Georgia's name card was a pitcher of water and several small glasses. Georgia set the box under the table and looked around the room, which had been set up with several round tables and chairs. On the far wall, glass-enclosed shelves housed hand-painted ceramic plates decorated in cerulean blue, red, and white. Off to the side was a table of appetizers—dishes of kalamata olives and large green olives, plates of feta cheese and warm pita bread, individual crispy *tiropites*, cheese pies, and next to this, a table of wine and coffee.

"Would you like some coffee before you speak?" Popi asked.

Georgia eyed the carafes of red and white wine, the glass chilled and frosty. *After the day I've had, I'd really like some wine,* she thought. "Yes, I'd love a cup of coffee."

"We have about fifteen minutes before we begin," said Popi. Georgia looked around doubtfully. Only some tables were occupied, and a few people milled around the food and drink tables.

"Are we expecting more people?" she asked.

"V*evaios*," replied Popi. "I need to go check on the sound system. Make yourself comfortable."

Georgia picked up the coffee pot and poured some coffee into a white china cup. The aroma of buttery baked cheese pies wrapped in crispy filo dough made her stomach rumble, and she realized that the last thing she had eaten was the cookie at *Kiria* Stavropoulou's house. She set her cup and saucer down on the table and picked up a cheese pie. Foregoing a plate, she held a napkin under the *tiropita* and bit into the flaky pie. She hadn't realized how hot it would be and waved her hand in front of her mouth, which was now covered in filo crumbs, to cool it off.

"Halloo," Georgia heard a voice behind her. She turned to face a large, smiling brown-haired man who appeared to be in his forties.

"Hello," she replied, wiping her mouth with the napkin.

"I'm Charles," he said, extending his hand. "I'm the children's book author," he added, his British accent apparent to Georgia.

"So nice to meet you," Georgia said. She held a napkin in one hand and half a cheese pie in the other. "Excuse me," she said, setting the cheese pie on the saucer and wiping her hand with the napkin. She put out her hand. "I'm . . ."

"I know who you are," Charles said, shaking her hand. "You're the American author."

"*The* American author?" Georgia asked.

"Well, you're the only one who came from the States, so, yes—the American author. You know several people are coming to see you tonight, don't you? It's not every day we get an author from America in the Peloponnese."

Georgia blushed at the unexpected celebrity. *I wish I could get that kind of recognition in the States,* she thought. She looked around the sparsely populated room. "Several people? I don't see several people here." *Come to think of it, where were Zoe, Demi, and Sophie?* She reached into her canvas bag for her phone. "Excuse me," she said, "I need to locate some people." "WHERE ARE YOU?" She texted Demi and then repeated the process with Zoe.

She received an instant reply from Demi: "Waiting for Aunt Zo and Soph."

"Greek time," Charles laughed.

"I'm sorry?"

"Greek time. People will get here eventually."

"I thought this was being put on for English-speaking authors and readers?" Georgia said.

"True," laughed Charles. "But we *are* in Greece."

Georgia's phone signaled another text message, this time from Zoe. "Waiting for the girls to get ready." She took a deep breath and let it out slowly. "Excuse me for texting," Georgia said. "I'm waiting for my family." She texted back, "Tell them it's not a beauty contest. We're about to start." Looking around the near-empty room, she had her doubts.

Popi approached one of the microphones on the table and tapped on it. "Excuse me," she announced. "Could I have the writers for the authors' panel on stage now?" Georgia gave her mouth one more swipe with the napkin, wishing she had time to reapply her lipstick, and ran her tongue over her teeth, just in case she had lipstick or filo crumbs on them. She set the napkin on the saucer under the cup and took her untouched coffee to the stage, where Charles introduced her to "the mystery writer" and "the romance writer." She guessed she was the "non-fiction writer." The authors pulled out their chairs and took their seats. The chatter in the room increased as more people arrived. Georgia checked her watch.

It was 7:15. Charles waved and caught her attention from the other end of the table. "Greek time," he mouthed.

Georgia glanced around the room and let out a relieved sigh when she saw that Zoe and the girls had arrived. Sophie was a younger, albeit taller, version of Zoe, with her dark hair, classic Greek nose, and large dark eyes. Demi had pulled her hair up into a bun, and the application of black eyeliner and mascara intensified her blue eyes. They set their purses down at a table towards the front of the room and went over to the table of appetizers. Georgia realized that they were probably as hungry as she was.

The mystery writer to her right leaned in towards Georgia. "It's interesting that you wrote a book about your Greek roots," she said. "You don't look Greek."

Georgia pressed her lips together and forced a smile. "Yes, I get that a lot," she said, unconsciously fluffing her short blond curls, "but I am definitely . . ."

"Now, *she* looks Greek," the writer said, pointing across the room at Demi, who was pouring a glass of white wine from the carafe. Her aquiline profile and curvy figure reminded Georgia, and apparently, the mystery writer, of the marble statue of Aphrodite that she had seen at the museum.

"Yes," Georgia admitted. "Yes, she does."

The microphone crackled. "*Kalispera,* good evening, everyone. If you will take your seats, we will begin in just a minute."

Georgia caught a movement at the other end of the table from the corner of her eye. Charles was waving both of his arms back and forth to catch her attention. He pointed to his wristwatch and raised both eyebrows. Georgia fought the inclination to roll her eyes and turned back to the mystery writer, hoping to avoid any further embellished references to "Greek Time."

The mystery writer touched Georgia on the arm. "Oh," she said, pointing to her top lip. "You have a little, uh, crumb on your lip. I hope you don't mind me . . ."

"Oh, my goodness, thank you so much!" Georgia wiped her mouth with the napkin on her saucer, removing any last traces of the lipstick she had so carefully applied. She reached for the pitcher to pour herself a glass of water. Taking a sip, she glanced around the room, surprised to find that most of the tables were full. Her heartbeat quickened, and she took what seemed to be her tenth deep breath of the day.

From the table in front of the stage, Demi caught her eye and smiled. "You've got this," she mouthed.

Georgia slowly exhaled, and she nodded to Demi, "Thank you."

"Welcome, everyone, to the first night of our "Celebration of Greece" literature festival," Popi announced. "We are so happy to have with us a talented group of authors representing several genres . . ."

CHAPTER 4

The hum of voices floated on the warm evening breeze, which blew softly through the taverna on the square. Lights from the city reflected in the bay in glowing waves. Waiters dressed in white shirts and black pants rushed across the street from the restaurant buildings to the tables in the plateia, laden with dishes of grilled octopus, fried potatoes, and Greek salads of cucumbers, juicy tomatoes, kalamata olives, and large slices of feta cheese drizzled in olive oil and sprinkled with fresh oregano.

"Excuse me," a waiter said, spreading a large sheet of white paper over the blue cotton tablecloth and securing it to the table on each side with metal clips. He returned a minute later with a tall bottle of water and four glasses, followed by a carafe of white wine, a carafe of red wine, and four small glasses. "It is our homemade wine," he said.

Georgia picked up the carafe of white wine and poured some into her glass. "Who else wants white?" she asked.

"I do," Demi and Sophie both answered.

"I guess this is all for me, then," Zoe laughed, pouring herself a glass of red wine. She lifted it towards Georgia. "You did great," she said. "I'm so proud of you!"

"Honestly, I'm glad it's over."

"Really, Mom? It looked like you were enjoying yourself up there." Demi took a sip of wine. "Oh, it's really dry!"

Sophie sniffed at the wine in her glass and wrinkled her nose. "Um, I didn't drink any of it yet. Can I pour it back into the carafe?"

"No, Sophie, don't do that," Zoe said.

"Why not?" asked Demi. "Here, give it to me." She took Sophie's glass and poured the wine back into the carafe. She then poured the rest of her wine into Georgia's glass.

"Well, I guess this is all for me, then," Georgia laughed, lifting her glass towards Zoe. "You know, once we did the presentations, it was fun answering questions. I didn't realize how many people have actually read my book. And how many want to—I can't believe I've already sold half of the ones I brought! It took me six months to sell that many in the States."

"I bet you'll sell the other ones tomorrow at your workshop," Sophie said.

"Here's to selling them all," Zoe said, raising her glass.

"Here's to not having to cart that box around anymore," Georgia said.

"Wait 'til Dad hears," Demi said. "He's going to be so proud of you."

Georgia shrugged. "I guess so."

"Mom, of course, he will. He doesn't always say so, but I know he's proud of you. Have you talked to him yet?"

"No, I didn't get a chance to call him today about the car incident. I'll call him tomorrow."

"It's seven hours earlier there—you can call him when you get back to the hotel."

Georgia thought back to their conversation about the Literary Festival invitation. *Why do you have to go to Greece to sell your book? Can't you just sell it here? Do you really think you're going to sell enough copies to pay for that trip? Come on, Georgia . . . you're being selfish. You know I can't leave work now.* "I'm tired, Demi. I'll call him tomorrow."

The waiter reappeared with a basket of freshly baked bread. He stood above the table. "What would you like?"

"We'll have a Greek salad," Georgia said, "and can you bring us a plate of *mezethes*? Some Greek meatballs, some *taramosalata* and pita, and maybe . . ."

"Yes, yes, I will fix you a nice plate," the waiter smiled. "And for you?" He turned to Zoe.

"Oh, uh, no. That's for all of us," Zoe said.

"I think he was kidding, Mom," Sophie giggled.

The waiter winked at Sophie and turned back to the restaurant.

"I think he was flirting with you, Aunt Zo."

"He was not," Zoe said. She turned to Georgia. "Was he?"

"So, Mom," Demi said. "What are you doing tomorrow?"

"Well, I have the workshop in the morning. Then they're having a couple of author talks in the afternoon. After that, they're having concurrent writing seminars. Aunt Zoe and I are both taking the fiction one to "Fleshing out Your Character." I'm sorry we don't have a car anymore, but I don't think it's worth renting another one while we're in Gytheio. There are beaches nearby—I'm sure you and Sophie can take a taxi to the beach. Unless you want to come to one of the workshops?"

"Oh, that could be fun!" said Sophie. "Which one should we take?" She saw Demi's look of disdain. "Or maybe we could do both?"

"You can go to a workshop. I'm going to the beach." Demi said.

"No, I'll go to the beach with you," Sophie said.

"Good. Stavros will pick us up around eleven." Demi took a piece of warm bread out of the basket and pulled it apart. "This smells so good. Do they have any butter or maybe . . ."

"What?" Georgia set down her wine glass. "On his motorcycle?"

Demi chewed the crusty bread and took a sip of water. "No, Mom. He has a car. Stavros said he knows a nice beach nearby that isn't overrun with tourists. He doesn't work until tomorrow night, so he can take us to the beach in the morning."

"Well, that's interesting," Georgia said. "I didn't know you were interested in Stavros. You didn't say anything when you got back to the hotel."

"Well, we didn't really have time to talk, Mom. And who says I'm *interested*? It's just nice to have someone show us around. The last thing I need after Andrew is another romance."

"Andrew was six months ago, Demi," Georgia said.

"It feels like six days ago." Demi's voice softened. "It hurts like it was yesterday." She took a deep breath and shook off the sudden melancholy. "Anyway, Stavros offered to take us."

"You don't even know him," Zoe said. "I'm not sure I want Sophie driving with someone she doesn't even know in a foreign country."

Demi looked at Georgia and nodded her head towards Zoe.

Georgia turned to Zoe. "Well, we know his grandmother. And he *did* rescue us from disaster today. I don't think it's a problem."

"Mom," Sophie said. "I'm 24, not 14. I think I'm capable of taking care of myself."

"It's not you I'm worried about," said Zoe.

"Then who are you worried about, Aunt Zo?" Demi said.

With a flourish, a large plate of *mezethes* appeared before Zoe—fried Greek meatballs, eggplant spread, warm pita, stuffed grape leaves, and *tiropita*. "For you, Miss," the waiter smiled. "It is nice, yes?"

"Oh—yes! It is very nice. Thank you. *Efharisto.*"

"*Parakalo,* it is my pleasure to serve you," the waiter said and left.

"Smooth," Demi said.

Georgia burst out laughing. "Looks like you've got yourself an admirer, Zoe."

"Hallooo," a booming British voice approached their table.

"Looks like you do, too," Demi laughed.

"Hi, Charles," Georgia said. "How are you?"

"Well, I'm fine now that that's over. Hate those panel discussions. Must do it for the exposure, but I could do without it. Say—that looks delicious."

"There's enough food here to feed an army," Zoe said, sliding a stuffed grape leaf onto her plate. She cut it in half and took a bite, the lemon sauce dripping onto the plate. "Oh, my goodness, this is delicious!' she said.

"Ah! Mind if I join you?" Charles said.

"Oh, I don't think we're going to be here that long," Georgia said.

"Not a problem." Charles pulled up a wooden chair and squeezed in between Zoe and Georgia. "I say, *Kirios,*" he waved his hand towards their waiter. "Might I get a plate and a fork?" He eyed the carafes of wine. "And a glass, if you please." He turned to Demi and Sophie. "I'm Charles Duckworth," he said. "Maybe you know me from 'Tales of the Duck?'" He looked at their blank faces. "No, no, perhaps you don't. British books—probably don't have them in the States."

"Oh, right—you're the one who writes children's books," Demi said.

"*Kalispera, Kiria*!" a loud Greek voice approached their table. "You have discovered my favorite restaurant in Gytheio!"

"*Kalispera, Yiorgo*. I'm surprised to see you here. Didn't you say you lived in Xirokambi?"

"*Nai,* yes, but I have nothing better to do. I am here with my friends." He nodded across the plateia, where tables and chairs were set up like theirs but with different colored tablecloths, and the waiters scurried in and out of a different building.

"If this is your favorite restaurant," Georgia said, "why are you sitting over there?"

"It is my favorite restaurant tonight because you are sitting here, *Kiria* Georgia."

"Unbelievable," Demi said, looking between Georgia and Zoe. "What is going on with my life?"

"Do you want to sit down?" Sophie asked.

"There's not really any room," Georgia said.

"Thank you, yes. It has been a long day." He pulled a chair from the next table and wedged it between Georgia and Charles.

"Hallo, I'm Charles. And you are?"

"I am Yiorgos." He looked around until he spied the waiter. "*Servitore,*" he called. *Mia beera, parakalo.*" He glanced at the table. "Miss Georgia, your wine is empty. "*Alo ena krasi, parakalo,"* he said to the waiter. "You must drink another wine. To celebrate."

"What are we celebrating?" Georgia asked him.

"Your *yiorti*—you enjoyed your party?"

"It wasn't a party," Georgia said, "It was . . ."

"The party was fine, Yiorgo," Zoe said.

The waiter returned with a beer and a carafe of white wine. Yiorgos filled Georgia's glass and went to fill Demi's.

"Oh, no," she said, putting her hand over the glass. "It's too dry." She lowered her voice. "It kind of tastes like nail polish remover."

"Hmm, I don't know what that is," Yiorgos said, "but this is not the same wine. *Oriste*, here." Demi moved her hand away from the glass, and Yiorgos poured the wine.

Demi took a sip. "Oh, this is much better. But," she said, pointing to the first carafe, "I thought that was the homemade wine?"

Yiorgo laughed. "Yes, that is the problem. You must ask for *this* wine. It is not so dry."

Deep men's laughter drifted over from the table at the restaurant next door. One of the men raised his glass of beer towards Yiorgo. "*Aide Yiorgo mou. Yiammas*!"

"What did he say?" Sophie asked.

"He say, 'to your health,'" Yiorgos said.

Zoe and Georgia lifted their glasses. "*Yiammas*!"

CHAPTER 5

"Are you *serious,* Georgia? You're letting her go off with someone you don't even know? Unbelievable." The voice on the phone was sprayed with static, but the rebuke came through clearly.

"What do you think is going to happen, Jimmy? You said yourself that things are safer in Greece."

"You don't even know this guy. What if he . . ."

"What, Jimmy? What if he does what? He is taking Demi and Sophie to the beach. Period. Demi's been on her own for years. She doesn't revert to being a teenager just because we're in a different country. Please calm down." Georgia glanced down at Demi, who was sleeping soundly. Sometimes, in her sleep, she still looked like the little girl who would fall asleep on the couch, arms spread wide, mouth open, not a care in the world.

"Calm down? You want me to calm down? You're in another country doing who knows what and letting our daughter run wild, and you want me to calm down?"

"Excuse me? Is that what this is about? I'm doing 'who knows what?'" Georgia lowered her voice to keep from waking Demi. "You know damn well what I'm doing. You didn't even ask about the panel discussion. You know how important that was to me. You have never taken my writing career seriously."

"Your career is teaching, Georgia. Your writing is a hobby."

Georgia clenched her teeth.

"Georgia?" The line was silent. "Okay, okay, I'm sorry. I didn't mean that. It's just that . . ."

She heard a light tap on the door. "Georgia?" Zoe called. "Ready?"

"I have to go. I'm late for the first session."

"Come on, Georgia. I said I'm sorry."

"Goodbye, Jimmy." Georgia clicked the off button and threw her phone on the bed beside her tote bag. "I'll be right there, Zo," she called. She stepped into the bathroom, turned on the cold water, and then splashed her face. She patted it dry with a thin white towel, looked in the mirror, and applied a bit of lipstick. She slid the cell phone into her canvas tote and slung the bag over her shoulder. She took a deep breath and opened the door.

Zoe looked closely at her sister. "What's wrong?" she said.

* * *

"How far is the beach?" Demi asked. They had been driving for about fifteen minutes on a windy road parallel to the water but now diverted away from it. The road, bordered on both sides by whitewashed apartments and hotels, now abutted a stone wall on the right, above which flourished large cactus plants with wide, flat leaves, and a cliffside on the left, lush with pine trees. Through the open spaces between the trees, Demi caught the sparkle of the water in the bay. "I thought it was five minutes from Gytheio?"

"Yes, of course, there are beaches closer to Gytheio. This one is better." Stavros downshifted the faded blue Toyota Celica as they snaked around a steep curve. The *komboloi,* or worry beads, hanging from the rearview mirror swayed right, then left.

"Um, could you go a little slower?" Sophie asked from the back seat. "I'm feeling a little carsick."

"Why is this beach better?" Demi asked.

"You will see, don't worry," Stavros replied. He downshifted again as they began to climb up a long hill.

"Aren't we going away from the water?" Sophie asked.

Stavros glanced in the rearview mirror at Sophie, who looked as if she had just sucked on a lemon. "Tss tss tss. Open the window and breathe some air. We will be there in ten minutes." He turned back to Demi. "You think I am stealing you?"

Demi burst out laughing. "Do you mean kidnapping?" She turned to look at Sophie who clutched her beach towel to her chest. "Sophie, are you okay? Do you need to stop?"

Sophie nodded.

"Well, which one is it?"

"I'll be okay if it's only ten minutes."

"Yes, yes. We will be there in ten minutes. I promise you, Sophia," Stavros winked at Sophie in the rearview mirror. Despite her discomposure, she smiled.

* * *

"Okay, why don't you finish the paragraph you're writing, and then we can talk about the exercise," the workshop leader interrupted the scratching of pens on paper. "Go ahead and grab a cup of coffee if you like, and we'll get back together in about fifteen minutes."

Zoe set down her pen, leaned back, and stretched her arms above her head. Georgia wrote the last sentence down in her journal, leaned back, and rolled her neck from side to side. "I haven't written this much at one time since I was working on my book."

"I know," said Zoe. "It feels good, doesn't it?"

"Let's get some coffee." The large conference room from the previous night had been divided into two separate rooms at either end. Carafes of coffee and hot water for tea decorated the long table between the rooms, along with a tray of Greek cookies and bowls of almonds. Georgia poured a cup of coffee, and Zoe selected a tea bag from the box of English teas. "I'm tired of the air conditioning," Georgia said. "Let's go get a few minutes of sunshine."

They pushed open the heavy red doors, surprised to find a few people from their workshop already sitting on the steps in conversation. "Let's head over there," Zoe said, pointing her teacup to a wooden bench across the square.

They walked over to the bench and sat down. "This feels so good," Georgia said, closing her eyes and lifting her face toward the sun. "I hate being inside when the weather is so perfect outside."

"I know," Zoe said, "but I'm really enjoying the workshop." She blew on the cup of tea and then took a sip. "Still hot," she said, fanning the cup. "What character did you invent for the exercise?" she asked. "Did you base it on someone like Maria said?"

Georgia smirked. "I based it on Jimmy." She pursed her lips and looked down at her coffee.

"Are you still mad at him?" Zoe asked.

"What do you think?"

"I don't think he meant to upset you."

"Zoe, that's exactly what he meant to do. And he knows how to do it. He always has."

"But why do you let him upset you so much?"

"Zoe, think about it. How would you feel if you were questioned about every move you made? When I went back to school to get my teaching degree, he said I was wasting money, and he didn't see why I couldn't be happy with being a secretary and his wife. You know that—you know how upset I was then."

"I remember," Zoe reflected, recalling the angry phone calls from Georgia. "But, in the end, he supported you."

"Yeah, after I landed a teaching job, and he realized that I could be home with Demi in the summer. When I went to school for my MFA, he said I was wasting money and time that I could have been spending with him and Demi—even though she was already in college—instead of spending my evenings writing. He said that I didn't need a degree to learn how to write books." Georgia got up and tossed the rest of her coffee into the bushes behind the bench. "Come on, they're going in."

* * *

"This is the beach?" Demi asked. They had pulled into a dirt parking lot, along with a few other cars, an old Vespa, and a rusted white van. She got out of the car and looked beyond the parking lot towards the narrow strip of sand between the lot and the water. "What is so special about this beach?"

Sophie climbed out of the back seat and took a deep breath of sea air, letting it out slowly. "Are there any bathrooms here?" she said, looking around at the near-empty parking lot.

"What do you think?" Stavros asked. "That I would not take you to a good beach?" He walked towards the sand, then turned and motioned them. "*Elate,* come. I will show you."

The girls looked at each other, and Demi shrugged. "Okay, let's go." They caught up to Stavros and tried to keep pace, their feet sinking into the pebbly brown sand.

"This isn't the kind of beach I saw on the travel channel," Sophie whispered to Demi. "Wait, look," she said, pointing at the water ahead of them. "Paddle boats!" She called ahead to Stavros, "Can we rent them?"

"*Vevaios*, of course," he said. He walked towards a shack where a middle-aged man was speaking to a younger man. "*Yeia sou Maki,"* he called to the older man, who grinned and waved. Stavros spoke quickly to him in Greek, then turned to the girls. "Put your things here," he said, pointing to the corner of the shack, "and come with me." He led them down to the shoreline, where the younger man was already pulling a paddle boat up to the shore. "Get in," Stavros said. "And don't go too far. I don't want to swim out to get you." The girls climbed in, and Stavros and the young man gave the boat a shove.

"This is so cool," Sophie said. They pedaled the boat parallel to the shoreline and noticed a long, low building beyond the shack with a bar and stools. Several occupied umbrellas and chairs sat closer to the snack bar, and a few boats were anchored in the sand.

"What a gorgeous day," Demi said. The clear, bright cerulean sky reflected in the dark blue water in front of them as they pedaled out towards the horizon.

"Don't go too far," Sophie said. "We don't want Stavros to have to swim after us."

"I guess you're right," Demi said, "although I wouldn't mind being rescued by him."

They moved parallel to the shoreline for a while, alternating between pedaling and floating until they were doing more floating than pedaling. Sophie said, "I feel like I'm biking through quicksand."

"Let's head back," Demi said. "I want to lay out for a while, anyway." The girls pedaled as they turned the half-wheel towards the beach and returned to the shore. The young man who had sent them off ran down to meet them. He waded into the water, grabbed the handle on the front of the paddle boat, and pulled it up onto the sand. Sophie and Demi climbed out. Demi glanced up at the shack, where Stavros stood talking with Makis.

"That was nice of him," Sophie said.

"Yeah, it was."

"He's really cute, Demi."

"I guess so if you're into that long-haired, brooding, macho Greek look."

Sophie burst out laughing. "Come on, Demi. You know he's cute."

"I didn't say he wasn't. He's just not my type." An image of Andrew crossed her mind—tall, slim, sandy, short blond hair, brown eyes. A chill raced down her spine despite the midday sun. "Come on, let's get our stuff and head to the snack bar."

Stavros saw them approaching and walked down to meet them. "That was great," Sophie said.

"Yes, thank you," Demi said. "I think I'm going to get a frappe and sit under one of those umbrellas."

"No, no, you don't want a frappe now," Stavros said.

"I don't?" Demi asked. "Why don't I?"

"It is better you do not drink anything yet."

"Why?"

"Come, I have a surprise for you." He turned back towards the shack, and once again, the girls followed him.

"*Ela re, Malaka*," he called to one of the young men who had gathered at the shack.

Sophie whispered to Demi, "Isn't that a bad word?"

"I think it's one of those words that's only bad if you say it when you're angry. I think it's like saying, 'Hey asshole, what's up?' to a friend."

"I would never say that to a friend," Sophie frowned.

"Well, no, I don't mean *you,*" Demi laughed.

"Come, *elate,*" Stavros said, holding two bright orange life vests.

"Um . . . what are those for?" Demi asked.

"Put them on." Stavros handed a vest to each girl.

"Why are we wearing life vests?" Demi asked. Stavros pulled an orange vest from the hook in the back of the shack and pulled it on. "Because you don't want to drown," he said, buckling his vest around his chest and waist.

"I can swim," Demi said.

"Of course," Stavros said, "but you will see. *Elate,* come." He led the girls to the shore, where a middle-aged man with darkly tanned skin and dark hair had pulled up with a speedboat. The boat rocked gently near the shore. Two thick yellow ropes were attached to a metal handle in the stern. Makis walked down to the shoreline, dragging two large inner tubes behind him.

"You are ready for some fun?" Stavros asked the girls.

"Um," said Sophie, "I'm not sure . . ."

"Yes!" said Demi, beaming.

Stavros took an inner tube from Makis and hooked it onto one of the yellow ropes while Makis hooked the other. "Okay," he nodded to Sophie. "Jump in."

"What?" Sophie said, looking at the large tube. "How?"

Stavros laughed. "Here," he said, lifting the heavy tube over Sophie's head and dropping it over her. Demi moved toward Sophie's inner tube to get in.

"No, no, no," said Stavros, "I think it's better to ride with one of us. Just in case."

"In case of what?" Sophie said, her eyes growing large.

"It's okay. We are stronger. Just so, you know, to help you hold on. You will be fine. Dino!" he called to one of the other young men from the shack, "get in the tube with Sophia." It took Sophie a minute to recognize the bellman from the hotel without his jacket on. She smiled and waved.

Dinos ran down the sand and into the water, his long legs splashing everyone. "*Ela re, Malaka,*" Stavros laughed, "You are a donkey."

"Sorry," Dinos said to Sophie. "Sorry."

Stavros turned to direct Demi to the other tube, but she had already climbed in. "Well," she said. "Come on. Let's go!"

* * *

"Shouldn't the girls be back by now?" Zoe asked, looking at her phone.

"Zoe, I'm sure they're fine," Georgia said. She slipped her journal and pen into her bag. "That's about the tenth time you looked at your phone in the last hour. I don't know how you even concentrated on the workshop."

"How do you know I looked at my phone ten times if *you* were concentrating on the workshop?"

Georgia ignored the remark. "They might even be back by now. They're not going to come here just to let you know they're back."

"I know, but I told Sophie to text me when she got back."

Georgia stood up, stretched her arms, then turned from side to side. "That was a lot of sitting. Come on, let's take a walk. I need some fresh air."

"Sounds good," Zoe said. "I wouldn't mind checking out the shops."

The late afternoon heat enveloped them in a drowsy hug, and they moved sluggishly down the street toward the few stores that remained open. "Oh," said Georgia. "How could I forget?"

"Forget what?"

"They close the shops in the afternoon."

"Well, you can see why they take siestas. It's too hot to move."

"Yeah," said Georgia. "I'm starting to think a siesta is a good idea. Let's go back to the hotel. We can check out the shops later."

By the time they arrived at the hotel, sweat was dripping from their brows. "I'm going to need another shower," Zoe said, pushing open the door to the lobby.

"*Yeia sas kiries*, hello ladies," They were greeted by the same desk clerk from the previous day wearing the same dour expression. He looked back at his computer screen and continued to type.

"*Yeia sas kirie*," Zoe said. "*Ti kaneis*? How are you today?"

The desk clerk looked up to see Zoe smiling at him. He stopped typing and stood up. "I am well," he said, nodding slightly. "Thank you for asking."

"May I ask your name?" Zoe said.

"It is *Mihalis.* Michael in English."

"Nice to meet you, *Mihali.* See you later. Have a nice evening." Zoe waved and turned towards the steps. She opened the door to the stairwell and held the door for Georgia.

"What was that all about?" asked Georgia once inside the stairwell. She plodded up the steps, followed by Zoe, feeling the effects of the day of writing and the afternoon sun.

"Well," Zoe said, "We're here for a few more days. Maybe he was just having a bad day yesterday. I don't think it would be a bad thing to try to make friends with him. I don't think you got off to a very good start with him."

"Me?" Georgia said. She stopped and turned around to look at Zoe. "I wasn't the one with the attitude."

"Okay, Demi," Zoe said.

"Excuse me?"

"Apples and trees, Georgia. It's no mystery where Demi gets her attitude from."

"Are you kidding? She gets it from Jimmy."

"Right," said Zoe. They walked the rest of the way in silence.

Zoe stopped at her door and rummaged through her purse for the room key. "See you around seven?"

"Make it eight," Georgia said. "I feel a serious nap coming on."

Georgia opened the door to find Demi sprawled out face down on her bed, a light red tinge to her shoulders and back. *Oh no*, she thought. *That looks painful.* Demi's tangled mass of hair resembled the pile of knotted ropes Georgia had seen on their walk by the docks. She shook her head, kicked off her sandals, and lay down on her bed, fluffing the feather pillow. The air conditioner hummed softly as she drifted off to sleep.

She awoke to the sound of the hair dryer and heard Demi mutter, "Are you kidding me?"

Georgia rolled over and sat up. "What's the matter?" she called through the bathroom door.

Demi paused the dryer and opened the door. "Oh, hi, Mom. You're up."

"What's wrong?"

"This hair dryer has about as much power as a push mower."

"Interesting analogy," Georgia said. "Why don't you just let your hair dry naturally?"

"Because it will look like a bunch of spaghetti, that's why. I'm not lucky enough to have hair like yours." She turned the dryer back on and pointed it at the round brush she was twirling her hair around.

"I wasn't lucky in high school," Georgia called over the whirring of the dryer. "Everyone made fun of my frizzy hair."

Demi rolled her eyes.

"I can see you in the mirror, Demi."

Demi shut off the dryer, picked up a travel-size can of hairspray, and sprayed her hair. "What time is it?" she asked.

Georgia looked at the clock on the bedside table. "Nine-thirty? Can that be right? I'd be thinking about putting my PJs on at home."

"Well, we're not at home, Mom, so wash your face, and let's go get some dinner."

"We were supposed to meet Zoe at eight o'clock."

"I'm guessing Aunt Zoe and Sophie are probably sleeping, too. Why don't you call them?" Still sleepy from the hard nap, Georgia felt around the bed for her cell phone. "Never mind, I'll go see if they're up." Demi turned and opened the door.

Georgia heard the muffled sound of her ringing cell phone from under the pillow. She retrieved it and saw her husband's name. "Hello?" she said.

"Hey, Honey," Jimmy said. "I had a quick break. Didn't know if I'd find you. Thought you might be out to dinner."

"Hi, Jimmy. No, we just woke up from our naps." Georgia yawned and swung her feet over the side of the bed.

"What? Isn't it around nine o'clock there?"

"It is," Georgia said, looking automatically at the bedside clock. "It was a long day."

"How's Demi?"

"She's fine."

"How was her day at the beach?"

Georgia stood up and opened the door to the balcony. The night air was still warm, but the sea breeze was refreshing. "I actually don't know."

"What do you *mean,* you don't know? Isn't she back yet?"

Georgia felt the muscles in her neck tighten. "She was asleep when I got back."

"Where is she now?"

"She just went to check on Zoe and Sophie. What's with the interrogation, Jimmy?"

"It's not an interrogation, Georgia. Can't I ask about my daughter?"

"Are you asking or accusing?"

"What would I be accusing you of?"

"Forget it, Jimmy." She shut the balcony door, cutting off the warm breeze. The air conditioner kicked on with a thunk and settled into its steady hum.

"Honestly, Georgia, I don't even know what to say to you. All you want to do is pick a fight. I just called to see how your thing went."

"Did you? I thought you called to chastise me because that's what it feels like."

Georgia listened to the silence on the line, wondering what direction the conversation would take. "So, how was it?" Jimmy said. "Is it worth the trip?"

Georgia breathed in deeply and exhaled slowly. "It was fine, Jimmy. I'm going to get ready for dinner. I'll talk to you tomorrow, okay?"

"*S'agapo*, Georgia."

She paused, then said, "I love you, too, Jimmy."

CHAPTER 6

"*Kiria Georgia! Kalispera*!" The now familiar voice of the taxi driver rose above the din of motorcycle engines and clattering plates, signaling his approach. The ladies were seated at a small white wooden table on the sidewalk in front of a fish taverna across the street from the seawall. Its legs wobbled on the concrete as a waiter set down glasses and a carafe of water. Georgia lifted the towel from the basket of warm, crusty bread in the middle of the cloth-covered table. The smell of freshly baked bread mingled with the already pleasant aroma of broiled fish, lemon, and oregano mixed with the salty sea air wafting in from the Gulf.

"*Kalispera,* Yiorgo. I see you're in Gytheio again."

"Ah, you are *paratiritiki yineka*."

Georgia shook her head. "I don't know what that is."

"You see things, and you, hmmm," he looked up and put his index finger to his mouth, tapping it a few times. He held his hand out, palm upward. "Maybe you know them?"

"I know that this taverna isn't your favorite restaurant in Gytheio. I'm surprised to see you here," Georgia added, although she was not surprised.

Yiorgos shrugged. "I like fish," he said. He glanced around, looking for an empty chair, but the restaurant was full.

Sophie looked up from her phone. "He said you're an observant woman, Aunt Georgia," she said, waving the phone at her aunt and grinning. "I downloaded the translate app."

"So that she can understand Dinos," Demi teased. "He doesn't speak much English."

"But *Stavros* does," Sophie taunted.

"What is going on here, girls?" Zoe asked.

"Nothing," the girls said. They looked at each other and smiled.

Yiorgos cleared his throat to speak. "*Kiria,* I see that you are busy."

"You are a *paratiritikos anthropos,* Yiorgo."

"Perhaps after dinner, you and your *parea* will join me and my *parea* for a drink? At my favorite restaurant, of course," he winked.

"Oh, no, thank you," Zoe said. "It's been a long day and . . ."

"Perhaps," Georgia smiled.

"*Endaksi, tha ta poume,"* he said, and left the taverna.

"He said, 'alright, see you . . .'"

Georgia placed her hand over Sophie's and smiled. "I know what he said, honey."

* * *

"That was delicious," Zoe said, setting her fork down on an empty plate. "Everything tasted so fresh."

"I know," Demi said, "I don't even want to eat a tomato when we get back to the states. The salads here are amazing. I swear you can taste the soil in the tomato."

"Euww," said Sophie.

"You know what I mean," said Demi. "It just tastes so earthy. Everything tastes better here."

Georgia leaned back in the wooden chair and looked out over the gulf. The darkness of the water merged with the darkness of the sky, blending invisibly on the horizon. She sighed.

"What's wrong, Mom?" Demi asked.

"Nothing, honey." She gave an unconvincing half-smile.

"Have you talked to Dad yet?"

"Yes, he called earlier. He's fine."

"That's good. I bet he misses us. Next time, tell him I love him."

"Of course, Demi."

The waiter returned with a dish of deep pink watermelon and four forks. "It is on the house," he said, setting the plate on the table and passing out the forks.

"*Efharisto*," Georgia said. "That looks delicious." She picked up one of the forks and stabbed a piece of watermelon. The sweet juice filled her mouth as she took a bite. "Oh, it *is* delicious!" The others picked up their forks and followed suit.

"So," Demi said, setting down her fork, "Sophie and I were going to check out the nightclubs."

"Do you think that's a good idea?" Zoe asked. "It's already past eleven."

"Mom," Sophie said, "it's right above the hotel. It's like a ten-minute walk if that. I'm sure we'll be fine."

"Yeah, don't worry, Aunt Zo. I'm pretty sure Dinos will walk us home if we need him to."

"Dinos? The bellman?"

"Yes, Mom," Sophie said. "I told you he was at the beach today."

"What about Stavros?" Zoe said.

"What about him?" Demi asked.

"Is he meeting you there?"

"No, he's working." Demi pushed back her chair and bent down to kiss her mother on the cheek. "We have our keys—don't worry about us."

"Have fun, girls," Georgia said. She signaled to the waiter for their bill. "The night is young, Zoe. We have miles to go before we sleep."

They watched the girls walk in the direction of the hotel. "Do you really think it's a good idea, Georgia?"

"Come on, Zoe. You know how safe Greece is. They'll be fine." The waiter brought over a shot glass with a small slip of paper rolled up inside.

"That's not what I'm talking about."

"Well then, what are you talking about?"

"Meeting the taxi driver."

"Yiorgos? You're kidding. It will be nice to talk to someone not involved with LitFest. I love writing, but I don't need 24 hours a day of talking about it. And I'm not going back to the hotel to sit up and wait for Demi."

"So, you *are* worried about the girls." Zoe reached into the small purse slung across her body.

"I've got this, Zoe," Georgia said, pulling a credit card out of her phone case. "Look, I always worry about Demi, whether we're in the

States or in Greece. I don't think a parent ever quits worrying about their kids, no matter how old they are. I used to think once they were grown up, that went away. I guess it never does." The waiter appeared as if out of thin air and took the bill and credit card.

"I don't know," Zoe said. "I think it's our generation. I don't think Mom worried about us when we grew up."

"Yes, she did, Zoe. She worried about you all the time."

"What makes you think that?"

Georgia leaned back in her chair and folded her arms. "Because every time I talked to her on the phone, she would say, 'Do you think Zoe is okay?'"

"I know she was upset about the divorce. That's why I didn't want to tell her."

"Well, she might have wondered where Walker was when he didn't show up at Christmas. I don't think the divorce itself bothered her. She just wanted you to be happy."

"Well, I am now."

"Are you, Zoe?"

"What do you mean?" She spread her arms open and looked around her. "Look at where we are. I have a good job . . ."

Georgia raised her eyebrows. ". . . that you complain about all the time."

Zoe ignored her. "I have a nice house . . ."

". . . that you keep telling me is too big."

". . . and I'm in Greece with my sister and our daughters. I do miss Marina, though—I'm so disappointed that her schedule didn't work."

"I know, but I'm so proud of my niece. When does she finish her certification?"

"Next month. She's already gotten some job offers. I think she'll be able to find a dietitian position quickly."

"I hope she can stay in Pittsburgh. I'm glad she and Demi were able to room together. Especially after Andrew . . ." her voice trailed off. The waiter reappeared with a credit card machine, handing it to Georgia. She signed off and handed the machine back to him.

"*Efharisto, Kiria,*" he said. "*Kali nihta.*"

"Georgia, I know that you and Jimmy really liked Andrew, but if he was right for Demi, they'd still be together."

"I just can't believe that after Demi turned down the job in Philadelphia to stay with him, he dumped her."

"Maybe he got scared."

"Maybe he should have thought of that before he convinced her to give up the job." Georgia and Zoe slid their chairs back from the table and stood up. Georgia brushed a few breadcrumbs from her sundress, then took her scarf from the back of the chair. A cool breeze blew in from the Gulf, and she wrapped the light blue scarf around her shoulders. "He's the one who said he couldn't 'do' a long-distance relationship," she said. "She stayed for him, and three months later, boom."

"Well, she seems to be doing okay." Tables crowded the sidewalk, and Zoe peered down the street to her right, then left, before stepping off the curb. At the sound of an approaching motor, heard but not seen, they dashed across the street and turned towards the main square. Waves lapped the seawall in a steady, soothing rhythm.

"I don't know, Zoe. I don't think she's long for that job. The country club would be lost without her, but the evening hours don't leave much room for a social life. Although I'm not sure she wants one right now."

"I get that. Marina said she doesn't want to date. Demi told her she's committed to her career."

"Maybe. I think she's put up a wall," Georgia said. "At least she seems to be having a good time here."

The sisters walked along the sea wall towards the plateia. Laughter and conversation floated in a crescendo as they approached the square. The bay reflected the lights of the city in long glowing fingers that stretched out far into the water until they disappeared into the darkness. The lights from the restaurants glowed, giving the plateia the appearance of a movie set. Georgia scanned the taverna for Yiorgos. "There he is," she pointed.

Zoe looked in the direction of the plateia and laughed. "So much for no 'shop talk.'"

Three four-tops had been pushed together; Yiorgos and his friends sat at one end, and several writers from the LitFest sat at the other end. Charles sat in the middle, a liaison between the two groups. He looked out towards the water and spotted the ladies. "Halloooo!" he called, getting up and knocking into the table as he waved. The drinks shook from side to side, and three hands sprang out to steady them.

"Ah," sighed Georgia. "This should be fun."

Georgia and Zoe walked over to the Plateia where Charles was already directing the others to move down as he squeezed a chair between himself and another writer. "*Kalispera,*" he said and motioned to Georgia to sit down. She looked at the empty chair at the far end of the table and said, "Thank you, Charles. I think I'll practice my Greek tonight." She turned towards her sister. "Zoe, why don't you sit there?" Georgia pointed to the chair next to Charles. Zoe's mouth opened, and she glared at her sister, but she was already introducing herself to the Greeks at the end of the table.

* * *

The girls walked past the Hotel Aktaion and turned up the hill towards the reverberation of clashing bass coming from separate doorways of separate clubs. The bright red door of the second club stood partially open, and several dark-haired young men stood in front of the club smoking cigarettes. They looked the girls over, and one of them called out to Sophie, "Hey, sexy lady, I buy you a drink?" Another openly leered at Demi.

"Let's go back to the hotel," Sophie said. "I don't think I want to go in."

"Dinos is waiting for you, Sophie. Let's just go in and find him. We don't have to stay if you don't want to." They passed by the young men, ignoring their comments, and through the red door. A blast of cold air greeted them, and they blinked as their eyes adjusted to the darkness. To the left was a long bar, occupied by mostly men, drinking mostly bottled beer and wearing tight jeans. At the back of the room, a bleached blonde DJ stood behind a table that held an assortment of technical equipment, his head nodding from side to side with the beat. To the right, down a few steps, was a dance floor, occupied by mostly women wearing very high heels and very short skirts.

Sophie looked down at her leather sandals and long cotton skirt and at Demi's blue jeans, sandals, and halter top. "I don't think we're dressed for this, Demi," she said, watching the woman in front of her gyrate in a tight black mini-skirt that may or may not have been painted on.

"Who cares?" said Demi. "Do you want to dance?" She slung her shoulder bag over her head and across her body and headed down the steps to the dance floor. "Come on, Sophie!"

Sophie hesitated a minute, scanned the room for Dinos, and walked onto the sticky wood floor to join Demi. The beat of the bass drowned out the lyrics. "I can't tell if this is English or Greek," Sophie called over the din.

"It doesn't matter," Demi smiled, weaving through the dancers to a spot in the middle of the floor. Her body relaxed as she melted into the music. "I can't remember the last time I went dancing." Sophie shuffled from side to side, her arms bent at the elbows and close to her body. Demi raised her arms and pumped her hips confidently. "Come on, Sophie, drop it low with me!" she said, bending her knees and shaking her hips.

Sophie laughed and attempted to emulate Demi's moves. Without Demi's natural confidence, she moved stiffly at first, but as one song faded into another, she relaxed and danced with assurance. She glanced around the floor and watched the girls next to them. "I don't think they're Greek. I hear them speaking English. I think they're tourists."

"We're tourists, Sophie."

"I know. I just meant maybe this isn't where the Greeks go. You know, the Greeks who live here."

Demi looked towards the bar. "I know one Greek who goes here. Look up there," she pointed.

Dinos stood with a small group of dark-haired, dark-eyed men and waved to Sophie. She motioned for him to join her on the dance floor. He raised his chin in the Greek gesture of "no" and waved at her to join him at the bar. Sophie turned to leave the dance floor.

Demi grabbed her arm. "Where are you going, Sophie?" she said. Sophie pointed at the bar. "Don't run the minute he waves." Demi moved towards Sophie with an exaggerated motion, beckoning with her hand in a come-hither gesture. Sophie laughed and followed her as she backed onto the dance floor. Their spot had been swallowed up by the growing crowd of dancers, forcing them to adopt Sophie's initial moves.

"*Signomi*," a woman behind Demi said, as her hip bumped Demi's.

Demi forced a smile. "*It's okay,*" she said. Scanning the floor, she could not find a spot where they wouldn't bump into other dancers. "Come on," she said, nodding at the bar. She and Sophie zig-zagged through the maze of dancers and walked up the steps towards the group of men.

Dinos was facing the bar and now turned towards the girls with a bottle of Mythos beer in each hand. "*Orieste*," he said, handing one to Sophie and turning to hand one to Demi.

"Oh, thank you," said Sophie.

"No thanks, Dino," said Demi. She waved at the bartender. "I'll have a vodka soda with lime."

Dinos looked down at the extra beer bottle, shrugged, and set it next to his half-full one on the bar. "Sophia, I am so happy you come."

"What?" she yelled as the music rose to new decibels. "Sorry, I can't hear you."

"Dino," Demi leaned towards his right ear. "Why aren't any of the men dancing? Why is it only the women who are dancing?"

He shrugged.

"Do you dance?" she asked.

He shrugged again.

"Do you know how to dance?"

Another shrug.

"Why don't you go dance with Sophie? I'm sure she'd love that." She put one hand on Sophie's back and one on Dinos' and gave them a gentle push towards the dance floor. Sophie handed her beer to Demi and led the way. Dinos followed, looking back at his friends as they laughed, before disappearing into the horde of dancers with Sophie.

"What's so funny?" Demi asked the group, setting down the beer and picking up the vodka from the bar. One of the men raised his eyebrows and stared at Demi. Another pursed his lips. The third put his hand out to shake Demi's. "Kostas," he said. "And you are?"

"Demi," she replied. "I don't get it. What's so funny? Do only the women know how to dance?"

"We know how to dance," Kostas said. "This," he said, nodding his head towards the dance floor, "is not dancing."

"Yes, but it is nice to watch," another man said, winking at Demi.

"If you want to see a man dance, you come to a Greek dance. Then you will see dancing," Kostas said.

Demi squeezed the lime into her drink and took a sip. "Where would I find a Greek dance?"

"Ah, there is a festival in Xirokambi on Friday. The birthday of the church. It is big festival, with food and music and dance."

"That could be fun," Demi said, more to herself than the group. The coolness that had greeted them at the door had evaporated, and the air was close and muggy now. "I need some air," she announced, but the men had turned inward and were talking among themselves. She wove her way through the crowd, pushed open the heavy door, and walked outside. The group of men that had been lurking at the doorway were gone, and Demi sat down on the steps. The noise of the club faded to a distant cacophony, and she realized that her head was throbbing. Demi closed her eyes and took a deep breath of fresh air. Small groups of twenty-somethings walked up and down the street, with an occasional older couple passing by. The door opened behind her, and a slim, blonde woman walked out. Demi had noticed the woman on the dance floor because of her shiny silver skirt and the bright lipstick, which echoed the red of her platform shoes. Her long hair was soaked with sweat at her hairline. She sat down next to Demi and combed her hair away from her face with her fingers, revealing roots several shades darker than the rest of her hair.

"*Kalispera*," she said, nodding to Demi. She reached into her purse and took out a pack of cigarettes. She held the pack out to Demi.

"Oh, no, thank you," Demi said.

The woman put a cigarette in her mouth, clicked a blue plastic lighter, and brought the flame up to the cigarette, inhaling deeply and blowing the smoke out in a long, slow puff. "You are American," she said. She slid the lighter back into her purse.

"I am," said Demi. "How did you know?"

The woman smiled. "You are with Sophia."

"How do you know Sophie?"

The woman smiled. "Dinos is my little brother. He has talked about the Americans at the hotel for two days." She held her hand out to Demi. "My name is Nadia."

Demi set her drink down and reached across the step to shake Nadia's hand. "Nice to meet you. I'm Demi."

"It is the first time I see Dinos dance. Maybe his friends will not make fun of him. I don't know." Nadia cocked her head to the side and laughed. "I think maybe they will." She took another drag of her cigarette, turning her head away from Demi to exhale. "No matter, I think for him it is worth it. She is pretty, your cousin."

"She is," said Demi. "I don't think she realizes how pretty she is."

The door behind them opened, and Dinos and Sophie came out. Dinos' black tee shirt was soaked with sweat under both arms, and the sheen on his forehead glistened in the beam of light over the door. "That was so much fun!" Sophie yelled.

"Shhhh," Demi said. "You don't have to yell out here."

"Oh, sorry!" Sophie said.

"It's okay," said Dinos. He turned to Demi. "You don't like the club?"

"It's fine," Demi said. "I just have a headache." She stood up and rolled her shoulders. "Sophie, I'm going to go back to the hotel. You can stay if you want."

"No, no, I'll come with you. It's late."

Gravity failed Dinos as his entire body and face sagged. "Sophia, you don't want to stay?"

"No, that's okay. Thanks for dancing. It was fun. Good night, Dino. *Kalispera*." She turned towards Nadia. "Bye-bye!"

"*Kalo vrathi*, Dino," Demi said. "It was nice to meet you, Nadia," she added.

"Yes," Nadia said. "Maybe we meet again."

The girls walked down the steps and turned to walk down the hill. Nadia stood up and watched a forlorn Dinos stare after Sophie. "*Ela adelfe,*" she put her arm around his elbow. "Let's go home. You will see her again. Of this, I am sure."

* * *

Demi turned the key in the lock quietly and opened the door. The shutters were still ajar, and the streetlight streamed in through the balcony window, revealing two beds—one with Demi's clothing strewn across it and one turned down with the feather pillow fluffed up and leaning against the wrought iron headboard. Her mother was not in bed. Demi took out her phone to text Sophie, but she was interrupted by a knock at the door. She opened the door as Sophie said, "My mom's not in our room!"

"What time is it?" Demi asked.

"It's almost two. Where are they? Do you think they're looking for us?"

"I doubt it."

"What should we do?" Sophie said, looking around the room as if her mother and aunt might materialize.

"I don't think we should do anything." Demi sat on the bed and unbuckled her sandals. "I'm sure they're just having fun."

"My mom doesn't stay up past ten, Demi. It's two in the morning."

"I'm sure they're fine," Demi said, massaging her foot.

"Will you come look for them with me?"

Demi sighed and flopped back on the bed, her legs hanging over the side. Sophie grabbed her hand and pulled her up. "Please . . ." she said.

Demi looked with longing at the bed. "Fine," she said. She took a pair of flip-flops from under the small table in the room. "Alright, let's go."

The moon had risen high in the sky, its reflection dissipating throughout the bay. The night was quiet now; the only sound on the street was the gentle swoosh of the moonlit waves as they lapped at the seawall. Sophie walked quickly along the promenade, her long legs taking her several paces in front of Demi. "Sophie, slow down!" she said. "Five minutes is not going to make a difference. If they've been kidnapped, it's too late anyway." Sophie stopped and turned back to look at Demi with wide eyes. "I'm just kidding. But seriously, slow down. It feels like I'm walking across hot coals."

The subdued sounds of late-night conversation reached them as they rounded the corner to the plateia. Streetlights illuminated the two tavernas that remained open. Several patrons sipped ouzo or Greek brandy—among them, their mothers. Georgia tilted back her head and laughed—a laugh that echoed down the dark street. Demi smiled. Her father called that Georgia's 'cackle,' smiling to himself whenever she laughed. "I told you they were fine," Demi said.

Sophie was watching her mother, who was leaning, chin in her hand, toward Charles, who had the attention of everyone at that end of the table.

"Come on, Sophie," Demi said, moving towards the plateia.

"No!" Sophie grabbed Demi's top and pulled her back. "I don't want my mom to think I'm checking on her."

"That's exactly what you're doing."

Charles looked towards the gulf and squinted. "Isn't that your daughter?" he asked Zoe.

Zoe peered into the dark. "Yes, it is." She waved. "Girls, over here!"

"Uh oh," Sophie said. They approached the table, and she summoned an enthusiastic smile. "Hi, Mom!"

"What in the world are you doing here? I thought you were going to the nightclub."

"We did. Mom. It's two in the morning. We went back to the hotel and were worried when you weren't there."

"What's this 'we' stuff?" Demi asked, raising her eyebrows.

"*I* was worried."

"It's two o'clock?" Zoe asked. "I guess we lost track of time."

"Demi!" Georgia called from the other end of the tables. "Hi, Sweetie. What are you doing here?"

Demi rolled her eyes at Sophie. "Just came to say goodnight, Mom."

Charles pointed to a couple of chairs that had been vacated by some of the writers. He stood up and pulled one away from the table. "Do have a seat," he said.

"Oh, no thanks," said Demi. "I have to get to bed. We're going to the Caves of Diros tomorrow, and I want to get some sleep. It's been a long day. This morning seems like a long time ago."

"Um, about that," Sophie said.

"Come on, Sophie. The caves are supposed to be amazing. The pictures of them are incredible."

"I just don't like the idea of being in a cave." Sophie crossed her arms tightly around her body.

"It's a cave, Sophie, it's not a closet."

"I'm sorry, Demi. I get claustrophobic just being in my laundry room. Anyway, I'm sure you and Stavros will have a good time without me."

Demi's mouth turned up in a slight grin, and Sophie smiled. "Aha!" she said. "You *do* like him."

"Maybe a little."

"Sophie," Zoe said, "Do you want to go shopping for souvenirs in Kardamyli with me tomorrow? Aunt Georgia has a couple meetings. We could get a taxi."

"I can take you," said Charles. "I have a car, and I've been hoping to get to Kardamyli. It's a lovely town. We can have lunch there if you like."

"Don't you have to go to the meetings?" Zoe asked.

Charles laughed. "I'm a children's book writer. They don't pertain to me."

"That would be nice," Zoe said. "Sophie?"

"Yes, I'd love to." She smiled at Charles. "Thank you!"

"I guess we'd better get to bed." Zoe looked at Georgia, who was deep in conversation with a woman at the end of the table. "Georgia, excuse me," she called. Georgia looked up. "Are you coming?" Georgia held her index finger up, then turned and said something to the woman, who smiled and nodded. Georgia stood up, and they clasped hands.

Their slow pace reflected the weight of the day as they walked towards the hotel. "Who was that woman?" Demi asked.

"Just someone from the festival," Georgia replied. *Someone who might just be able to make something happen.*

CHAPTER 7

A loud rapping at the door worked its way into Demi's consciousness as she lay with her head embedded in the confines of her feather pillow. She opened her eyes slowly, blinking herself awake. She glanced at her mother's empty bed and reached for her cell phone on the nightstand. The rapping continued. "Demi!" she heard a male voice outside the door. "You are awake?"

The screen on the cell phone read ten forty-six. "Oh, shit," she mumbled. She jumped up and looked in the mirror. Her hair, matted on one side, stuck out in wayward clumps on the other side. Her oversized yellow O.A.R. tee shirt from last summer's concert hung loosely to her mid-thighs. "Just a minute, *ena lepto*!" she called. Demi ran into the bathroom, opened the faucet, and splashed cold water onto her face. She grabbed one of the hair ties that sat on the bathroom sink, finger-combed her hair and quickly twisted it into the hair tie. "Ugh," she said and splashed her face again, cupping her hands to swish some water around in her mouth. She dried her face, threw the towel on the bed, and opened the door.

"I see you are ready," Stavros said. His eyes moved down to her legs, lingered there for a second, and then back up to her face.

Demi pulled the hem of her tee shirt down. "I'm sorry. I can be ready in five minutes." Stavros raised his eyebrows. "Ten minutes," she said. "I'll meet you downstairs in ten minutes."

"*Endaksi,* okay. Make sure to bring a jacket. The caves are cold."

* * *

At eleven o'clock, Demi emerged from the stairwell.

"*Kalimera, Despinis,*" the desk clerk greeted her from behind his computer.

"*Kalimera, Mihali.*"

"You are going to the caves?" he asked.

"Yes," she said, looking around the lobby.

He nodded towards the front door. "Your friend is waiting outside."

The aroma of baked goods wafted in from the dining room, and Demi's stomach growled. She contemplated the breakfast bar, but she had already kept Stavros waiting long enough. She walked into the bright sunlight and blinked. Stavros was leaning against the car, holding a cup of coffee. "*Oreiste,*" he said. He handed her the coffee and reached through the open window into the car. He pulled out a flaky pastry wrapped in a napkin and handed it to her.

"Oh!" she said, with a mixture of surprise and pleasure. "Thank you."

"*Tipota,*" Stavros said. "It's nothing." He noticed that Demi wore no makeup. Her hair was now pulled up into a tousled top knot of sun-bleached waves. The blue from the gulf reflected in her eyes, which took on a blue-green cast. She had put on denim leggings, a clean white tee with the word 'Karma' in large grey script, and grey tennis shoes.

"What are you looking at?" Demi asked, self-consciously patting her hair for any wayward strands.

"*Tipota,*" he said. "Where is your jacket?"

"It's like ninety degrees out. I don't need one."

"Eh," Stavros said. "Just like an American."

"What's that supposed to mean?"

"You are stubborn." He opened the passenger side door. "Get in." Demi sat down, still holding her pastry and coffee, and slid her legs around to the front. Stavros shut the door and came around to the driver's side. He leaned his head in through the window. "*Ena lepto,*" he said and ran back into the hotel.

He reappeared a minute later, opened the back door, tossed something into the back seat, and got in behind the wheel. "*Pame,*" he said. "We go."

* * *

Georgia poured herself a cup of black coffee from the now-familiar pot on the table at the Center. A space had been sectioned off at either end of the large room by a series of partitions. Each divider was decorated with black and white unframed photos of artifacts that had been excavated from various sites and were now housed at the Archeological Museum in Sparta. Georgia walked over to the room at the far end of the hall where a chart on an easel read 'Publication Symposium' in large block letters. She set her coffee cup down in front of the open seat next to Gloria, the mystery writer, and caught a whiff of jasmine, unsure of whether it had come through the partially open window or from Gloria's perfume. Gloria's red hair was teased into a bouffant style, and her long eyelashes and red lips reminded Georgia of an actress of another era, perhaps Lucille Ball, and seemed out of character for someone who appeared to be in her early forties. Six other men and women sat at the large round table, chatting among themselves. Georgia took a notebook and pen out of her bag and set it on the floor next to her chair. "*Kalimera,*" she addressed the group.

"*Kalimera,*" several voices echoed.

"We'll get started in a few minutes," one of the authors said. "Popi is in the other room doing an introduction." Georgia looked at the beam of filtered sunlight streaming in through the window glass. The morning walk to the Center had been delightful. The sun rising over the gulf promised to roast the city with strong afternoon rays, but the cool morning breeze tempered its power, and Georgia was comfortable in her blouse and pants. She had brought a sweater with her for the air conditioning that had run constantly during the LitFest, but she was pleased to find the room a comfortable temperature, and she hung the sweater over the back of her chair. Her box of books was in the corner. Only four books remained.

Gloria followed her glance. She pointed to the box with the silver pen in her hand. "Did you sell all of them?" she asked.

"All but four," Georgia replied. "I don't want to take them back with me."

"No worries," Gloria said. "The LitFest will buy them from you and sell them online or at the book table next year."

"Oh!" Georgia said, "If I had known that, I would have brought another box!" She took a sip of her coffee and realized Gloria was staring at her. "I'm just kidding," she smiled.

Gloria wove her pen between her fingers, moving it back and forth. "Oh, of course," she said.

"*Kalimera,* writers." Georgia glanced up to see Popi looking somewhat like a moving garden of daisies as she entered the room in a brightly flowered sundress. She suppressed a giggle and leaned over to Gloria. "It's like Birnam Woods moving to Macbeth's castle," she whispered. Gloria looked at Georgia and furrowed her brows. "Never mind," Georgia said. "It's an allusion."

"To what?" Gloria asked.

"Shakespeare," Georgia said, failing to keep the condescension out of her voice. How many times had Demi told her that she sounded condescending? She sighed and leaned her chin on her palm. Gloria shrugged and turned back to Popi. Georgia opened her notebook and started to doodle letters of the Greek alphabet, savoring the smooth roll of the black gel pen as it glided over the page.

"I'm glad to see you all here," Popi said. "We'll be discussing the differences between self and independent publishing and the pros and cons versus traditional publishing methods. In the second hour, we'll have breakout sessions. I've arranged for representatives from two publishing houses to join us."

Georgia's pen stopped in mid-letter, and she sat up. *Publishing houses? This was going to get interesting.*

* * *

"*Kalimera*!" The enthusiastic voice of Charles greeted the women as they emerged from the hotel. "Good morning, Zoe. Good morning, Sophie! Lovely day." He opened the passenger door of the small blue Opel and motioned to Zoe.

"Uh, Mom," Sophie said, "Do you mind if I sit in front? I got pretty car-sick on the way to the beach. I don't do well on these windy roads."

Zoe pondered the two-door car for a second before replying, "Of course not, honey. You need more legroom than I do, anyway."

Charles' face fell slightly, but he summoned his jolly countenance. "Of course, Sophie. Do get in front. Wouldn't want you to lose your lunch!"

Zoe pushed the seat forward and crawled into the back of the sub-compact, and Charles got in on the driver's side. Sophie squeezed into the front. Her knees brushed the dashboard. "Oh dear," Charles said. "I think there's a lever on the side to push the seat back. Sophie felt around with her right hand until she located the lever. She pulled on it to no avail. "You really have to give it a tug," Charles said. She tugged at it, and the seatback flew backward, landing Sophie in Zoe's lap.

"Ouch!"

"Oh, sorry, Mom!" Sophie looked above her at her mother's chin. "Are you okay?"

"Whoops-a-daisy!" Charles said. "I think you pulled the wrong lever, Sophie."

Sophie pulled up on the lever, and the seatback shot forward, projecting her until her head was suspended four inches above the dashboard.

"Cripes!" Charles looked at Sophie with alarm. She pulled the lever slightly and pushed the seatback up to a comfortable sitting position—as comfortable as possible with her knees on the dashboard. "Come to think of it, I think perhaps the lever to move the seat back is actually under the front of the seat," Charles said, reaching under his seat and patting the underside of it. "Ah, yes, there it is. So sorry."

Sophie reached under the seat and tugged on the lever. Her seat slid backward into Zoe's knees.

"OUCH!" Zoe repeated, with more emphasis.

"Sorry, Mom!"

"Oh my, my," Charles said. He looked back at Zoe, who was folded up like a closed accordion. "We're not off to a very good start, are we?"

Zoe glared at Charles. Sophie pulled the lever up slowly and used her leg muscles to glide the seat forward several inches to reach a happy medium between the dashboard and Zoe's knees.

"Well, never mind," Charles said. "All good?" He looked at Sophie and then back at Zoe, who was rubbing her knees. "Seat belts?" He started up the car, put it in gear, and started to pull onto the main road.

Zoe heard the hum of a motorcycle approaching from around the bend and caught a flash of red through the rear window. "Charles, look out!"

"Bollocks!" he exclaimed, stalling the car as a bright red Vespa sped past. Sophie gasped. Zoe clutched the back of Sophie's seat. "Everyone alright?" Charles asked. He mistook their silence for agreement and re-engaged the clutch. "Off we go, then!"

* * *

Stavros turned off the main road and stopped in front of a small ticket booth at the top of a long hill. Demi unbuckled her seat belt. "No, no, this is just to get the tickets. We will park over there," he pointed to the bottom of the road.

"I'll buy the tickets," Demi said. "You drove."

"Yes, I drive, so I will buy the tickets," Stavros said, opening the car door.

Demi got out and followed Stavros to the short line at the ticket booth.

"I can buy my own ticket," Demi said.

"Of course, you can," Stavros said. "But not today." He walked up to the cashier who, despite the warm afternoon, wore her dark hair long.

She smiled at Stavros. "*Boro na sas voithiso*—may I help you?"

"*Thio sitiria, parakalo*" he said, reaching into the back pocket of his jeans for his wallet and passing the requisite number of euros under the plexiglass partition.

Demi sighed and folded her arms.

"*Orieste*," the cashier handed him the tickets. "*Na perasete kala.*" She smiled in amusement, with a barely perceptible glance towards Demi.

"What did she say?" Demi asked, fully aware of the nuanced motion.

"She say you are very beautiful," Stavros said.

Demi rolled her eyes. "She did not." *Where were Sophie and her app when she needed them*?

"*Ela*," Stavros said, and they got back into the car. At the bottom of the hill, cars were tightly wedged into parking spaces that paralleled the road, so he pulled into the first space that he saw along the side of the road under a row of pine trees. "We are too late," he said.

"Too late? Didn't you just get tickets?"

"Yes, too late. I think morning is better." Stavros said. "But it's okay. We are here." He got out of the car and flipped the car seat forward. He reached in back and grabbed a dark blue hoodie.

They walked down the hill behind the main entrance to a large shelter overlooking the sea. Several picnic tables sat on a concrete platform under a wooden slat roof. Most of them were occupied. Stavros looked at the time on the tickets. "*Yamoto*," he said. "This is not good."

"What?" said Demi.

"We have to wait."

She looked across the bay from the cliffside. Across the harbor, the topography transformed from rocky cliff to a long, flat, white sand beach. Behind the beach, a grey mountain towered over the foothills, which were thick with pine trees. A dozen small fishing boats dotted the harbor with splashes of red, white, and pale blue. The water, blue-green below them, darkened into a deep indigo where it met the horizon. Demi inhaled, tasting the sea and the forest. "It's so beautiful. Do you want to sit in the sun?"

Stavros raised his chin, and Demi recognized the subtle expression for 'no.' "It's too hot," he said.

Demi held her forearm up to Stavros' arm. Her tan looked pale in comparison to Stavros' olive hue. Her slim arm brushed his muscular forearm, and she caught her breath at the slight chill running up her spine. She pulled her arm away. "I need some sun," she said.

Stavros pointed to a table in the corner of the shelter. The sun's rays caught one end of the empty table; the other end sat in the shade. "*Ela*," he said.

He sat down at the picnic table in the shade of the roof. Demi sat down across from him, the sun on her back. "Do you want a frappe?" Stavros said.

"That sounds great. I'll get it," Demi said. She untucked her leg and swung her legs around the bench, but Stavros was already on his way to the café.

Unbelievable, she thought. She turned her attention to the table beside her, where two pale young blond girls ran in circles around their equally pale blond parents. Each time they completed a circle, the mother reached out to catch them, and they shrieked, their squeals rising above the underlying chatter of the other tables. *I hope they're not with our group,* Demi thought. The afternoon sun baked her back and arms, and rivulets of perspiration formed on her forehead and in the middle of her back. Her dark leggings sucked in the heat, and the bottoms of her thighs began to sweat.

Stavros returned with two frappes and held one out to Demi. "Your frappe, Madam."

"*Efharisto,*" Demi said. She took a sip of the cold, frothy coffee. "This is perfect."

"*Telios,*" he said.

"*Telios?*"

"Perfect."

Slowly, covertly, Demi slid down the bench an inch at a time towards the middle of the table. Stavros gasped in mock surprise. "Demi, you have lost the sun!"

"It's too hot," she admitted reluctantly.

"Yes, didn't I say this?" he asked.

Demi set her frappe down and put her elbows on the table, resting her chin on her folded hands. She looked directly at Stavros. "Why did you bring me to the caves? You've been here before. I'm sure you don't want to see them again. You must have better things to do."

Stavros folded his arms on the table and leaned forward. "*Mayia.* I bring you to see magic. The caves of Diros are said to be . . ." Stavros held his hand palm upward, searching for a lost word, "*thavmata tou kosmou.* There are seven. This is the next one."

"Wonders of the world? The eighth wonder of the world?"

"Yes. When something is so special, you want to see it again. You don't get tired of it." He took her hands in between his and looked into her eyes. "I want to show this to you."

* * *

"How cool is this one, Mom!" Sophie held a glass bead up to the light streaming in from the open doorway. Inside the translucent turquoise bead, a silver channel caught the light, and the bead sparkled. She bent over the tray of beads, sifting through them with her fingers like a bird foraging for food.

Zoe peeked out from behind the rack of gauzy sundresses and kaftans nestled among the trays and tables of beads and jewelry. "Sophie, could you please make up your mind? We've been here for almost a half hour." She held up the paper bag with a blue and white striped sundress inside and waved it at Sophie. "I've already checked out, and I'm sure that Charles is tired of looking at beads."

"Not a problem," Charles said. "The beads are quite lovely. However, I do have a suggestion—why don't we have tea while we wait for Sophie? She can meet us when she's done."

Sophie glanced up from the wooden tray of beads, which were partitioned into small squares of assorted blues and greens. Some of the slots held 'mati' beads—the traditional blue and white 'eye' design, reputed to ward off evil. She looked at Zoe. "That's a good idea, Mom. Then I won't feel rushed."

"How will you know where to find us?" Zoe looked around the room as if Sophie might disappear behind a tray of beads.

Charles put his hand behind Zoe's back and steered her past a rack of organic incense towards the door. A hint of sandalwood, rose, and lavender infused the air. "Mmm, lovely," he said and breathed in slowly. He looked back at Sophie. "We are turning right, Sophie. We'll be at the first *kafenio* you come across."

"Okay," she said, absorbed again with the vast assortment of beads, clasps, and wires.

"Sophie!"

"What, Mom?"

"Did you hear Charles?"

"Yes," Sophie said. "You'll be at the first coffee shop. On the right. I will find you. I'll see you in an hour."

"An hour!" Zoe said.

"Just kidding, Mom." She looked over at the table of small glass tumblers, which held a rainbow of tiny seed beads from bright yellow greens and vibrant reds to deep violets. "I think . . ."

Charles guided Zoe out the door and into the bright sunshine. Zoe took her oversized sunglasses out of her bag and put them on.

"You look quite glamorous," Charles said. He pointed to the breezy patterned scarves loosely knotted over a wooden rack outside the door. "Add one of those scarves, and you could be mistaken for Audrey Hepburn."

"Hmm. More like Barbra Streisand," Zoe laughed.

"Well, I am partial to Barbra," Charles said. They walked single-file down the narrow sidewalk past old stone shops and whitewashed buildings until they came to a *kafeneio* where patrons occupied most of the round tile-topped tables on the patio. "Here we go," Charles said, ushering Zoe to a table in the shade of a green awning and pulling out the wooden chair for her. She sat down and slung her purse strap over her head and across her body.

"You shouldn't do that, you know," Charles said.

"What, wear my purse like this?"

"No, no. You shouldn't be so self-deprecating. You're a lovely woman. I meant what I said."

"Oh, thank you. I guess I'm not used to compliments. I've never been very confident in my appearance. My husband was always criticizing me—my clothes, my makeup, or lack of it, my body."

"Was?"

"I'm divorced."

A serious-looking young waiter approached the table. "Two hot teas," Charles said. "And some biscuits."

"We don't have biscuits. We have *finikia, galatobourika, diples*, no biscuits." He turned and walked away before Charles could reply.

"I'd say I'm sorry, but it sounds like you're better off without him," Charles said. "My husband makes cracks once in a while, but I give it right back to him."

"Your husband?" *Huh*, Zoe thought, *didn't see that coming.*

"Yes—Peter. We've been married eight years in November. He's in finance; I'm a writer. Of course, he thinks I'm wasting my time, but I do alright. We don't always see eye to eye, but it works. We both love Greece. We met here. Unfortunately, he couldn't come this year, but we're already planning a trip to the islands next year.

Zoe was quiet.

"So sorry. Didn't mean to carry on. Have I upset you?'

"No, not at all. I was just thinking about Georgia. Her husband thinks she's wasting her time, too. But she loves writing. She comes alive when she talks about it."

"I noticed that at her book talk. Now, *there's a woman who loves what she does*, I thought to myself. Pity her husband doesn't see that."

"Yes, it is."

The waiter returned with a tray of cups, a bottle of amber honey, a small ceramic pitcher of cream, and a glass carafe of hot water. He set these down, along with a box of assorted English teas and a plate of butter cookies. "No biscuits—*koulourakia*."

"*Efharisto*," said Charles. He pointed to Zoe's cup. "May I?" he asked. He selected two English breakfast teas, poured hot water into their cups, and stirred a teaspoon of honey into each. He handed Zoe a cup and saucer. "What about you, Zoe? What do you do when you're not traveling the Greek countryside with a hapless romantic?"

"Um, isn't it a hopeless romantic?'

"No, no, quite meant to say hapless. Play on words, you know. Never mind. Tell me about Zoe."

Zoe looked across the street at a park where several benches surrounded a cobblestone courtyard. The benches were empty, but a group of children laughed and chased each other around a large stone fountain. A stray orange cat watched them from the top of a tall green garbage can. The *coo-coo-ri-coo* of a mourning dove sounded from the trees. Zoe looked back at Charles. "I work for Benton and Bruin—it's a large advertising agency. I've worked in their Public Relations department for about ten years."

"Do you enjoy it?"

"I love collaborating with clients. I've never really felt comfortable at the company. It's pretty much an 'old boys' network, and I'm one of the token females. I'm good at what I do, but I don't know how far I can go until I hit the glass ceiling."

"No chance of shattering it?"

"Highly unlikely."

"Why stay, then?"

Zoe lifted her cup and blew on her tea. She didn't answer.

"Sorry if I'm too blunt. Peter says I ask too many questions."

"No, it's okay. I've tried to figure that out myself. I have a decent salary and good benefits, and the work itself is fulfilling."

"But. . ."

"I don't want to go to another agency. Most of them are still male-dominated. At least where I am, I have credibility. And the clients respect me, even if the owners don't."

"Have you thought about starting your own PR business?"

"I have. It would be a lot of work, and I'd have to take a pay cut. I can't afford to do that and keep my house at the same time."

"You love your house," Charles said in more of a statement than a question.

"It's the one the girls grew up in." Zoe dunked a cookie into her tea and shook the excess liquid from it. She took a small bite. "It's their home."

"They still live there, then?"

"No, of course not," Zoe said. "Marina lives with Demi, and Sophie lives downtown, close to work.

"I see," Charles said, pausing before continuing. "Pardon my manners, but as I told you, I can be blunt. I was terrified of quitting my sales job to become a full-time writer." Charles wrote in the air with an imaginary pen, which he then pointed at Zoe. "That's right, I was a salesman—sold industrial cleaners, and I was pretty good at it. But I took the plunge. It took a few years, but once 'Tales of the Duck' took off, I knew I'd made the right decision."

Zoe held her teacup up to her mouth with both hands. She looked over it at Charles. "But, what if 'Tales of the Duck' hadn't taken off?"

"Well," he paused, resting his chin in his hand. "Then, at least, I would have tried."

"It's not that easy doing it alone," Zoe said.

"No, I don't suppose it is. But nothing worth pursuing ever comes easy. Just ask Peter," he winked.

* * *

Demi and Stavros joined the group of ticket holders and walked down the corridor of steep steps to a large room with racks of flotation devices. Once again, Demi found herself wearing an orange life vest. The guide ushered the patrons through a doorway and down another set of steps to the docking area, where the cool, humid air was in stark contrast to the hot, dry air outside. They were guided in groups of five or six to blue and white rowboats, which stood out from the darkness of the passageways beyond.

"*Prosekse* Demi," Stavros said. "Be careful." He took her by the elbow, and she stepped into the front of the boat with one foot. It wobbled, and she stabilized herself before putting the other foot in. Stavros jumped into the boat and joined her in the front seat, barely wide enough for two people. "We are lucky," he said. "Here, we have the best view."

"I'm not sure we're that lucky," Demi said, looking behind her. The family from the gazebo was boarding the boat. The father lifted one of the little girls and placed her in the seat behind Demi and Stavros, then lifted the other daughter and sat her next to her sister. Dad and Mom sat behind them. The girls squealed as the boat rocked gently. A man with an oar boarded the boat in the stern. "*Ta heria sas mesa*," he said. "Keep your hands inside the boat at all times." That was the last English they would hear from their Greek guide. He pushed off with the oar, and the boat slipped into the darkness.

The guide spoke, his voice echoing through the stillness of the caves, but his words were lost on everyone in the boat except for Stavros. "We are in *Vlychada*," Stavros translated. "The largest cave at Diros. The caves they are very long, 33,000 square meters, maybe as far as Sparta." The guide pushed his oar gently against the cave wall, guiding the boat down the dark passageway and around the stalagmites whose mounds and columns had been formed by calcium salts deposited by dripping water over tens of thousands of years. Spotlights placed at intervals illuminated the turns in the passage and cast shadows of dense grey stalactites on the cave walls. Suspended from the roof of the cave, they resembled icicles, although they were thick and opaque compared to the translucence of ice. Beads of water trickled from the stalactites, echoing throughout the caves as they plopped onto the water.

The passageway narrowed, and the guide spoke. "*Valte ta kefalia sas kato*."

"Put your heads down," Stavros turned and spoke to the other passengers. "Now!" he emphasized, as the roof of the cave suspended within inches of their heads. The passengers obeyed. The little girls screamed, their voices piercing the eerie stillness.

"It's alright," their mother spoke in what sounded to Demi like an Australian accent. "You're fine."

"It's like a fairy tale where the princess is kidnapped, and the prince goes through a maze to find her!" one of the little girls said.

"No, no, it's like Beauty and the Beast, but the Beast lives here, and Beauty brings him food on the boat!' The girls started chatting between themselves, their voices at odds with the serenity of the caves.

"Girls, be quiet," their father said. They giggled and continued to talk.

Stavros turned around and spoke to them in a whisper. Their eyes got large, and they peered over the sides of the boat. They were silent.

"What did you tell them?" asked Demi.

"I tell them they must be quiet, or they will wake the monster who live in the caves."

Demi giggled. "That was clever," she said.

"What you mean?"

"Coming up with that story."

Stavros stared at Demi. "Is not a story, Demi. You don't know about Hades? Read your *mythologia*." He turned to face forward.

Demi looked closely at Stavros for a trace of a smile but saw none in his profile. The girls behind them remained silent.

They wove through vast formations of rock, where some of the stalactites and stalagmites had joined to form dense pillars. Several times, they ducked their heads. "I think Sophie made the right choice," Demi said. "She would not have enjoyed this."

"But you are enjoying this?" Stavros asked.

"Yes, it's amazing!" Demi said. They traveled deeper into the caverns, where the colors of the caves changed from caramel and yellow ochre to a deep red-brown. *It looks like the underside of a portobello mushroom*, Demi thought. The air became cooler, and she shivered.

"You are cold," Stavros said.

"No, I'm fine," Demi replied.

"Of course," Stavros said, looking at the goosebumps on Demi's arms.

"Okay, it's a little chilly in here," Demi said.

Stavros unbuckled his life vest and took it off. The guide said something to him. "*Ena lepto*," Stavros said, holding up his index finger. He took off his hoodie and offered it to Demi. Her mouth opened, then closed again. She removed her life vest to admonishment from the guide, and put on the hoodie, then replaced the life vest.

"Thank you," she said. The hoodie enveloped her in warmth and a mild, fresh scent, perhaps aftershave or soap. Demi breathed it in.

The guide turned the boat into a passageway where the caves now appeared to transform into shades of mint, sage, and mossy green. Using his oar to push away from the cave walls, he steered the boat around large pillars draped in white crystal. He spoke again, his words echoing in the chambers of the caves. "What did he say?" Demi asked.

"He say there is another cave, *Alepotrypa*—it mean fox hole. We do not go there today, but they have explored this cave. They find beads, *angia,"* Stavros made the shape of a vase with his hands, "and *kokkala*." Demi recognized the word for bones. Stavros continued, "And *skeletous* of two people. They are in a, how you say?" He hugged himself tightly.

"Embrace?" Demi said.

"Yes. It is 5800 years this way."

"That's so sad," Demi said.

"No, it's not," Stavros said, looking intently at Demi. "It is beautiful."

"How is it beautiful?" she asked.

"Because they are together forever."

* * *

"Oh, my goodness," Zoe said, glancing down at her watch. "We've been here almost an hour. I wonder what's keeping Sophie. What if she got lost?"

Charles smiled. "It's doubtful that she would get lost walking down the street. Perhaps she stopped at one of the other stores."

"I don't think she'd do that when she knew we were waiting for her." Zoe stood up and pulled at her cotton skirt, which had stuck to the backs of her thighs. She looked down the street. "I don't see her. I'm going back to the bead shop."

"I can't imagine she'd still be there," Charles said. "How long does it take to pick out a few beads?"

"You don't know Sophie," Zoe laughed. "Although, this would be a record. I'm sure she's okay, but I'd feel better finding her."

"Of course," Charles said. "I'll head down the street and peek into the stores on the way, just in case. He called to the waiter, "*Parakalo*," then turned to Zoe. "I'll get the bill—go ahead, I'll be right behind you."

Zoe picked up her pace despite the midday heat. In the five minutes it took her to reach the bead shop, rivulets of sweat had begun to run down her back. She walked through the open doorway and stopped. A tall woman in a flowered dress stood by the door, holding a stick of incense up to her nose. Beyond her, Sophie stood at the counter with a rainbow of beads on the tray in front of her. At the bottom of the tray were bright red and coral beads; the top of the tray was filled with turquoise beads and blue shades of glass. Off to the side was a small pile of patterned beads with delicate designs etched into the glass, along with a few of the *mati* designs. Zoe stared at her daughter.

From the shadow blocking the light, Sophie sensed someone at the doorway and glanced up. She squinted at the backlit form and realized that it was Zoe. "Oh, hi, Mom," she smiled. "I thought you were going for coffee."

"Hmm, she is having a bit of trouble making up her mind," said the shop owner behind the counter. She smiled indulgently at Sophie and then shrugged her shoulders at Zoe. "Maybe you can help her?"

Zoe walked over to the counter. "Mom, look at these," Sophie said, pointing to the tray. "I can't decide which ones to pick."

"Maybe you should buy them all?" the owner offered.

"Oh, I don't have time to do that much beadwork," Sophie said. "But they're all so pretty."

"Why don't you pick out the ones that remind you the most of Greece?" Zoe suggested.

"Oh, that's a great idea!" Sophie peered closely at the tray of beads. "The red ones remind me of those fiery sunsets we saw in Santorini." She picked up one of the coral beads, then set it down and picked up a bright blue bead. "But the blue ones remind me of the sea. And the *mati* is so traditional." She sighed.

"Excuse me," the woman in the flowered dress approached the counter. She walked up between Zoe and Sophie with a tray of beads topped with a dozen sticks of incense. "May I?"

"Oh, of course," Sophie said. She slid her tray to the side of the counter and moved out of the woman's way. The woman set her tray down, and the shop owner rang up her purchase. The woman glanced at Sophie's tray.

"Those are lovely," she said. "Why don't you take all of them?"

"Oh, I'd love to, but I don't need that many beads."

"There you are!" Charles' voice boomed into the doorway. "You haven't run off to join a traveling circus then. Happy to see you're all in one piece." He traded places with the woman in the flowered dress as she left the shop, then looked down at Sophie's tray. "You've had some success, I see."

Zoe looked at Charles. "She's having a little trouble making up her mind."

"I can see why," Charles said. "They're lovely." He pointed his index finger up. "I have an idea," he said. "Why don't you take them all? You'll think of Greece whenever you're making jewelry with them—and whenever you're wearing it."

"Oh," said Sophie. "That's a great idea!"

Zoe rubbed her temples with her hands and shook her head.

"Perfect," said the bead shop owner. "Do you need any clasps or rings?" Zoe looked directly at her and shook her head surreptitiously.

"Oh. Um, yes, I do."

"Silver or gold?"

* * *

Georgia wove her fingers together and pushed her hands, palms upwards, towards the ceiling, leaning back in her chair for a deep stretch. She brought her arms down and raised her shoulders, circling them backward, then forward. She looked left, then right, then repeated the shoulder circles.

"I can find you a chiropractor," Gloria said, watching Georgia closely.

"Oh, no!" Georgia laughed, "I'm just stiff from sitting here. I need to take a walk."

"We have a break before the next session," Gloria said. "Would you like to get a coffee?"

"I think I've had enough coffee, but thank you. Actually, I think I'm going to skip the next session. I'm not really into writing poetry."

"In that case, do you want to have lunch?"

Georgia hesitated, not wanting to hurt Gloria's feelings. "Thanks so much, Gloria, but honestly, between the LitFest and my family, I haven't had any time alone. I think I just need to clear my head a bit. I'll see you this evening."

Gloria tilted her head and smiled a close-lipped smile. "I understand," she said. "No problem."

Georgia rolled up her sweater and stuffed it into her bag along with her notebook, which was now full of publishing information and some contacts. Her mind was brimming with ideas, and she couldn't wait to talk them over with Zoe. She got up from her chair and slung the bag over her shoulder. She followed the other authors out of the room and into the brilliant afternoon. The outside air was hot and dry, and Georgia paused on the steps, not sure what to do with her afternoon. A walk? Lunch? A siesta? Some sun? She looked at her watch, wondering if it was too early to call Jimmy. Seven hours difference put him at five a.m. He might not appreciate the early wake-up. She would phone him later. She walked across the square past the main plateia, where a few tourists were sitting down for an early lunch. *Too early to have lunch,* she thought. She wasn't hungry yet, although the tangy aroma of sizzling souvlaki generated a slight rumble in her stomach.

"*Kiria Giorgia*," called a male voice from across the street, where several small outside tavernas and *kafenieos* bordered the gulf. She turned her head to see Yiorgos sitting with three other men. He waved at her.

"*Kalimera*, Yiorgo," she waved.

"*Ela*," he waved her over. "Come to have a coffee."

She crossed the street and approached the group. One of the men she recognized from the previous evening. She did not know the others, and he introduced her. "This is the famous American writer," he said.

"I'm not," she said. "Famous, I mean. But I am a writer."

One of the men pulled a chair over from the next table.

"Oh, no, thank you," she said. "I've had enough coffee already this morning."

"Then stay for the *parea*," Yiorgos said with a wide smile, spreading his arms to encompass the group.

Georgia smiled. "I appreciate the offer, but I really need some time to myself."

"Time to yourself?" Yiorgos asked. "You are in Greece. Take time for yourself when you are home. Here, you must see everything, do everything. Please, sit down," he said, pointing to the empty chair.

"Only for a few minutes," Georgia said and sat down. The other men turned back to their conversation, speaking in rapid Greek.

"Where are the *koritsia* today?" Yiorgos asked.

"Sophie is with Zoe and Charles, the British writer. They went to Kardamyli to do some shopping."

"Ah, yes. Chaarlos," he said, drawing out the first syllable.

"What do you mean?"

"Nothing, *Kiria* Georgia. I just say, Charlos. He is a little—how you say—*piestikos*?"

"Pesty? Pushy? *Charles* is pushy?" She looked at Yiorgos and shook her head, laughing.

Yiorgos ignored the inference. "And the beautiful Demi?"

"She went to the Caves of Diros with a young man."

"Stavros," he nodded.

"You know Stavros?"

"*Vevaios,* I know him. He call me to take you to Gytheio."

"Well, yes, of course, but I didn't realize that he was calling *you*, specifically."

Yiorgos continued. "When a beautiful American girl comes to the village, Stavros will find her."

"I see," Georgia said, a knot of concern taking shape in her stomach.

Yiorgos saw her frown. "No, no, no. Is okay. Stavros is a good boy."

"And you, Yiorgos? Are you a good boy?" Georgia leaned toward Yiorgos and raised her eyebrows. "Or do you also look out for American women?"

"Beautiful American women," Yiorgos corrected. "Of course. What kind of man would I be?"

Georgia laughed. "Not a Greek one, I suppose."

Yiorgos reached for her hand, but Georgia drew it away. "Yiorgos, I told you. I'm married."

"Ah, but you are in Greece," he began, reaching again for her hand.

"*Vre, Malaka*," his friend said, laughing. "She don't want you. Maybe she want me," he said, puffing out his chest and pointing to it. A barrage of rapid Greek ensued, and Georgia leaned back in her chair and looked out at the marina. Several small wooden fishing boats tied to metal plates on the concrete docking area bobbed on their moorings. On the sidewalk, dozens of octopuses dried in the sun, draped over thick ropes attached to tall metal poles. Behind the string of tentacles, Georgia saw a flash of red hair.

"Gloria!" she called. She realized that Gloria must have seen her as she walked past the coffee shop. "Gloria!" she called again.

Gloria stopped and peered through the string of octopuses. "I guess you changed your mind."

"Oh, Gloria," Georgia said. "Come here, join us, please."

Gloria walked towards the tables. She hesitated, looking back and forth between Georgia and Yiorgos. "I don't want to interrupt anything."

"You aren't," Georgia said. "Please, sit down."

"Yes, *vevaios, kathiste*," Yiorgos said, getting to his feet and pulling another chair over to the group.

"I thought you had enough coffee," Gloria said, still peevish. "I thought you needed time to yourself."

Georgia laughed. "I've found that being in Greece doesn't permit either of those things!"

* * *

The guide steered the boat to a makeshift dock and spoke to the group in Greek. "From here, you walk," Stavros told them. "It is about 15 minutes." The little girls stood up quickly, and the boat rocked. "*Prosekse*!" the guide shouted, and they sat down again.

"Come on, here we go," the father said, lifting one of the little girls and handing her to the mother, who had gotten out of the boat. He repeated the process with the second daughter, and the girls began to run down the slippery stone path. "Oi, girls, for God's sake, slow down!" their mother said, her words echoing in the caverns. "Roger, stop them," she yelled at her husband, who was already upon the girls.

"Here we go," their father said, scooping them both up, one in each arm. "What is the hurry, girls?"

"We want to get away from the monster!" one of the girls said. The other nodded, her eyes large.

"What monster?" the father asked.

Demi looked at Stavros and giggled. "Uh oh, you're in for it now," she said.

"In for it?"

"Never mind," Demi said. She stood up, and the boat rocked again. Stavros hopped out of the boat and put his arm out to Demi. He clasped her arm and pulled her onto the dock area. The guide pushed off with his oar and drifted towards the canal. The Australian family had disappeared down the path, and Demi and Stavros stood alone, surrounded by the cool stillness of the caves. Stavros still held on to Demi's arm. She didn't know if it was the cold air in the cavern or the nearness of Stavros that took her breath away. With his free hand, he brushed a loose hair from her forehead and smiled down at her. She smiled back and held his eyes. He bent his head down, his lips close to hers.

"Euuww! They're kissing!"

Stavros and Demi broke their gaze to see the little Australian girls.

"No, they're not," the little blond girl said to her sister. "They're just hugging."

"Girls, come back here!" Their father's voice preceded him as he rounded the corner. "What in God's name are you doing?"

"I forgot Dolly!" the younger one said. "I left her in the boat." She looked at the dock where the boat had been. Her lower lip trembled, and she took several short breaths in preparation for the wail that was about to burst from her mouth.

Stavros squatted to face the girl and held a finger to his lips. "Shhh!" he said and nodded his head towards the water. "The boat will go back to the entrance. I'm sure you will find your *koukla* there."

The little one backed away slowly from Stavros, then turned and ran, followed by her sister, who ran to her father and grabbed his leg. "Don't you run away from me again!" their father scolded, hugging them both. Once again, they rounded the bend and disappeared.

Demi looked at Stavros, a question on her face. In answer, he grasped her arms and pulled her towards him. He leaned down a second time.

"We are at the end of our tour," a woman's voice echoed in the chambers as the next boat pulled up to the small docking area. "Please watch your step, *prosekse*."

Stavros put his palms upwards and shrugged. "Eh," he said, "what can you do?" He took Demi by the hand and walked towards the path that led to the exit.

CHAPTER 8

"Wait, so he *didn't* kiss you?"

"Well, not at that exact moment." Demi wiped the steam from the bathroom mirror with a white hotel towel. She wore another around her body and a smaller one turban-style on her wet hair.

Her cousin Marina's impatience burst through the cell phone speaker. "So, what happened?"

"Well, it was pretty awkward after that." Demi unwrapped the towel from her head, picked up a wide-toothed comb, and ran it through her damp hair. "He didn't say anything on the path out of the caves, and I wasn't sure what was going on. I felt like, I don't know, maybe the moment had passed or something for him. Not for me—I was super nervous, and I felt like my heart was going to explode. I was sure he could hear it!"

"So, then what happened?"

She squirted a dollop of mousse into her palms and massaged it into her hair. "*Ipomoni*, Marina. *Ipomoni*."

"You know I don't speak Greek."

"Patience, Marina. We'll get there." Demi paused and smiled again as she ran the mousse through her hair with her fingers. "So, we came out of the cave exit, and the sunlight was blinding. It was so hot out, and I was still wearing his hoodie. I took it off, and I was going to give it back to him . . ."

Marina burst out laughing. "Oh my god, you didn't! How many hoodies have you stolen?"

"I prefer 'borrowed,' thank you."

"Anyway . . ."

"Anyway," Demi continued, "I was going to give it back, but I tied it around my waist. So, we were walking back to the car, and the woman who was selling tickets . . ."

"The one who was flirting with Stavros?"

"Yes. There was no one in the ticket line, and she was outside of the booth, having a cigarette. She looked over at us and called out something to Stavros in Greek."

"What did she say?"

"I have no idea—she talked too fast. But he said something back to her, and she winked at him. And when I asked him what she said, he gave me some BS about how she hoped we enjoyed the caves."

"Couldn't that be what she said?"

"I don't know—she looked kind of snarky to me." Demi picked up the phone and took it to the bed, where she sat down and crossed her legs, still wrapped in the damp towel. "So, we got in the car, and Stavros asked me if I wanted to go to the beach. I told him I didn't have a bathing suit, and he said it didn't matter; we could still go enjoy the sea. There was a public beach right by the caves—you could see it from the mountain, and I thought that was where we were going, but we drove for about fifteen minutes, and he pulled off the side of the road, and we walked down a rocky path into a little cove. The water was so clear. It was gorgeous. It was so hot out. So, he said he was going to go for a swim. And then, he took off his jeans and tee shirt." Demi thought back to Stavros's muscled body.

"So, um, what did you do?"

"Well, it *was* hot out. So, I stripped down to my underwear."

"Oh . . . My . . . God . . ." Marina stopped. "Wait. Which underwear?" As Demi's roommate, she was familiar with the contents of Demi's underwear drawer. "Not the 'Hello Kitty' combo?"

"No," Demi laughed. "Just your standard blue thong."

"What! Oh my god, what did he do?"

"Nothing. He was already in the water."

"Guarantee he was watching you."

"Duh."

A brief silence hung on the line while Demi mulled over the events of the afternoon, and Marina waited for the next part of the story.

"So, then I went in. The water was incredible. It was so refreshing, and you could see down to the bottom of the rocks. I walked out to where Stavros was, and then all of a sudden, the water got deep, so we just swam for a while."

"Wait, *you* were swimming?"

"Well, not exactly. More like treading water. Anyway, I didn't last that long—I got kind of tired. I guess I haven't worked out in a while. Luckily, I had the hoodie with me, so I didn't have to get my butt sandy. And then I figured, well, it's just sand, and I'm tired, so I decided to lay down. And the next thing I know, Stavros is lying down next to me . . ." As if to demonstrate, she plopped back on the bed.

"And?"

Demi turned over onto her stomach and talked into the speaker. "And then he leaned on his elbow and stared down at me." Demi closed her eyes and pictured Stavros with sand coating his damp body. "His hair was dripping onto my face, and I started laughing. Then he smiled at me, and I swear my breath caught in my throat. He brought his face down to mine . . ."

"And then two little Australian girls came running from around the rocks."

Demi laughed. "Nope. Not this time."

* * *

"*Kali spera, Kiria Karras,* good evening," Mihali glanced up from where he was bent over his computer to greet Georgia.

"*Kali spera, Mihali,*" Georgia replied. "How are you?"

Mihali sat up, surprised at the pleasantry. "*Kala, Kiria, Efharisto.*"

"Do you know if my sister has returned yet?"

Mihali raised his chin and eyebrows to indicate 'no.' "I have not seen *Kiria* Zoe and Miss Sophie, but I believe your daughter has returned."

"Thank you, Mihali. *Efharisto.*"

Georgia walked through the door and up the marble staircase, dragging from the late afternoon heat. *So much for alone time,* she thought.

Coffee had turned into lunch, and lunch into wine. She didn't know which she wanted more—a nap or a shower.

She reached the room and turned the key quietly in the lock in case Demi was sleeping. Upon opening the door, her suspicions were confirmed. Demi lay sprawled across her bed in her white bath towel, her face smashed into the pillow. A wave of nostalgia caught Georgia's breath short as she remembered so many times that Demi, as a little girl, would pass out on the couch in the same position, head smooshed into the pillow, when she had insisted that she wasn't sleepy.

Georgia peeled off her pants and blouse and went into the bathroom. She let the shower run until the water was tepid. The stream of water from the shower head was cooling, and as much as she hated to waste water, she let it run over her body for a few minutes before washing her hair and scrubbing her body. She slid open the shower curtain and reached for her towel. The rack was empty. She walked out onto the floor mat and glanced at the towel racks, but there were no towels on them. *Dammit, Demi*, she thought.

A knock sounded at the door. "*Ena lepto*," Georgia called. "One minute!" She grabbed her robe and wrapped it around her wet body. She opened the door a crack to see the housekeeper at the door. "You call for more towels," she said. "I'm sorry they are late—we just finish the washing."

"*Efharisto*," she said, mentally apologizing to Demi. She removed her now-damp robe and wrapped one towel around her body, hanging her robe up to dry, and one towel around her head before collapsing on the bed herself.

* * *

"*Kali spera, Kiria* Zoe. *Kali spera,* Miss Sophia." Mihalis spoke from behind his computer; then, as an afterthought, he stood up and nodded. "*Ti kanete*? You had a nice day in Kardamyli?"

"Yes, thank you, Mihali," Zoe smiled. "It was lovely. Do you know if my sister is back yet?"

"*Kiria* Karras arrived about an hour ago."

Sophie glanced eagerly around the lobby, then peered into the dining room.

"You have lost something, Miss Sophia?" Mihalis said, straight-faced.

"Um," she said, still scanning the small lobby. "No, nothing . . ."

"Ah, good," Mihalis said. "Because, if you had, I have no one here to help you look for it. Dinos is not working tonight."

Sophie's face flushed, and Zoe pressed her lips together to suppress her smile. *Clever man*, she thought. "Let's go get a nap before dinner," she said to Sophie.

"Just a quick one," said Sophie. "Not one of those marathon naps like yesterday. I'd like to eat before ten o'clock."

"It's only five now, Sophie. I think we'll be fine." Zoe opened the door to the stairwell. "*Kalispera*, Mihali. See you later."

"Yes, *tha ta poume*, Kiria. See you later."

* * *

Once again, Georgia woke to the whirring of the hair dryer. Outside the window, the evening sky was a hazy blue, but it was not dark yet. She was chilled from the air conditioner, and she knocked on the bathroom door. "Demi? I need my robe," she called from the bedroom. She heard the hair dryer stop, and Demi opened the door a crack, handing Georgia the robe through the opening. "*Efharisto*," she said. The dryer clicked back on. Georgia removed the damp towel from her hair, which was almost dry, and fluffed her hair with her fingers. She knocked on the door again. "Demi, I need the mousse before my hair completely dries." Once again, the door opened, and Demi handed her the can of mousse. "Oh, for goodness' sake, Demi. Since when don't we share a bathroom? Let me come in so I can rinse my hands off."

Demi turned off the hair dryer and opened the door. "Geeze, Mom, I'm almost done." She still wore her towel wrapped around her body.

"I thought you were going to the caves today," Georgia said, noticing the tinge of red on Demi's shoulders and chest.

"We did, and then we went to the beach." Demi unplugged the dryer and plugged in the curling iron.

"Well, how was your day? Did you have fun?"

"It was fine." Demi's mouth turned up in a half smile. "The caves were amazing!"

"And?"

"And what? The beach was nice, too."

Georgia looked closely at her daughter. "Since when don't you tell me about your dates, Demi?"

"Since I haven't been going on dates, Mom. I'm out of practice, remember? And this wasn't a date."

Georgia raised her eyebrows and looked directly at Demi.

"Okay, fine. Maybe it was kind of a date. Just don't make too much of it."

"I'm not making anything out of it," Georgia replied. "Did you have a good time?"

"Yes, I had a good time," Demi said. She looked sideways at Georgia, then closed the toilet lid and sat down. "Okay, fine," she said, and Georgia knew she was in for a story.

* * *

Stavros sipped a strong Greek coffee in the plateia under the enormous plane tree whose thick, gnarled branches reached out to shade a large area of the square. His friend Elias leaned back in his chair as he sipped an ouzo and scanned the plateia. At this hour of the evening, there were few women in the square. Men sipped coffees or ouzos at *kafenios* along the perimeter of the square where they played *tavli*, as they called backgammon, in quiet concentration, the only sounds the rattling of the dice and the clacking of the game pieces as they were collected. "So, you have found another one, eh?" he chided Stavros, raising his dark eyebrows.

"This woman is different," Stavros said.

Elias set down his glass and looked at Stavros. "Yes? What is so special about her?"

"I have never met anyone like her before. She is stealing my heart."

"*Vlakies*!" Elias said. "It will end like all the others. Spare her the misery."

"Stavro!" a voice called from inside the restaurant. Stavros looked up to see the furrowed brow of Dimitris, a stocky, middle-aged man, in the frame of the doorway. "The meat is not going to grill itself!"

"Okay, okay, I'm coming." He took a sip of water and set down the glass. "Tomorrow, you will meet her, and you will see what is so special about her."

"Is she pretty?" Elias asked.

"Pretty?" Stavros asked. "No, she is beautiful."

Elias shook his head and laughed. "That's what you say about all of them."

"No," Stavros said. "Dimitra is different. She is beautiful in the way a wild violet is beautiful. At first, it blends in with the others." He leaned over his coffee cup, put his elbows on the table, and pointed to his eyes. "But, when you look closely at this one, you see the face of the violet—soft yellow in the middle and deep blue petals that fade to white along the edges of the flower. Only then, when you realize the beauty of the violet, you are captivated."

"*Vre, Malaka*, is she a flower or a woman?"

Stavros smiled. "She is both."

* * *

The late afternoon sun had dissipated, rendering the sky a soft, dusky grey. Georgia, still in her robe, opened the balcony doors, letting in a warm gulf breeze. She turned back and called to Demi, who had finished her story and was now using the curling iron on her hair. "We better pick up the pace—we have an early start tomorrow, so I don't want to be out too late tonight." She glanced at a mound of dark blue material on the floor next to Demi's bed. Georgia picked it up by the hood and held her arm straight out, dangling the large hoodie in front of her. "Demi? I don't remember you packing a hoodie?"

"I didn't."

"Then where . . . oh, for goodness' sake." Georgia laughed, remembering the grey Harvard hoodie hanging from the hook in Demi's apartment and the faded black "Skater Boi" hoodie still in Demi's old closet at home, along with a few random sweatshirts. "You could dress a football team with the number of hoodies you've 'borrowed.'"

Demi came out of the bathroom, smiling. "Maybe just the defense," she retorted. She traded places with Georgia, who went into the bathroom to finish her hair and makeup while Demi dressed. "Mom," she called, "have you talked to Dad today?"

"Oh, crap! I forgot to call him. I was going to call earlier, but I didn't want to wake him up. I guess I lost track of time."

Demi glanced at the small clock on the nightstand, doing a quick calculation. "It's two o'clock at home now."

"Oh, good," Georgia said. "Why don't you call him on my phone? He'll be glad to hear your voice. I can talk to him when you're done."

"Sounds good," Demi said. She picked up Georgia's phone from the end table and hit Jimmy's number on speed dial.

"My unlock is "Demi90," Georgia called from the bathroom.

"Yeah, I know, Mom."

Georgia peeked around the doorframe. "How do you know?"

"Hello?" Demi spoke into the phone.

"Georgia? Where the hell have you been?" Jimmy's voice resonated through the phone. "I've been waiting to hear from you all day."

"Geeze, Dad, chill. It's Demi."

"Oh, hi, honey." His voice softened. "How are you?"

"I'm fine, how are you?"

"Where's Mom? Is everything okay?"

"Everything is fine. Mom's been busy with her workshop." Demi glanced towards the bathroom, where Georgia was peering closely at the mirror and plucking a stray eyebrow. "She's just fixing her hair. I just wanted to say hello."

"Fixing her hair? For what? Isn't it after nine o'clock there?"

"Yes, Dad. It's after nine o'clock. And it's Greece. I know you've been here. I know you know that people don't even go out to dinner until ten. What is all this about?"

"Nothing, Demi. Nothing. I'm glad you wanted to say hello. Are you having fun?"

"I am." She sat down on the bed and propped the pillow against the headboard.

"What have you been doing while Mom's in her workshops?"

"Oh, going to the beach, hanging around Gytheio. Oh, I went to the Caves of Diros today. They were amazing!"

"The Caves? Did they have a tour?"

"No, I went with Stavros. He's the one who got us a taxi when our car broke down."

"You went with a stranger to the caves? Did Sophie go with you?"

Demi considered a small white lie before answering. "No, Dad, Sophie did not go with me. I can take care of myself. You know that." Demi waited through the silence for her father's reply.

"I know, Demi. You always could. Sorry. Put your mom on the phone."

Demi whispered into the phone. "*Only if you're nice to her. Otherwise, I'm hanging up*."

"Of course, I'll be nice to her."

"You better," she warned. "Bye, Dad. I love you."

"I love you too, Demi."

Demi slid off the bed and called to Georgia. "Dad wants to talk to you."

Georgia came out of the bathroom, and Demi handed her the phone. "Wow, Mom. You look really pretty. I like your hair that way."

"Thanks, Sweetie." She put the phone to her ear. "Hi, Jimmy."

"What did you do to your hair?"

"What?"

"Your hair. I heard Demi say she likes your hair that way."

Georgia took a deep breath. "I smoothed it out. The humidity is low today. I thought I'd try something different."

"You never try anything different here."

"I do, but you don't notice. Seriously, Jimmy, is this how you want to start off this conversation?" Demi shook her head and reached for the phone, but Georgia waved her off.

The pause on the phone was followed by a quiet "No."

"Good," Georgia said. "So, how are you? How are things at home?"

Demi pulled on her halter top and long skirt while her parents' conversation hummed in the background. The tenseness which had accompanied Georgia's first few lines had evaporated. *Why do they argue so much*? Demi wondered.

"Alright, bye, honey," she heard her mother say. "I love you, too."

Georgia clicked off the phone and turned to Demi. "Okay, let me slip a dress on, and I'll be ready in a minute. Why don't you go knock on Zoe's door?"

"Okay," Demi said, but she hesitated.

"What's wrong, Demi?"

"Mom," she paused before continuing. "Is everything okay between you and Dad?"

"Of course it is," Georgia said. "Why do you ask?"

"It's just that . . . I don't know. Sometimes, you seem really frustrated with him. And sometimes, he's so short with you."

"Demi," Georgia said. She sat down on the bed and patted the spot next to her. Demi sat. "Thirty-five years is a long time to be with someone. You're not always going to agree with them. In fact, sometimes you're not going to agree with them at all. Yes, I get frustrated with Dad—he's stubborn and opinionated, and he's pretty set in his ways."

"Understatement of the year," interrupted Demi.

"But," Georgia said, "he loves me. And he loves you. Fiercely. And anything he does or says is with that love in his heart, even if it's misguided sometimes. As long as I remind myself of that, I can put up with him."

"But is that what you want?" Demi said. "Just to put up with someone?"

"Maybe I put that wrong, Demi. You take the good with the bad. You put up with someone's negative traits if their positive ones outweigh them. Dad is funny and clever; he'd do anything for me, and he's pretty sexy, too."

Demi covered her ears. "Don't want to hear that, Mom."

Georgia laughed. "Okay, okay, but Demi. Love—deep, lasting love—is more than just the heart palpitations you get when you first meet someone. Yes, it's physical, but it's a partnership. It grows—it has twists and turns. A lot of people don't weather those twists and turns—that's why the divorce rate is so high. And some people just aren't meant to be together."

"Like Aunt Zoe and Uncle Walker?"

Georgia sighed. "Sometimes high school sweethearts aren't meant to be. Uncle Walker and Aunt Zoe are very different people—time showed that. Zoe is driven and ambitious. She loves to travel and try new things. Walker was happy with a beer and his favorite TV show. Those are things you don't understand when you're in your twenties. You believe that love conquers all."

"I thought I understood Andrew," Demi said. "We were compatible. We had fun together. I really loved him." Demi closed her eyes to hold back the tears that were threatening to fall.

"Ah, Sweetheart," Georgia shook her head. "Don't put yourself through this again. Andrew got scared. He was afraid of commitment."

"Well, why didn't he say that when I got the job offer?" Her sadness turned to anger. "Why didn't he figure that out before I turned the job down? Before I stayed in Pittsburgh? Before I fucked up my career for him?"

Georgia looked directly at her daughter. "Demi, you turning down that opportunity for him was the ultimate sacrifice and the ultimate commitment. You are a romantic—there's nothing wrong with that." She smiled at Demi and continued. "Andrew wasn't ready for that."

Demi opened her mouth to object, but Georgia held up her finger. "I'm not condoning what he did. It was insensitive and hurtful. But you didn't fuck up your career—you're still gaining valuable experience. You're just on a different trajectory. And, if you weren't, you wouldn't be here in Greece right now, hanging around a handsome Greek man and about to go eat some delicious *kalamari* with your family." She hugged Demi and kissed her on the forehead.

"Thanks, Mom," Demi said. "I love you." She stood up, inhaled deeply, and let her breath out slowly. "I just need to give it some time." She picked up her shoulder bag, slung it across her body, and paused. "Um, Mom, about tomorrow . . ."

"Yes?"

"Would you be upset if I didn't go with you guys?"

"Upset?" Georgia looked up at Demi and shook her head. "No—but why? I thought you wanted to see Monemvasia."

"I do. I mean, I did. Well, I still do. But . . ." Demi shrugged. "I want to spend the time with Stavros. He's working tomorrow night and the next day, so tomorrow is the only time I can see him, and . . ." Her voice trailed off into the stillness of the room.

"Demi, it's okay. Do what makes you happy."

"Do you think Sophie will be upset?"

"Sophie will be fine. It's Aunt Zoe you have to worry about. She's been reading up on Monemvasia ever since we got here!"

* * *

"What do you mean you're not coming to Monemvasia?" Zoe's voice rose above the din of the nearby tables. The traffic around the plateia had increased as the weekend approached, and the throbbing of idling motorcycles not only raised the noise level but scented the air with whiffs of gasoline.

"Demi has other plans, Zoe," Georgia said, lifting her hand, palm forward, to ward off any further conversation about the matter.

"But, Demi," Zoe said, "It's supposed to be amazing. The fortress was built in the 13th century—parts of it are still standing today. And the town . . ."

"Mom!" Sophie said. "What looks good on the menu?"

Demi winked at Sophie. "That Greek salad looks amazing," she said, nodding toward the table next to them.

"Mihalis said that this place is known for their sardines," Georgia said.

"Sardines?" Sophie said.

"Mihalis?" Zoe said. "You were talking with Mihalis?"

"Yes," Georgia laughed. "Why shouldn't I talk to Mihalis?"

"I don't know," Zoe said. "I didn't think you got along with him."

Demi was happy for the diversion. She leaned over to Sophie. "I hope you don't mind, Sophie. It's just that . . ."

"Of course not!" Sophie said. "I'll take lots of pictures."

"I'm sure you will," Demi smiled.

CHAPTER 9

Demi woke to the smell of fresh rain. A warm breeze blew in through the open balcony door. She inhaled and opened her eyes slowly. Outside, the grey of the bay blended with the dark clouds that hung over the horizon. *Shit*, she thought, thinking about her plans for the beach later that day. She rolled onto her side and reached for her cell phone on the nightstand. "Good morning, Sweetie. Have a good day. We'll miss you <3," read the message from her mother. Nothing from Stavros yet, but it was only nine-thirty. "Oh crap," she muttered. Breakfast ended at ten. She was not going to miss it this morning. Five minutes later, face splashed, hair in a ponytail, dressed in a black tee shirt and jeans, she was on her way down the stairs, the slap of her flip flops echoing with each step.

"Good morning, Miss Demi," Mihalis spoke from behind his computer.

"Good morning, Mihali."

"You did not go with your family to Monemvasia?" he asked. His voice took on a note of concern. "You are not well?"

"No, no, I'm fine. I just have other plans." She looked through the rain-spattered window in the front of the lobby. "Well, I did. I was going to go to the beach, but . . ."

"No problem, Miss Demi. This rain, she happen." Mihalis pointed towards the window. "In one hour, you will see the sun."

"Thank you, Mihali," Demi said. "That makes me feel better."

"Yes, this rain, we did not have in the summer for many years. "Now," he looked up as if looking at the sky above the ceiling, "it is not so unusual."

Demi furrowed her eyebrows. "But I thought the streams and rivers were drying out. The riverbed in Sparta was almost completely dry."

"Yes, of course," Mihalis nodded. "This happen over many years. Many people take water from the *Potamos Evrotas*."

"But how can they take water from the river if it's dry?"

"No, no, no. The water, she is under the ground. From this they take to grow their food." Mihalis made a digging motion. "*Eskapsan pigadia*."

Demi processed Mihalis' pantomime. "They dig wells?"

"*Nai, nai*, yes. They dig wells. For the oranges. And the *elies*."

"The olives?"

"*Nai*. The river, she is dry in summer. But sometimes in winter, too much rain." Mihalis pushed his chair back, stood up, and smiled at Demi. "But today, you are okay. You will go to the beach."

"*Efharisto*, Mihali. But first, breakfast before it's all gone!" Demi smiled at Mihalis and walked into the dining area.

* * *

"The only way to reach Monemvasia was by boat. A paved pathway was later constructed to connect the castle entrance to the mainland," Zoe read from the guidebook as they drove through town on the road leading to the fortress. "This is how the name was derived, meaning 'single passage.'"

"Ah, well, lucky for us, they built this," Charles said as they approached the causeway, "otherwise, we'd be swimming across." Sophie laughed politely while Georgia elbowed Zoe in the back seat and shook her head slightly. Zoe suppressed a laugh. "How are you two sardines doing back there?" Charles glanced into the rearview mirror. "Perhaps it's a good thing Demi didn't come today. We might have had to put her in the boot!"

For a second, Georgia wondered whether she should have taken Yiorgos up on his offer to drive them to Monemvasia in his taxi rather than squeezing into the Opel, but Charles had been so eager to go. She lowered the window, letting in the hum of motorcycles as they left the town, and drove across the causeway towards the mountain in front of them. Anchored off to the left, a streamlined white yacht sparkled against the deep blue of the sea. As they neared the base of the mountain, the road widened on both sides, leading to rocky areas of shoreline, then narrowed again at the base. A restaurant at the foot of the hill sat empty with white cloth-covered tables awaiting lunch patrons. A few smaller whitewashed buildings with closed doors and blank windows stood silent at the mountain's base while the sea lapped the rocky shoreline on the right.

Zoe looked up from the guidebook. "Did you know that the history of Monemvasia dates back to the thirteenth century?" she asked. "There's a history of Byzantine, Ottoman, and Venetian occupation."

"Well, we don't have to fret about that now, do we?" said Charles. He downshifted as they began to climb the narrow road. A few cars were wedged into the left where the road met the mountain. Progressing uphill, cars were squeezed in nose to bumper where the road cut into the steep cliffside. As they neared the top, cars lined either side of the road, leaving little more than a single lane. A grey Peugeot approached them from the top of the hill. "Good grief!" said Charles. He froze momentarily. "I have nowhere to pull over!"

"Charles," Georgia said. "Just put it in reverse and go back a few feet. They'll be able to go around you."

"Right you are!" said Charles, shifting into reverse and moving backward. The group watched as the Peugeot narrowly passed their rental. Charles let out the breath he'd been holding in a huff. "Well then," he said. "Onward." They were greeted at the top of the mountain by a dark archway built into a large stone wall. "I don't see anywhere to park," said Charles. "I'll let you off and try to find a space along the way down."

"I'll go with you, Charles," Zoe said, getting out of the back seat and stretching her legs. "Georgia, why don't you and Sophie go in? We'll meet up with you."

"Where?" she asked.

Charles looked at her and smiled. "Don't worry," he said. "Something tells me you won't get too far."

* * *

Demi stepped outside. The rain had subsided, leaving large puddles on the uneven road. The air hung humid, and she reached subconsciously to pat her hair, which she had smoothed out with the straightener. Already, the strands had begun to frizz, each strand expanding from the humidity in the air. *Well, so much for that*, she thought, as she reached into her beach bag for a hair tie, picking through sunglasses, sunscreen, and a small make-up bag containing lip gloss, some euros, and a random lighter. She turned to go back to the room when she heard the whirr of a motorcycle as it pulled up to the hotel. Stavros pulled up to the entrance, turned off the motor, kicked down the kickstand, and jumped off. "*Kalimera koritsi*," he said, a grin lighting up his face.

"Good morning," Demi said, feeling her pulse quicken. *What the heck,* she thought. *What is wrong with me*? "You brought the bike," she said, stating the obvious.

"I did?" He looked at his bike as if seeing it for the first time, then feigned surprise. "Oh, yes, I did!"

Demi crossed her arms and attempted a stern look. He approached her and grasped her arms while he kissed her on each cheek, then looked into her eyes. "You are happy to see me?" he asked.

"Of course I am," she said. "Otherwise, I'd have to call a taxi to take me to the beach."

Stavros laughed, letting go of her arms but still standing close. "I'm sure Yiorgos would take you wherever you want to go," he said. "However, you might not have as much fun with him."

"You never know," laughed Demi.

"You have had something to eat?" Stavros asked. "At the beach, we can get frappe, but no food until this afternoon."

"Yes, I actually made it up in time for breakfast today," she said. "You don't have to worry about me being hangry!"

"It's not hungry?" he asked, stretching out the first syllable.

"No, *hangry*," Demi said, putting both palms up as she explained. "It's when you're crabby because you're so hungry."

Stavros shook his head and frowned. "I am sorry, my English is not so good."

"No, no, it's slang—your English is fine." Demi touched his forearm. "Much better than my Greek."

"Ah, your Greek would be much better if you would stay here for a while." Stavros looked closely at Demi. "You would learn very fast, I think."

Demi sighed and glanced out over the gulf. She turned back to Stavros. "I'm sure you're right."

He paused and looked down at Demi. The straps of her blue bathing suit were tied around her neck, peeking out from her tee shirt. "You are ready to go?"

"I was just going back to the room to get a hair tie."

He shrugged.

"A hair tie." She pantomimed putting her hair in a ponytail.

"Why? Your hair is beautiful."

Demi smiled and turned to go back to the hotel, but Stavros gripped her arm. She turned back to face him. "Demi," he paused, his expression serious. "Your family—they have gone to Monemvasia?"

"Yes, they left early this morning."

Stavros' eyes met Demi's. "Do you want me to come with you?"

"To the beach? Of course—I thought . . ." Her breath caught in her throat, her mouth suddenly dry. *Be calm*, she told herself. *Be sure*. She held Stavros' gaze while her mind shifted into overdrive. *This is crazy. You hardly know him. This is reckless*. And then, *This is what I want*. "Yes," she said. She turned around and opened the door to the lobby. Stavros followed.

"Miss Demi," Mihalis said. "You have forgotten something?" When he saw Stavros behind Demi, he discreetly turned back to his computer.

Inside the stairwell, Stavros grabbed Demi's arm and pulled her towards him. Leaning her against the wall, he cupped her face in his hands, then bent down and kissed her. Demi wrapped her arms around him, feeling the heat of his body through his thin white tee shirt. Stavros pulled away to look at her and ran his strong fingers through her hair, bringing her face close to his. "*Ela,*" he whispered and took her hand. Together, they climbed the stairs.

* * *

Charles navigated the car back down the narrow road away from the fort. "Ah, marvelous!" he said as he passed an empty spot. He brought the car to a sudden stop and stalled the engine. "One moment," he said, pressing the clutch and bringing the car back to life. He backed up, cutting the car towards the cliffside, but he cut it too sharp and had to begin again. After three attempts, he eased the car into the small spot. "There we are!" he said to Zoe.

"Um, Charles," Zoe said, but Charles had already unbuckled his seat belt and was heading out the door. "Charles!" she yelled.

"Yes? What is it?" He bent down to peer in through the driver's side. "Oh, crikey!" he said, realizing there wasn't enough room for the passenger door to open. "I don't suppose you'd like to come out this way? I don't know if I could squeeze into this space again."

"I guess I should have stayed in the back seat," Zoe said. She lifted her long leg awkwardly over the gear shift, then paused to contemplate her next move.

"Oh dear," said Charles. "Perhaps you should crawl out instead?" Zoe lifted her right leg to join the left and lay with the gear shift under her bent knees. And then, she began to laugh. Legs sprawled over the hump in the middle of the car, head halfway down the back of the seat, her giggle turned slowly into a guffaw as the tears streamed down her cheeks.

"Oh dear," Charles repeated, unsure what to do with the hysterical Zoe. "You've gotten yourself in a bit of a pickle! Let me help you," he said, offering a hand, but Zoe was unable to move, constrained by the laughter emanating from deep inside her belly.

"Ch-charles," she managed to say through guffaws. "You have to move the car. I can't get out!"

"Well, that might be a problem," said Charles. Your legs are in the way—I can't sit down." Now, it was Charles' turn to laugh. "What shall we do?"

A middle-aged couple walking up the hill paused and peered into the car. "Can we be of assistance?" asked the man. "I'm a doctor."

Charles and Zoe again burst into laughter. "Oh, no thank you," said Charles. "We'll have to work this out ourselves." He turned to Zoe. "Alright, up you go," he said, sliding into the driver's seat under her legs.

The couple shook their heads and continued up the hill. Charles started the car and wedged out of the tight parking spot. He put the car in neutral and engaged the emergency brake. Then he went over to the passenger side and opened the door. "Let's get you out of there."

* * *

Demi opened her eyes to the sun pouring through the open balcony door. She felt the warmth of Stavros' body embracing her under the crisp white hotel sheet and turned to face him. "The sun is out," she began, but his mouth covered hers with a slow, soft kiss.

Stavros pulled away and smiled at Demi. "We fell asleep."

"What time is it?"

He reached over Demi and picked up his phone from the nightstand. "*Mia kai misi*—one-thirty," he said, setting the phone back down and embracing Demi again. "You are hungry?"

She smiled. "I could eat."

He kissed her forehead and hopped out of bed. Demi watched him pull on his shorts, noting his strong calf muscles. "Do you work out?"

"Work out?" he asked.

Demi pantomimed bicep curls with her arms. "You know, lift, work out."

"Ah," he said. "No, I play football. It is good for the legs."

Demi slid back and pushed herself up to lean back on the headboard. She pulled the sheet up to cover her breasts. "I didn't know they had football in Greece."

"No, no. Not your American football. European football. *Pothosphairo.*"

"Soccer?"

"Yes, soccer. I have played for many years. Now, only on Saturday, maybe Sunday, because I work at night." He looked closely at her. "Dimitra, you want to talk about soccer?"

"Well, no, I . . ."

Stavros sat down on the bed. "Why you cover yourself? You are cold?"

She shook her head.

Stavros reached for the sheet and pulled it down. The stream of sunshine revealed the contrast of Demi's white breasts and tan body. Stavros leaned over her and lowered, bracing himself with his forearms. "You are beautiful," he said, watching her eyes. She wrapped her arms around his body and pulled him to her.

* * *

Georgia and Sophie walked through the large stone archway into a surprising flash of color and life. Small storefronts on either side of the narrow cobblestone street were adorned with jewelry hanging from pins on the walls, from braided ropes of small seed beads to 24-karat gold handmade bracelets and necklaces. Overhead, grapevines stretched from one side of the street to the other. Underfoot, the stones were worn smooth from centuries of foot travel. A large white cat sat regally on the stoop of a wine shop as if guarding the door. Another thin gray cat scooted across the street in front of them and disappeared behind the wall of a café.

"Aunt Georgia, aren't these gorgeous?" Sophie walked towards a display of brightly colored silk scarves suspended alongside hammered gold and silver metal jewelry.

"Yes, they are," Georgia said.

The shop owner materialized from inside the store. "These are hand-painted," he said. He swept his hand to include the entire store. "Everything we sell is handmade and authentic." He turned to Sophie. "Do you see something you like?"

"Oh, um, yes, I . . ."

"*Efharisto*," Georgia said. "We'll look around for a bit."

"*Opos thelete*," the man said. "As you wish. Please let me know if I may be of assistance." He turned around and went back into the store.

"Oh, Aunt Georgia, isn't this one beautiful!" Sophie said, lifting a red and orange scarf with infusions of bright yellow.

"That would look lovely with your hair, Sophie. Why don't you buy it?"

Sophie grimaced. "Oh, I don't think I could pull that off."

"Pull *what* off?"

"You know—that look." She looked at the scarf again.

"Sophie, what are you talking about?"

"You know, Aunt Georgia. That kind of boho look." She looked behind Georgia and pointed to a small group of young women coming through the entrance. Their laughter echoed in the narrow passageway. "Like that. Look at her."

Georgia turned to see a young woman wearing a white muslin shirt, a red hat cocked sideways over her tousled blonde hair, large gold hoop earrings, and short suede booties. She turned back to Sophie and sighed. "Of course you can." Georgia pulled the scarf from the rack and reached up to wrap it around Sophie's head, forming a large, floppy bow on the side. She pulled Sophie's long dark hair and gently tousled it around the scarf. She turned Sophie around to face the tiny mirror suspended next to the scarves and then turned her face to face. "Listen, my beautiful niece. My *smart* and beautiful niece. You are on vacation. Wear the scarf. Wear what makes you happy. *Do* what makes you happy. Dance, run, sing—and don't worry about what anyone else thinks. You don't have to conform to anyone's notion of beauty."

Sophie turned back to the mirror. Her large brown eyes conveyed their approval. "Thank you, Aunt Georgia," she said, beaming at her reflection. She turned around and hugged her aunt.

* * *

Zoe and Charles trudged up the hill toward the entrance to the fortress—an ascent made more difficult by the amount of paraphernalia Zoe carried: a camera bag; a large straw tote bag filled with a water bottle, snacks, a sunhat, an umbrella, and a sweater; and her purse, containing wallet, makeup, and passport.

"May I carry something for you?" Charles asked.

"Oh, no, that's okay." She shifted the bags for balance. "I've got it under control."

"Did you confirm your reservations, then?" Charles asked.

"Reservations? For what?" Zoe looked alarmed. "Was I supposed to make reservations for something?"

Charles grinned. "For your hotel. With all your luggage, I presumed you were planning to stay the night." He looked at the camera bag slipping from Zoe's shoulder. "Here," he said, "at least let me take this for you."

"Thanks, Charles. Maybe I overdid it."

He peered into her tote bag. "Well, I suppose you never know when it might rain again. However, I'm pretty sure you won't be needing that sweater." He fanned himself with his hand as beads of sweat formed on his brow. "I think we're in for another hot one today."

"That's true," Zoe said. She stopped, reached into her tote bag, and pulled out her straw sunhat. She gave it a shake and placed it on her head. They approached the entrance to the fort and walked through the cool, drab archway. Zoe stopped in awe at the burst of color and sound that greeted them. Traditional Greek music from a restaurant in the distance blended with the mix of languages as tourists navigated the street. "Oh!" she said. "I didn't expect this. I thought this was just a fortress!"

"The guidebook didn't prepare you for this?" Charles smiled.

"No. I didn't realize there were stores. I thought it was a historical place."

"It is. You'll see as we progress. Now, let's find your daughter." He looked up the street, pointed, and chuckled. "I didn't suppose they'd have gotten too far."

"Mom!" Zoe called and walked down to meet them. "What do you think?" She twirled around, fluffing her hair with her hands. A pair of gold spiral-shaped earrings dangled from her ears. "Aunt Georgia bought them for me!"

"The earrings?"

"And the scarf! What do you think?"

"She shouldn't have bought . . ."

"Don't worry about it, Zoe." Georgia approached them with a shopping bag in her hand. "It was my pleasure."

"My dear, you look radiant," Charles said. "That scarf makes you look absolutely badass." Zoe's mouth opened, and her eyebrows shot up. "Oh dear," Charles said. "I do hope I'm saying that in the right context. It was meant to be a compliment."

Sophie beamed. "Thank you, Charles. I *do* feel a little badass."

Charles nodded towards a café where a red-haired waitress carried a tray filled with water and coffee. Patrons sipped Greek coffee and frappes at small, round, blue metal tables facing the street. He pointed to an empty table. "Shall we have a cup of coffee before we begin our adventure?"

The strong smell of coffee beckoned Georgia. "Sure," she said. "Sounds good to me."

"I don't really want anything," Zoe said. "You guys enjoy your coffee." She looked down the street at a display of carved wooden spoons and decorative boxes on a table outside a bright blue storefront. "Sophie, want to go over to that store with me?"

"Okay!"

"Do you mind if I leave this bag here?" Zoe asked, dropping her tote bag next to Georgia. "And maybe this one," she added, setting her camera bag on the extra chair. "I don't think I'm going to take any pictures yet."

"Of course not. Go ahead."

"Thanks," Zoe said. "We'll be back." She gave a small wave, and they headed towards the store.

"Is she always so . . ." Charles began, then paused.

"So . . . ?"

He pressed his lips, searching for the right word, but it continued to elude him. "So . . ." He leaned his chin onto his hand, looking up as if the word might appear above Georgia's head.

"Anxious? Over-protective? Worried?" Georgia suggested.

"I was thinking more . . . cautious. Perhaps that's the right word."

The red-haired waitress came over to set cold glasses of water on the table. "*Efharisto*," said Georgia. "*Thio kafethes, parakalo*," she ordered. She took a sip of water and set the glass down, then put her elbows on the table and rested her chin on her clasped hands. "Zoe is awesome," she said. "She's got a great sense of humor, and we laugh every time we're together."

"Yes, I've certainly seen that side of her," Charles said.

"But ever since having kids, she's been a worrier. Her ex wasn't much of a father in that . . ."

"Walker."

Georgia sat up. "She told you about Walker?"

"Briefly," Charles nodded. "Enough to know that he wasn't right for Zoe."

"Right. I don't think he did much for her self-esteem. And she's basically raised her kids herself. He told her that the kids were her domain." Georgia shook her head. "It took a lot for her to leave him, and she's worked hard to maintain the lifestyle they had when they were married."

"But they're adults now."

Georgia sighed. "You have no children, do you, Charles?"

Charles shook his head. "No, not so fortunate."

"Children are wonderful. Demi is my treasure. I'm thankful every day for that girl. But, Charles, when you have children, you never stop worrying about them."

"But Sophie is a lovely young lady. What does Zoe have to worry about?"

"When you've spent over twenty years worrying, it's hard to let go."

CHAPTER 10

Demi sliced into the large piece of feta, topped with oregano and drizzled with olive oil, and scooped a large spoonful of tomatoes, cucumbers, olives, and onions onto her plate, along with the cheese. She lifted the cloth napkin from the crusty loaf of bread and pulled a large piece away. She dipped the bread into the oily dressing and took a bite, followed by a bite of tomato. "Oh, my goodness," Demi said. "This is amazing." She took another bite.

Stavros laughed. "It is only a salad."

"No, it's so much better than the salads we have at home." As proof, she broke off a piece of the feta with her fork and waved it at him.

"How this can be?" He shrugged. "A tomato is a tomato."

Demi shook her head. "Maybe it's the soil here. Or the sun."

"Or maybe it is because you are in Greece, and everything is better in Greece."

"Is it?" Demi rested her chin in her hand.

"Of course," Stavros said. He held his arms out to encompass the large stone patio, the wood chairs with rattan seats, and the turquoise-painted tables. "Look," he said and pointed beyond the covered patio of the restaurant, past a strip of grass on which lay unoccupied wooden sunbeds lined up between thick-trunked palm trees with wide green palm fronds. Blue and red umbrellas dotted a strip of beach that gently sloped to the sparkling turquoise water of the sea.

"It's beautiful," Demi said. "But . . ."

"*Alla*?"

She sighed. "It's not reality. It's a postcard." Stavros frowned. Demi waved her hand towards the water. "All this is amazingly beautiful. *You* are amazingly beautiful." She sighed. "If I could freeze time, I'd do it right here, right now, with you. But I can't."

Stavros leaned towards her, clasping his hands together on the table. "Why not? Why you don't stay here?"

"Because my life is in the States. Everything I've worked for—my career, my family, my friends."

"But no *filos*?" He raised his eyebrows.

"No," Demi half-smiled. "No boyfriend."

"So, you can make new friends, find a new job."

"It's not that easy. Is it, Stavro? Is working in a restaurant what you want to be doing? Or do you have bigger dreams?"

Stavros looked out over the sea. His jaw clenched.

"Stavro," Demi said. He looked back at her, unsmiling. "I'm sorry."

"It's okay," he said. "Why I would not want to work in a restaurant? There are beautiful women every night."

"Oh," she bristled. "I see."

"Dimitra," he laughed. "I am joking. I work in the kitchen. No beautiful women there. Just Dimitris. He is not beautiful."

"You're a cook?" she said, tilting her head to the side. "I figured you were a waiter."

His eyebrows furrowed. "Why you say this? I study cooking in the army."

"You were in the army?"

"Of course. All men in Greece must go to the army for a year."

"You were a cook in the army?" Demi pictured the mess halls she'd seen in movies and television.

"No," Stavros said. "I go to *Scholi Mayeron*. It is the army cooking school in Gytheio."

"Wait," she said. She leaned on the table, absorbing the information. "So, you served in the army here. Like, a half hour from your home? And learned how to cook?"

"Yes. I told you. I am lucky."

A stocky, bearded waiter approached the table, a dish in each hand. He set down a plate of french-fried potatoes sprinkled with oregano and feta and another with white, flaky grouper drizzled in oil and lemon. "This is *rophos* from the Mani."

"That smells delicious," Demi said.

"Yes, this is why I bring you here," Stavros said. "They make this almost as good as I do. But mine is better."

Demi squeezed the lemon over the fish and served herself a small filet. "Why is yours better?" she asked. She picked up the plate of french fries and slid some onto her dish.

"Because I catch the fish, then I cook it. How you can get better fish than this?"

Demi recalled seeing the fishing poles and tackle boxes in the taxi driver's trunk. "Do you fish with Yiorgos?" she asked.

"You think I fish with a pole?" He patted his chest. "This is not fishing—to sit on a dock and wait for the fish to bite."

"Well then how . . ."

"With a *psarotoufeko*, how you say?" He made a shooting motion with his hand.

Demi put down the plate of potatoes and stared at Stavros. "A gun? You shoot fish?"

"*Vevaios.* This is the challenge. It is more a hunting game than to sit on a dock and wait for the fish."

"Then where do you sit? On a boat?"

"What you are talking about, Dimitra? We dive in the water. How you can *kamakonei psari* when you are sitting on a boat?"

"Your gun works underwater?"

"Of course. It is made for this."

"But don't the bullets blow up the fish?"

"Bullets?" Stavros burst out laughing. "You think I am shooting fish 'bang bang' like John Wayne?" He sat back and laughed from deep inside his belly.

Demi folded her arms. "Then what are you talking about, shooting fish?"

The waiter had returned with a plate of fried eggplant and joined in the laughter. "*Signomi, koritsi*, he is talking about a speargun. He uses a speargun to shoot the fish."

At Demi's expression of annoyance, Stavros and the waiter attempted to hold back their amusement, but she was unable to maintain a straight face. The three of them burst into laughter.

* * *

The party walked past small boutiques and terraced cafes on the cliffside, catching glimpses of red and orange tiled rooftops below and the sea sparkling in the distance. The narrow road became even narrower, interrupted by short flights of uneven steps, built centuries past to help people ascend the steep hillside. There was little shade in the full afternoon sun, and drops of sweat trickled down their foreheads. Small stone houses, some with modern glass windows, replaced the shops and restaurants. A pure gray cat stared at them from the stoop of one; a spiky aloe plant potted in a large clay vessel decorated another. Ahead of them, a couple dressed in khaki pants and sweat-soaked white shirts that clung to their backs dragged suitcases whose wheels rumbled loudly over the uneven cobblestones. They lifted and lugged their suitcases up a short flight of steps and turned into an alleyway. "Where do you think they're going?" Sophie asked.

"There are dozens of hotels wedged into the mountainside," Charles said. "Some of them are quite lovely. Peter and I looked at dozens online when we were planning our vacation, but we didn't make it here. I'm delighted I was able to join you today." The group passed a faded, whitewashed building with decades of blue paint peeling from the short, arched wooden door.

"I could never fit in that door!" Sophie said.

"I don't think any of us could," added Georgia.

A lean tabby cat slithered from around the side of the building and brushed against Sophie's leg. "What a beautiful face," she said. "Look at those green eyes!" The cat looked up at her, and she bent down to pet it."

"Sophie, don't!" warned Zoe. The cat scampered back behind the building at the sound of her voice.

"Mom, you scared her," Sophie said. She looked around the side of the building. "She's gone." She folded her arms and pouted.

"You don't know what disease that cat might have. It's probably feral."

"Mom . . ."

"Actually, your mother is probably right," Charles said. "Feral cats have existed in Greece for centuries. They do an excellent job of fending for themselves. You don't know what they may have eaten."

"Probably table scraps around here," said Georgia, waving behind them towards the cafes.

"Or vermin," said Zoe.

Georgia shook her head and smiled. "Come on," she said, falling into step with Charles, who had already resumed his walk.

The path began to zig-zag in a long upward slope, past trees with gnarled trunks that appeared to be growing sideways out of crumbling walls. "Oh, look!" Zoe said. She stopped and pointed to the top of the mountain, where a formidable 12th-century Byzantine Church clung to the edge of the cliff. Sections of the greyish stone façade had crumbled, while other parts of the church, including a massive dome, appeared intact.

"There's so many windows!" Sophie said.

"I believe those were so the occupants could look out for marauders," said Charles.

"Who were the occupants?" asked Sophie.

"In the 14th century, the fortress was a Byzantine trading center," Charles explained. "It changed hands a few times over the centuries. It wasn't until the early 1800s that the church was re-dedicated." He turned to Sophie. "Do you know the name of the church?"

She shook her head. "No, I don't."

"It was named *Ayia Sofia*— Saint Sophia, dedicated to the wisdom of God."

"Saint Sophia?"

"Yes, Sophie. Your name means wise one," Charles smiled. "Which, I believe, suits you nicely."

Zoe looked up from her guidebook. "It says here that Monemvasia was occupied by the Venetians until 1540 when it was taken over during the Turkish occupation. They painted the walls with lime and used it as a mosque. It wasn't until the Greek War of Independence that they regained the church, and it became a Christian place of worship again."

"It's hard to believe that it's withstood all of the occupations for so many centuries," said Sophie. "Not to mention weather. I don't think there's any churches in the U.S. that have been around since the 13th century."

Zoe shook her head, and Georgia laughed. "Well, considering that the only inhabitants of America in the 1300s were Native Americans, I'm pretty sure there weren't any brick-and-mortar churches in the U.S. in the 13th century. But I bet if you go to Massachusetts, you might find a few that have been around since the 1600s."

"Oh, good point." Sophie giggled as she imagined Demi saying, *maybe not-so-wise*. "I wish Demi were here," she said.

"I hope she made the right choice staying behind," Zoe said.

"Ah, Zoe," Georgia sighed. "When do we ever know if we've made the right choice?"

"Oh, my," said Charles. "This is getting quite philosophical. Anyway, I know I made the right choice by coming here today with you lovely ladies. Shall we continue?" he asked, nodding towards the church.

Zoe pulled the camera out of her bag and unhooked the lens cap. "I hope my zoom lens is strong enough to get a good picture of the church."

"You don't want to walk up there?" Charles asked.

Zoe squinted at Saint Sophia's, distinct in the distance against the background of the cloudless blue sky. "How long do you think it would take?"

"I'm guessing twenty minutes, maybe a half hour?"

"I think I'll pass, Charles." Zoe wiped the perspiration from her forehead with the back of her hand. "I'm already sweating like crazy. You guys go if you want to."

"I'll go, Charles," Sophie said.

"I think I'll stay with Zoe," Georgia said. "We can explore some of the churches in the lower town." She turned to Charles and Sophie. "Why don't we meet at that café with the red awning in an hour or so? No hurry—we'll have a glass of wine if we get there first."

"First class!" said Charles. "See you then."

* * *

Demi had drifted off to sleep to a symphony of clinking plates and glasses, soft chatter from the restaurant patrons, and laughter from the beach below. The sun had shifted, and the wide palm fronds no longer shaded the sunbeds. Her frappe sat half-empty, froth lining the glass, on the wooden table beside her.

"You are awake?" Stavros asked. She opened her eyes and turned her head towards him. He was sitting, facing her, on the sunbed next to hers.

She stretched her arms far above her head and yawned. "Yes."

"You enjoyed your siesta?"

"*Vevaios,*" she smiled.

"Come," Stavros said, holding out his hand to her. Demi reached for her sundress. "No, you will not need this. You can leave your things here. He nodded at the towel on the lounge chair. "We will go for a swim." Stavros took her hand and led her along the stone path and down a short flight of cement steps. They crossed a makeshift bridge of wooden planks and rope railings that spanned a gully formed by beach erosion. They ran across the short expanse of warm sand and into the sea.

"I can't believe how clear the water is here," Demi said, observing small silver fish circling her feet.

"Here is not so clear," said Stavros. "In the islands, the water is even better. They have *petres*, not sand. You can see many meters below."

They walked out until the water was waist-high. Demi sank into it and leaned back, soaking her head. She ran her hands over her hair and squeezed out the water. About 100 yards to their left, she saw a ship moored close to shore.

"What is that?" Demi asked. "It looks like an old pirate ship."

"Ah, this is what I want to show you," Stavros said. "Come, you will see." They left the water, and he took her hand as they walked along the shoreline, leaving footprints in the moist sand. To their left, sea grasses dotted the beach, interrupted by mounds of rocks. The large ship was run aground about 20 feet from the shore, its bow pointed toward the beach.

"What's it doing here?" Demi asked.

"There are many stories," Stavros said. "Some people say it was *lathreborie* who were taking cigarettes from Turkey to Italy."

"Smugglers?"

"Yes, yes. And they were captured. The ship stay in port, but then it break free, and it come here." He paused, looking out beyond the gulf, then continued. "Another story we have is with the captain. He is very sick, and they come to Gytheio so he can go to the hospital."

"That doesn't explain why the ship is here."

"Because the captain does not return. And the people on the ship, they don't get paid. So, they abandon the ship."

"Oh, that makes sense."

Stavros stopped walking and dropped Demi's hand. "Yes, it is too easy."

"What do you mean?"

He leaned towards Demi and spoke with intent. "This is what people say who do not want to believe the real story."

"Which is?"

"Look, Demi." Stavros turned Demi by her shoulders. "Look at this ship. How it comes here from Gytheio? Why it does not go out to sea and sink?" He turned Demi back to face him. "It is a *plio fantasma*. A ghost ship." Demi grinned. "You don't believe me? Wait. You will see." Against the backdrop of the distant faded blue mountain, the ship tilted slightly towards the sea, a metal skeleton corroded by decades of exposure to the elements, its mast reaching towards the sky.

"*A phantom ship with each mast and spar across the moon like a prison bar,*" Demi whispered.

"What?"

"It's a line from a famous poem, 'Paul Revere's Ride.'" As they neared the ship, Demi could see holes in its rusted hulk. A cool breeze ran across their damp skin, forming goose bumps in the heat.

"You feel this?" Stavros asked.

Demi nodded, slowing her pace. "But who are the ghosts?"

The beach widened slightly underneath the ship as if the sand had extended a hand to reach out and grasp it. Demi shuddered.

"No one knows. Maybe the people die on the ship, and they cannot go home. There is a story about a woman who came to find her husband. Her footprints went out to the ship, but there were no footprints coming back."

"But thc tide would have washed them away."

Stavros shrugged. "Maybe. Or maybe, she find her husband's ghost, and she stay with him."

"Do you really think the ship is haunted?"

"Of course. Why you think the ship is still here? Why it did not sink like other abandoned ships?" Stavros raised his eyebrows for emphasis. "Because it is haunted."

They walked back up to the sunbeds in silence, lost in their own thoughts. *Mom should write a story about this*, Demi thought, as she pictured a young Greek bride hopelessly searching for her seafaring husband. Stavros's thoughts were closer to the heart. *Erotevome. I am falling in love.*

* * *

"Let me hold one of those bags, Zoe," Georgia said. "They have to be weighing you down."

"That's alright." Zoe set the bags down and shook out her arms. "I really feel like leaving the umbrella and the sweater here. I don't know what I was thinking."

"Well, at least let me lighten your load. I can put the umbrella and sweater in my shopping bag."

Zoe reconsidered. "Okay, thanks." She reached into her bag and handed the items to Georgia. "Every little bit helps, I guess."

They retraced their steps and approached the lower town. The smell of rosemary and thyme was replaced by the tantalizing scent of onions and garlic sizzling as restaurants prepared lunch. "Let me see your map," Georgia said. "I want to check out the birthplace of Yiannis Ritsos."

Zoe fished the map out of her bag and handed it to Georgia. "Who's he?"

"One of the greatest poets of Greece. I've taught some of his poetry in my creative writing classes."

"Hmm." Zoe shook her head. "I've never heard of him."

"Ritsos is not an everyday name in American poetry circles. He's most well-known for his political poems. He spent time in prison for siding with the Communist Party. He was also exiled from Greece for several years for being a member of the EAM."

"The EAM?"

Georgia pulled Zoe to the side to avoid a collision with a large group of tourists coming up the narrow path, then explained. "The National Liberation Front. They were a powerful group in the resistance movement against the Nazis in World War II. ELAS was their military arm. Ritsos wrote poems about the Greek resistance.

Zoe contemplated the information. "But why would he be exiled for working to resist the Nazis?"

"Because the resistance movement also included groups from the far right and center as well as the left. Towards the end of the war, there was a power struggle as to who would govern Greece. This resulted in the Greek Civil War. I've read that 50,000 people were killed fighting in the Civil War."

"That's really sad," Zoe said. "I didn't know that."

"Most people don't. I only know because of Jimmy. His great uncle was killed by ELAS."

"Oh, that's terrible!" Zoe was quiet for a moment. "But you still teach Ritsos' poems in creative writing?"

Georgia pointed to a small alley to their left. "I think it's that way." They waited as a small group of women walked by, then crossed the road and turned down the path. Georgia continued. "Is it any different than writing Japanese haiku, or celebrating Oktoberfest, or eating Southern fried chicken? The world moves on. We forgive our enemies even if we don't forget."

"True, but the poets who write haiku aren't the people who bombed Pearl Harbor."

Georgia raised her eyebrows. "That you know of . . ."

"I'm just surprised you'd teach political poems in creative writing."

"Not all of Ritsos' poems were political. His use of imagery is beautiful. He had a way of bringing everyday events to life with vivid descriptions. He's famous for his metaphor of Monemvasia. He called it a 'ship of stone.'" Georgia consulted her map and followed the path that led them to a gently sloped flight of worn steps, ending at a concrete courtyard. Short walls of crumbling stone bordered the quiet courtyard, which abutted the smooth façade of a small tan house. Close to the house, on a concrete pedestal, stood a large bronze bust of Yiannis Ritsos. The bronze had oxidized to a dark green patina, but the poet's features were bold, and the sculpture was formidable. While the bust cast only his head and the top of his torso, he carried his head proudly.

"No wonder he was a great poet," Zoe said. "Can you imagine the inspiration he got from this view? It's incredible." The bust of Ritsos looked keenly past the concrete fence over red tile roofs and the sea, as far as one's eyes could travel.

"It's so peaceful here," Georgia said. The sounds from the main path were muted by the buildings bordering the courtyard. "Imagine what this was like 100 years ago, without the tourists." She sat down on the border wall and looked out towards the sea.

Zoe set her bags down and sat next to Georgia. Imagine how quiet it would be at night when the only light was the moon shining over the sea."

Georgia closed her eyes and recited:

In the warm blue twilight of evening
You sailed me straight into the stillness of the Milky Way.

"That's Ritsos?" Zoe asked.

Georgia opened her eyes and nodded. They sat in silence, each lost in her thoughts. *I have to make more time to write,* Georgia thought. *No more excuses. If I'm going to be a writer, I need to write.* Zoe's thoughts were similar. *She needs to recognize that she is a writer. It's not a hobby. It's her passion.*

CHAPTER 11

Stavros downshifted the Vespa as he approached the Aktaion Hotel. He wedged the bike between the tightly parked cars, put it into neutral, and shut off the engine. Demi set her left foot down, raised her right leg over the seat, and lifted herself off the motorcycle. Stavros repeated her motion and hit the kickstand with the side of his foot to park the bike. He turned to Demi. "I'm sorry I must work tonight. I want to stay with you."

Demi unbuckled the helmet and handed it to Stavros. "It's fine," she said and smiled at him. "I had a great time today."

"Yes," he said. "Today was perfect." Stavros lifted the seat and put the helmet away. He glanced up at her balcony and smiled to himself. They stared at each other, silent for a moment, neither ready to say goodbye. Stavros spoke first. "Why you don't come to dinner at Dimitri's tonight? You will see where I work. And you will taste my cooking. Come with me."

Demi looked down at her tee shirt and shorts. Then she remembered her hair, flat on top from the helmet. "I can't." She fluffed up her hair and then pointed to her clothes. "I'm not dressed for it. And I need a shower."

Stavros shook his head. "Dimitra, I'm sorry. I cannot wait for you. Already I am late."

Demi glanced behind the hotel at the sun beginning to dip behind the mountains. "What time is it? I thought you didn't need to be there until seven."

He winked at her. "Maybe I lie. A little bit." He took on a serious expression. "I don't want to leave you." He moved closer to her and grabbed her by her shoulders. "You must come to dinner. I want you to see the Plateia at night. And enjoy my food, of course."

"I don't have a car."

"Yiorgos will bring you. I will call him now." A small gray Citroen came whizzing around the corner, close enough for them to feel the breeze it created. They scooted to the steps of the hotel.

Demi's phone buzzed, and she peered into her beach bag. "It's from my Mom," she said, glancing at the message: *Leaving shortly. Stopping for dinner on the way.* "I should be here when she gets back."

"Why?" Stavros asked. "You will see her every day. You will not see me after this week." He paused. "Unless you stay . . ."

Demi sighed. "I told you that I can't."

"Okay, okay," Stavros put his hand up. "We will not talk about this tonight. But you must come to dinner."

"Maybe," Demi felt herself yielding, "but I don't like eating by myself."

"You will not be by yourself," Stavros assured her. "Everywhere is *parea*. And I will be there. And you will eat my delicious dinner."

Demi smiled. "Alright, fine. I'll come."

"Good," Stavros nodded. "I will tell Yiorgos to pick you up at nine." He sprinted towards the bike, then stopped suddenly and returned to Demi. He took her chin in his hand, bent down, and kissed her softly on her lips. "*Tha ta poume*," he said. "See you soon, Dimitra."

Demi inhaled deeply and exhaled slowly, attempting to quell the butterflies wreaking havoc in her stomach. She pulled her phone out of her bag. Six thirty. She read the rest of the message from her mother: *Hope you had a good day*. Demi smiled to herself.

* * *

"*Yiayia*!" Stavros called as he opened the door of his grandmother's house.

Kiria Stavropoulou called to him in Greek from the kitchen. "*Ela*, Stavro. In here."

Stavros darted down the hall and kissed her on the cheek. "I have to take a shower. I don't have time to go home," he explained. "I have to get to work." He reached for a piece of cheese on the counter.

"*Aide*, Stavro, go take your shower." Kiria Stavropoulou waved him towards the doorway. "I will fix you a plate."

"No, *Yiayia*, I don't have time. I'm already late. Don't bother for me."

"It's no bother, *agape mou*," she said, opening the refrigerator door. "Go."

Stavros ran up the steps and grabbed a towel from the closet in the narrow hallway. He returned a few minutes later in a fresh shirt. A plate of pita bread, hummus, and feta cheese sat beside a glass of water on the kitchen table.

"Sit down, Stavro. Dimitris can wait five more minutes for you."

Stavros shook his head and laughed as he pulled a chair from the table and sat down. "Okay, *Yiayia*. I will sit for five minutes." He dipped a piece of pita into the hummus and took a bite.

Kiria Stavropoulou sat down across from Stavros. His wet hair was pulled into a ponytail, and his face was flushed from the shower or perhaps the sun. "Why you are so late for work tonight?"

Stavros waved off her concern. "I lost track of the time." He focused on the plate of food, scooping up the hummus with the triangular pieces of pita.

"How you do this?" Kiria Stavropoulou persisted.

"*Yiayia*, I went to the beach today. I didn't realize what time it was."

She raised her eyebrows. "Again, you go to the beach?"

"Yes, *Yiayia*. Again, I went to the beach."

"You are seeing the American girl," she stated.

Stavros pushed his chair back from the table and stood to leave. He bent down and kissed his grandmother on her cheek. "Thank you for the snack. I must go."

"Be careful, Stavro. She is here to fall in love."

"No, *Yiayia*," Stavros replied. "She is not." He opened the front screen door.

Kiria Stavropoulou called after him. "Be careful with her heart."

"Yes, *Yiayia*. I will," he answered. *Her heart?* He thought. *What about mine?*

* * *

"*Efharisto*, Yiorgo," Demi said as the taxi driver slowed the car in front of Kiria Stavropoulou's house. "Thank you for stopping here."

"Is no problem. I will take some fares, and I will be at the Plateia tonight when you want to go home. Is a five-minute walk from here. You want me to wait you now?"

"Is it safe to walk?" Demi asked.

"*Vevaios*," said Yiorgos. "*Prosekse ta aftokinita*, be careful the cars."

Demi peered into the fading light of the quiet street and wondered what Yiorgos was talking about. "Thank you," she said. "I'll see you later." She opened the passenger door, got out, and shut the door behind her.

Yiorgos leaned over to crank down the window, and Demi peeked in. "Did I forget something?"

Yiorgos pointed at the street ahead. "You go this way, then turn right. You will hear the noise from the plateia, and you will find it. *Yeia sou, koritsi*," he said and drove away.

The smell of onions sizzling in tomato sauce tickled Demi's nostrils as she approached the house. She tapped lightly on the screened door. "Hello?" she called. "*Yeia sas. Kalispera*."

"*Ena lepto*," she heard from inside the house. Kiria Stavropoulou came to the door, wooden spoon in hand, her apron over a light green house dress. She peered through the screen at Demi, who wore a short pale blue sundress. Her hair was loose and wavy, and her eyes reflected the hue of the dress. She wore a thin silver chain around her neck, echoed by the thin silver bracelet around her left ankle, and flat leather sandals. A smile lit up Kiria's wrinkled face. "Dimitra! *Ela,* come in." She opened the door and waved Demi in. "How nice to see you." She peered behind Demi. "Kiria Georgia is not here?"

"No," Demi replied. "They went to Monemvasia today."

"Ah, Monemvasia. It is one of my favorite places. Why you did not go with them?"

Demi hesitated, surprised at feeling uncomfortable. "I went to the beach."

Kiria Stavropoulou pressed her lips together and nodded.

Demi held out the small cardboard box she had brought with her. "I wanted to thank you for rescuing us the other day."

"*Efharisto*, Dimitra. It is not necessary. Come," she said, waving Demi into the kitchen. "I am cooking dinner. You want to eat?"

"Thank you so much," Demi said, "but I'm going to eat in the plateia."

Kiria Stavropoulou set the box on the counter and stirred the sauce with the wooden spoon still in her hand. "You are meeting someone?" she asked.

Demi considered a white lie but changed her mind. "Not exactly. I'm going to have dinner at the restaurant where Stavros works. He said he wanted to cook for me."

Kiria Stavropoulou nodded slightly, more to herself than to Demi. "So, you are keeping company with my grandson," she stated. She set the wooden spoon on the counter and untied the string around the box of cookies. "Sit," she said to Demi. "Stavros can wait." She poured a glass of water for Demi out of the tap and got a small plate from the cupboard upon which she set four golden honeycakes. "Ah, *melomakarona*. These are my favorite. *Efharisto, koritsi mou*." She placed the plate in front of Demi with a napkin and sat down across from her. She motioned for Demi to take a cookie.

Demi bit into the honey cake. The rich, moist cookie burst with honey's sweet, syrupy taste and a hint of orange. "This is delicious!" she said. "Maybe not as good as yours, but I wanted to bring you something to thank you for your kindness."

"You are sweet, Dimitra. Too sweet, maybe, for my Stavros." Kiria Stavropoulou raised an eyebrow and looked at Demi.

Demi set the other half of the cookie down on her napkin. "Why do you say that?"

"My Stavros, he is very handsome. He has many girlfriends."

Demi felt her face flush. She had suspected this, but hearing it from Stavros's grandmother clarified her suspicions. "Kiria Eleni, I'm not trying to be his girlfriend. I'm only here for a week."

Kiria Stavropoulou observed Demi closely. "But I think you like him very much."

Demi shrugged and tried to make light of this. "Of course I like him. He's charming. I enjoy his company. It's nice of him to take me places."

"What places he take you?"

"We went to the beach today, but I think you know that."

"Ah, yes. The beach." Kiria Stavropoulou thought a minute, then continued. "He show you the shipwreck Dimitri?"

Demi nodded.

"*Koritsi mou*, this he show to all the girls he meet from America."

Demi felt a knot in her throat. "You make it sound like there are dozens."

Kiria Stavropoulou shrugged her shoulders. She immediately regretted this as she watched the color drain from Demi's face.

"Does he take them all to the Caves of Diros, too?"

"*Tis spilies*? No, they are too far." She smiled kindly at Demi. "So maybe you are special to Stavros." She patted Demi's hand but then regained her warning tone. "*Prosexe, koritsi*. Do not give your heart away."

"Not a chance," Demi stated, with more conviction than she felt. Avoiding Kiria Stavropoulou's gaze, she glanced at the wall behind her and noticed a small painting of bright yellow lemons in a wicker basket. "What a beautiful painting," she said. "I hadn't noticed it before. I love the contrast of the lemons and basket with the blue tablecloth."

"*Efharisto*," said Kiria Stavropoulou.

Demi pushed her chair back from the table and looked more closely at the painting. She saw *ES* written on the bottom right-hand corner. "Did you paint this?" she asked.

"*Nai*, yes, I paint this a long time ago."

"Do you have other paintings?"

"Yes, come, I show you." Kiria Stavropoulou got up, stirred the sauce again, and then turned the heat down to simmer. She motioned for Demi to follow her into the living room. On the wall around the corner from the entrance were two small paintings—one of a rowboat moored next to a rocky beach and the other of a sunset over the sea. The water in the paintings was the same vibrant blue-green as the tablecloth in the other painting.

"I love your choice of color," Demi said. "Do you still paint?"

Kiria Stavropoulou lifted her chin in the now familiar motion of "no."

"Why not?" asked Demi. "These are lovely."

"I stop paint when my husband get sick," she said. "And then when I . . ." she stopped. "No, no, I do not paint now."

"But you're so good," Demi insisted. "May I take a photo of these?"

"*Vevaios*," Kiria Stavropoulou replied.

Demi returned to the kitchen to retrieve her phone from her bag and spotted Georgia's book, which she had tucked into it. She grabbed the bag and walked back to the living room. "I almost forgot," she said. She handed the book to Kiria Stavropoulou. "Mom had wanted to give this to you, but she wasn't sure if she'd see you again."

"*My Heart's Path*," Kiria Stavropoulou read from the cover. "By Georgia Karras. I not read English so good, but I will have my Veatriki read this to me when she come home. Say to your mama thank you."

"She signed it for you," Demi said. She took the book from Kiria Stavropoulou and flipped open the front cover to show her the inscription. "*Yia tin Kiria Eleni, o filakas angelos mas*." She looked at Kiria Stavropoulou. "What does it mean?"

Kiria Stavropoulou smiled. "It mean something very nice."

Demi raised her phone to the paintings and zoomed in to capture the photos. "I want to show these to my mom," she said. "She'll love them."

Kiria Stavropoulou was quiet as she looked at her painting of the sunset. "*Ela koritsi*," she said to Demi. She ushered her to the front door. "Thank you for come to see me. When you go home?"

"We're leaving Gytheio on Saturday morning. Our flight leaves Saturday night."

"*Krima*," said Kiria Stavropoulou. "A pity. It is too soon. *Ena lepto*," she said and walked back through the hallway. She returned and held something out to Demi. "To remember me."

Demi took the item from her, a smooth stone with the *mati* design hung from a short leather strip. She cradled the stone in her palm. "I would remember you without the *mati*, but I love this. Thank you."

"*Tipota,*" Kiria Stavropoulou said. "You are coming to the festival tomorrow?"

"Yes, we are."

"Ah, then I will see your mama again." Kiria Stavropoulou waved Georgia's book at Demi. "No books for this festival. Only food, wine, and dance."

Demi laughed. "I'll be sure to tell my mother not to bring hers."

Kiria Stavropoulou kissed Demi on her right cheek, then on her left. "*Yeia sou, koritsi mou*. Enjoy your dinner." She paused, then added, "*Prosekse tin kardia sou.*"

Watch my heart? Demi thought. *A little too late for that.*

CHAPTER 12

"I think we may have lost them," Charles said, nodding at the back seat. Georgia was in repose with her head resting on the headrest, and Zoe's head was leaning on the window. Both of their eyes were closed.

"It was a long day," Sophie said.

"The wine may have played a role," Charles chuckled. "I think they had quite a head start on us by the time we got back to the café."

"Definitely," agreed Sophie. "I was so thirsty; all I wanted was a glass of water. Or two."

"Yes, it was quite warm today," Charles said.

"That might be the understatement of the year," Sophie said. "What a beautiful night." The air was cooler now in the twilight, and lights from a remote village twinkled from a distance.

"You don't seem tired, Sophie."

"Oh, I'm not," she replied. "I feel like I could run a 10K." She inhaled the scent of sage that floated in through the open windows.

"Are you always this energetic?" Charles asked. "You're a right giddy kipper today!"

Sophie laughed. "Oh, no. I usually crash by nine or ten at home. I have to get up so early for work."

Charles realized he had not considered Sophie in any role other than American abroad. "What is it that you do?"

Sophie answered with pride in her voice. "I'm a copywriter for Sunstyle Magazine."

"How interesting," he said, then added, "I'm not familiar with it."

"Not too many people are," she replied. "Right now, we're regional, but we're growing. I've been there for two years, and we've tripled in size."

"You must be excited to be on the ground floor."

"Actually, we're in the basement," Sophie said.

"No, I meant . . ."

"Oh!" Sophie giggled. "Well, anyway, it's a really nice place to work. It's an old school building that they converted into offices. When I look out the window, I can literally see the legs of the people walking by. If we open the windows, I can hear their footsteps."

"Interesting," said Charles. "So, then, are you following in your *mother's* footsteps?"

"How so?"

"Wouldn't that be part of her job? Writing copy?"

"I guess so, to some degree. She writes press releases, and mostly, she markets her clients. I just write copy. Hopefully, I can work up to copy editor."

"Who edits *her* copy?"

"My mother's?" Sophie scrunched up her face. "Hmm. I'm pretty sure they have a whole department at her agency that does that."

"I see," Charles said. "Have you ever thought of working for them?"

Sophie shook her head. "Oh, my goodness, no. I'd never want to work there. Mom hates it there. I don't know why she stays. I mean, I know she makes good money. But they're not very nice to her. And she works her, uh, butt off but doesn't get the recognition she should. I guess she's been there for so long, it would be hard to leave."

Charles was quiet for a moment. "Sophie," he asked. "Do you think perhaps she needs to earn enough money to maintain her lifestyle?"

"Oh, no. Mom lives pretty simply. I mean, she wears nice clothes and everything, but she doesn't really splurge on herself."

"What about her house?" he ventured.

Sophie nodded. "She loves that house. I don't think she'd ever get rid of it."

Charles downshifted again as he slowed at the intersection. The sky was now a deep indigo, and the headlights of the cars on the main road signaled their approach. He waited as they passed and turned left onto the main road to Gytheio. He prompted, "Why do you think that is?"

"I don't really know. She kind of rattles around in it now that Marina and I are gone. Maybe it's full of memories." Sophie appeared to lose herself in one of the memories and added, "It's got a really nice kitchen."

"Sometimes people hang onto things for the sake of others. Perhaps your mother holds onto the house for you and your sister. It's where she raised you. Sometimes it's hard to let go."

Sophie looked closely at Charles. "Of the house? Or of us?"

"I'll let you ponder that."

The wheels turned in a steady rhythm on the blacktopped road. Zoe shifted her position against the window. *Is that what I'm doing*? She thought.

* * *

Darkness had descended upon Xirokambi, but the moon and stars had yet to fully emerge. Demi switched on the phone's flashlight and walked towards the plateia. She was still unsettled from her conversation with Kiria Stavropoulou, and when she heard a car engine approaching, she jumped to the side as the car whizzed past her. With each step she took, the laughter and conversations of the plateia grew louder, along with the background hum of motorcycles and car motors. Demi turned the corner and walked up the narrow street towards the bright lights that revealed the plateia. The busy road bordered the large town square on all four sides as drivers entered through the offshoots, cruised around the plateia once or twice, and exited. Across from each side of the square were *kafenios*, small groceries, a bakery, a butcher shop, and several restaurants distinguished by the style of tables, chairs, and tablecloths. About half of the tables were occupied. Demi paused and scanned the square for the blue chairs and white tablecloths Stavros had told her to look for.

Stavros turned the flame down on the stew and wiped his hands on his white apron. He left the kitchen to peer through the front door of the restaurant.

"Stavro," Dimitri teased. "What you are doing? You are waiting for the lambs to walk in the door?"

"Eh, no. I was taking some fresh air. It is hot in the kitchen tonight."

"It is hot in the kitchen every night."

"Well, tonight is especially hot," he said. Wiping his brow in exaggeration, he returned to the kitchen. "Ela *malaka*," he said to the line cook. "You have not made the potatoes? How I am going to serve the stew?" He put his hands in the air in frustration.

Dimitri walked out the door and scanned the plateia. He smiled when his eyes lit on the young American woman across the plateia.

Demi noticed the stocky man in the open doorway of the restaurant, under an awning that read *Dimitri*. Across the street from the restaurant, most of the tables were occupied. She felt her heart pounding as she waited for the stream of cars to slow before crossing over to the plateia and heading towards an open table. "Demi!" she heard a woman's voice rise over the chatter. She squinted at the nearby tables but didn't see anyone she recognized. "Demi, over here," she heard. Demi looked in the direction of the voice. Three women around her age sat at a table near the curb. The one who had called to her had her blonde hair in a loose bun and wore no makeup save for a subtle cat's eye. She wore jeans, a short white sweater, and espadrilles. Demi looked at her without recognition. "*Ela*," she said, waving Demi over with her left hand and taking a deep puff of her cigarette with her right. She slowly exhaled away from the table.

"Oh," Demi said. "Nadia!" She walked the few steps to the table. "I'm sorry, I didn't recognize you."

"I am not dressed for the club tonight," Nadia laughed. She looked behind and around Demi. "You are meeting someone?" she asked.

"Um, no, I . . ."

"*Ela*," she said, pointing at the empty chair across from her. "*Katse*."

"Thank you," Demi said. She pulled out the chair which faced the plateia, her back to the restaurant.

"*Prosexe*," Nadia said, pointing to the curb. "It is a little bit dangerous," she warned. "This is Demi," she said. She nodded to the woman beside her, a dark-eyed brunette wearing a tight red blouse. "This is Maria," she said, "and this is Elena." The petite woman to Demi's left smiled and nodded.

"*Harika pou sas gnorisa*," Demi said, practicing her Greek for "nice to meet you."

"Nice to meet you, Demi," Elena said.

"You are the American," Maria observed. "Nadia has told us about you and your sister."

"You mean my cousin," Demi corrected, and Maria shrugged. "There isn't much to tell."

"I hear Dinos is a little bit crazy for your cousin," Elena teased.

"Oh . . ." A clever reply eluded Demi.

"Anyway," Nadia said, "My brother *is* just a little bit crazy. Demi, you want something to drink?" A half-full carafe of white wine stood in the middle of the table. She signaled for the waiter. "I will get you a glass."

"Thank you," said Demi. *I definitely want something to drink.*

"Why are you here by yourself?" Maria asked.

"My family went to Monemvasia today."

"So? Why are you *here?* In Xirokambi? Don't they have restaurants in Gytheio?"

"Maria, you are being rude," Elena said.

"It's okay," Demi said. "I wanted to take something to Kiria Stavropoulou. She rescued us when our rental car broke down."

"I hear it was *Stavros* who rescued you," Maria said.

Does everyone know everything here? Demi wondered.

"It's a small town," Nadia explained, as if hearing Demi's thoughts.

Nadia glanced up to see the waiter bringing an empty glass for Demi and a tray of *mezzethes.* Behind him, in the doorway of the restaurant, she watched Stavros break into a grin when he spotted Demi. Nadia put her elbows on the table, rested her chin in her clasped hands, and smiled. The waiter set down the tray of appetizers and the glass and poured some wine for Demi. He went to pour some into Maria's empty glass, but she covered it with her hand.

"No, we are leaving," she said.

"We are?" asked Elena.

"Yes. Let's go to Mystras. I don't want to eat here." She lay ten euros on the table and stood up to go, wobbling slightly as she adjusted her high platform shoes to the cobblestone of the plateia. "Are you coming?"

Elena stood up reluctantly. "Sorry, Demi. It was nice to meet you. I hope you are liking Greece."

"Nadia?" Maria said.

"I think I will stay and keep Demi company," she turned to Demi, "if she wants me to?"

"You don't have to stay for me," Demi said, hoping for the opposite.

"Of course, I will stay," Nadia said.

"Whatever you like," Maria said. She looked down at Demi, then turned away and left without another word.

What a bitch, Demi thought.

"Sorry," Nadia said. She picked up the carafe and poured some wine into her glass.

"What was that about?" Demi asked.

"Demi," Nadia began. "You are with Stavros?"

Demi sighed. "I wouldn't say I'm *with* him."

Nadia glanced at the restaurant, where Stavros was again staring at their table. "Well, he is with you," she said, pointing at the restaurant.

Demi turned around to follow Nadia's direction and spotted Stavros. Her heart quickened, and she broke into a large smile. He grinned and nodded at her, then turned around and went back inside.

"Ela re, Malaka," Dimitri said, "You are going to burn the lamb chops. The girl is not going to disappear."

Nadia resumed her conversation. "Stavros is what I think you call a player. Mostly, he likes to flirt with the tourists. It is never anything serious. But I think he likes you. And Maria knows this. She is waiting for Stavros."

"Waiting?"

"She waits for him to fall in love with her."

"How long has she been waiting?"

Nadia pulled a pack of cigarettes out of her purse. "Since they were in high school." She rummaged for her lighter and pulled out the blue plastic one that Demi recognized from the club.

Demi's eyes widened. "Wow," she said. "That's a long time to wait."

"Yes, this we keep telling her," Nadia said, pausing to light the cigarette. "She is waiting for a bus that is never going to arrive."

"Did they ever . . ."

"Ah, this is the question. I think maybe when he was home from college in the summer, maybe they were together, but it was nothing serious. At least, not for Stavros."

"Wait. Stavros was in college?"

Nadia gave Demi a sideways glance. "You think he was always a cook? Stavros went to University in Patras for three years. Then his grandmother got sick. Her daughter—Stavros's mother—lives in Athens with her husband and their daughter. She has a very good job and could not leave. Stavros is very close to his grandmother, so he left school and came to stay with her. He took her to her doctor's appointments and her radiation. When Kiria Eleni got better, Stavros served his time in the army at the cooking school. He stayed close to home."

"He never went back to college?"

Nadia raised her chin. "He worked for Dimitri as a waiter while he took care of his grandmother. After cooking school, Dimitri offered him a job as head cook, and he took it."

So that's why he was offended when I thought he was a waiter. Demi shut her eyes and rubbed her temples.

"Demi, you are alright?"

"Yes, I am. I just . . ."

"Stavros is a good man. I think you are a nice person. Maybe your hearts will hurt, but you will be fine. You are young, and you are in Greece. Enjoy your summer romance." She lifted her wine glass. "To summer love," she said.

"What you are toasting to?" Stavros asked as he approached their table. "*Yeia sou* Nadia. Hello Dimitra. He clicked his fingers, and the waiter approached with a steaming dish of *stifatho* and two plates. "I make some lamb stew for you."

"We are toasting to love," Nadia said. She pushed her chair back, "Excuse me, I must use the toilette." She got up, and Stavros sat in her chair.

"I am glad you are here," he said. He pointed to the *stifatho*. "*Parakalo*, please taste."

Demi held a forkful of stew up to her nose, sniffing in the aroma of onions, cinnamon, and cloves, and took a bite. The meat was tender, moist, and flavorful. "Oh, my goodness, this is delicious," she said.

Stavros grinned. "I am happy you like it." He rested his chin on his hand and watched Demi enjoy her food.

"Stop watching me eat!" she laughed. She set her fork down.

"I like to watch you eat," he said. "You are enjoying my food, and this makes me happy."

Demi noticed a basket that the waiter must have brought at some point and lifted the towel to reveal warm, crusty bread and pats of butter. She picked up a piece and began to butter it.

"Dimitra," Stavros began. "How you know Nadia?"

"I met her at the club in Gytheio."

"You went to the club?" Stavros frowned.

"Yes." She bit into the soft bread, wiping the crumbs of crust from her mouth.

"When?" Stavros asked.

Demi set the bread down and leaned back, folding her arms. "Why does it matter?"

Stavros spoke in a sharp tone that Demi did not recognize. "Who else did you meet?"

"I didn't meet anyone. I went with Sophie. What is this about?"

"Nothing." Stavros shoved back the chair and got up as Nadia approached the table. "Enjoy your dinner. I must get back to the kitchen."

Demi sat with her mouth open at the sudden switch in mood. Nadia sat down and raised an eyebrow.

"What in the world?" Demi began. "I think he's jealous."

Nadia waved dismissively towards the restaurant. "Eh, he is a Greek man."

"That's no excuse for poor behavior," Demi said, her arms still crossed.

"Ah, no," Nadia said. A truck rumbled past them, its loud motor interrupting Nadia. ". . . but it is an explanation," she continued. She looked at the stew. "It's good?"

"Yes," Demi said. "Have some. I'm not hungry. I've lost my appetite."

Nadia's phone buzzed, and she pulled it out of her jeans pocket to read the message. "No, it's okay. I will eat something at home. Dinos is asking me to pick him up from work. Would you like me to take you back to the hotel?"

"Yes, thank you. Just a moment." She took her phone out of her bag and sent a text: *Thanks for dinner. Please tell Yiorgos that I don't need a ride.*

CHAPTER 13

A soft knock at the door roused Demi out of her sleep. Georgia rolled over and picked up her phone. "Nine forty-five? How did that happen?" She set her phone down and started to get up, but Demi was already answering the door. Dinos stood in the doorway holding a large wooden tray. On it sat a carafe of American coffee, two white ceramic cups, and a plate of assorted Greek cheese, meat, olives, and bread.

"*Kalimera*," Dinos said. "Is from Mihalis. He did not want you to miss breakfast. May I?" Without waiting for an answer, Dinos came into the room and set the tray on the desk. With a slight bow, he left.

"That was really thoughtful of Mihalis," Demi said. "I wonder if Dinos was so suave delivering Sophie's breakfast."

Georgia sat up, stretched her arms high, and yawned.

"You must have had quite a day yesterday," Demi said. "You were asleep when I got home, and it wasn't even midnight."

"I did," Georgia said. "I think I heard you come in. I was too tired to move."

"How was Monemvasia?" Demi asked.

"It was amazing," Georgia said. "I hope someday you'll be able to go."

"Me too," Demi said. "And how was Charles?"

"You know what, Demi? He was delightful. I'm glad he went with us. He's actually a very interesting man." Georgia got up and poured herself a cup of coffee. "I need to get ready. I have a meeting at eleven, and then we have our final breakout sessions at noon." She put some meat and cheese on a piece of bread and took a bite. "Mmmm, I don't know why we don't eat breakfast like this at home," she said.

"Probably because you don't have a butler," Demi said.

"Good point." Georgia went into the bathroom. Demi's phone buzzed, and she grabbed it to check the message. It was from Sophie. "Breakfast in Bed—smiley face!" "Same," replied Demi, checking to see if she had any other messages.

"How was dinner?" Georgia called.

"If, by dinner, you mean, 'how was the food,' it was delicious," Demi said. "I stopped by to see Kiria Stavropoulou. I gave her your book. She really appreciated it." Demi heard the shower turn on and turned back to her phone. Mentally, she calculated the time in Pittsburgh. *Too early to call Marina. What the heck had happened with Stavros last night?*

The phone on the bed stand rang, and Demi climbed over her bed to pick it up. It was Sophie. "Hi!" she said.

"Easy!" Demi said, holding the phone away from her ear. "I just woke up."

"Oh, sorry," Sophie said. "Mom is going to the breakout session today, and I think they have lunch afterward. Do you want to do something, or are you hanging out with Stavros?"

"Stavros is working today so that he can have the night off. He's helping to set up for the festival. Either way, I'm not hanging out with Stavros today."

"Oh, good. I mean, not good, if you wanted to hang out with Stavros. But good for me. Not that I didn't want you to hang out with Stavros if you wanted to, but . . ."

"Sophie!"

"Well, anyway, I thought maybe we could go to the beach or for a hike or maybe do some shopping?"

"I'd really like to relax today," Demi said. She leaned back on the headboard and pulled the phone closer to her with the cord. "And we have to pack. Why don't we meet around noon? We can shop a little and walk a little and get something to eat. I'm going to want to get a shower and do my hair before the festival."

"Sure. Maybe we can walk over to the tower and get some pictures. I can't believe we've been here for five days and still haven't gone over there."

"Yeah, we've been pretty busy."

"I can't wait to hear about your day!" Sophie said. "See you later."

Demi set down the phone. *My day*? She thought back to the previous morning and smiled despite her annoyance at Stavros.

"What are you smiling about, honey?" Georgia asked, coming back into the room. "Did you have a good time yesterday?"

"That's a long story," Demi said.

Georgia poured herself some more coffee and sat on the bed. "I've got an hour," she said.

* * *

The plateia was quiet compared to the previous night. Stavros was among a group of young men moving tables and chairs from the square to make room for the night's festivities. An old pickup rumbled down the road adjacent to the plateia, and the driver braked and shouted to a man having a coffee in front of the Patisserie. "Marko! What's up?"

The stocky man, dressed in denim coveralls and a white tee shirt, raised his coffee cup. "*Ela*, Niko," he called back. "Come to have a coffee."

"First, I need to deliver these watermelons," the driver shouted, pointing with his thumb to the bed of the truck, which was filled with ripe melons in variegated green stripes.

A horn blared from the taxi behind the truck. "*Vre, Malaka*," shouted the driver, leaning out of the window. "Move! You are going to talk all morning?"

Markos laughed as the truck driver waved and put the truck in gear with a clunk and a clatter.

"Stavro!" Dimitri yelled. "Move those chairs over here. We must make room for the dancers. *Ela*. At this rate, we will never finish."

"Alright, alright, just let me sit for a minute." At noon, the sun was already boring into the plateia. Stavros wiped the sweat from his brow with the bottom of his tee shirt, revealing his muscled stomach.

Elias approached, carrying a stack of chairs. "Eh, *Malaka*. Why you showing off? The American is not here." At the look on Stavros's face, he backed off. "It's okay, I'm just kidding. She is coming tonight?"

"I don't know," Stavros said. "I think I ruined everything."

"Don't worry, it won't be the last time," Elias said, laughing. "*Ela Vre, Malaka,* what can be so bad?"

Stavros shook his head and picked up a stack of chairs. He carried them past the musicians who had arrived to do a sound check and review the set lists. Stavros nodded at the young man who was plugging in his keyboard. An older man came over and clasped the young man on the shoulder. "Nice to have you with us," he said. He looked up to see a tall brunette woman approach the group. "Ah, good, our singer has arrived."

"Stavro, Louie!" Stavros looked past the musicians to see Yiorgos sitting at the kafeneio across the street. Next to him, under an awning, two white-haired mustachioed men hunched over a *tavli* set. Demitasse cups of Greek coffee sat half empty next to the game board. "*Elate*, come to drink a coffee with me."

"It's too hot for coffee," Elias shouted.

"Then come have a frappe. Or a beer," Yiorgos replied. "*Elate*."

"*Ena lepto*," Stavros said. He took his stack of chairs inside the restaurant. "I'll be back," he called to the empty room in case Dimitri was in earshot. He crossed the plateia to the small table where Yiorgos leaned back in a wooden chair with his legs crossed at the ankles.

"*Yeia sou*, Stavro."

"*Yeia sou*, Yiorgo. You are not working today?"

"Eh, I had an early fare to Kalamata this morning. I am tired. No more work today until I pick up the Americans in Gytheio tonight. He motioned to the empty chair. "*Katse*." Stavros pulled out a chair and sat down.

"So, what happened to the *kopela* last night? Demi?"

Stavros sighed. "I think she is angry with me."

"How she is angry with you? You only know her for what, four, five days? How you can make her angry already?" Yiorgos laughed, but when Stavros failed to crack a smile, he stopped. "Listen, *file mou*, whatever you did, you must apologize. You are a fool if you don't go after her. She is beautiful, and life is short. What you are waiting for?"

"Apologize?" Stavros said. He folded his arms. "For what? I have done nothing wrong."

"Ah, but if she thinks you have done something wrong, then you must apologize."

"This is what you would do?"

"Ah, me?" Yiorgos said. He looked over at the fruit market, where an attractive middle-aged woman was examining bright green peppers, then turned back to Stavros. "I am not so young. If it doesn't work, I move on to the next." He picked up a candied nut from the small dish and popped it into his mouth. "But you are young and have much life ahead of you. Don't miss a chance to fall in love."

* * *

"Come on, there's someone I want you to meet." Georgia led Zoe to the corner of the large room, which partitions had sectioned into small meeting areas. Large posters of Greece in bright blues and yellows hung on each partition. A short-haired woman wearing oversized designer glasses was already sitting at the round table. She got up to greet the sisters, and Georgia introduced her. "Ellie is a publisher based in London," she explained. "She may have an opportunity for you."

"Nice to meet you," Zoe said. "You look familiar. Have you been at the LitFest? I don't recall seeing you at any of the sessions."

Ellie replied in a British accent. "Lovely to meet you. I'm actually on the committee. We're always looking for new talent. I don't believe we've met, although you also look familiar."

"When you and I were chatting the other night," Georgia explained, "Zoe was at the other end of the table talking with Charles."

"Ah, Charles," said Ellie. "Delightful man."

"Yes, he is," Georgia agreed. "Shall we sit down?"

"You said you might have an opportunity for *me*?" Zoe asked. "I'm not the one who's the writer. Georgia is."

Ellie smiled. "I'm aware of that. I enjoyed Georgia's book, and I'm looking forward to her next one. That's where you might come in."

"How so?"

"I understand that you are in public relations?" Zoe nodded, and Ellie continued. "I work for a literary agency in London. We're looking to expand. I think that you might have the relevant experience to help us with our promotions. We're hoping to increase our marketing efforts to offer authors not only a publishing opportunity but a publishing and promotional experience. Give them the publicity and support they need to increase book sales."

"From what I've seen," said Georgia, "that's the way the industry is headed."

"I think it's a great idea," Zoe said, "but I don't see how it pertains to me. You're in London. I live in Pittsburgh."

"Exactly," Ellie said. "We're looking to expand internationally. With so much being done on the internet these days, we don't see the necessity to all work out of corporate headquarters. We've already staffed agents in Toronto, Seattle, and Dallas. Why not Pittsburgh?"

"Dallas?" Zoe asked. "Why Dallas?"

Ellie laughed. "We hire talented agents who have worked with national PR or advertising firms. It doesn't matter where they live if they have connections beyond their cities. We're not a small firm, Zoe. You can look us up. If you need to travel to meet with a client in, say, New York or Philadelphia, we'll take care of travel expenses. We'll either support an office in your home or fund a shared office space. Are you interested in discussing the opportunity?"

Georgia interrupted. "I'll leave you two to your discussion. I have another session to go to. Ellie, so nice to see you again." She leaned down to hug Zoe and whispered in her ear. *Do not start playing devil's advocate. Listen to what she has to say.*

* * *

Marina, groggy and with her eyes barely open, patted the bedside table next to her in search of her ringing phone. She unhooked it from the charger and spoke. "You know it's only six a.m. here, right?"

Demi and Sophie huddled around the screen on the phone, waiting for the video to stream. Marina's thick dark hair stuck out in wayward curls around her face. "You look like Medusa," Sophie giggled.

"I can hang up, you know," Marina said. "What is so important that couldn't wait a couple hours?"

"We just missed you," Demi said. "I wish you were here."

"Yeah, me too." Marina sighed. "Someday." She peered closely into her phone. Behind Demi and Sophie stood a small white chapel against a bright cobalt sky. "Where are you guys? It looks beautiful there."

"We're on an island!" Sophie said.

"An island? I thought you were in Gytheio." Marina propped the phone on her nightstand and disappeared from the screen, leaving the pale yellow wall of her bedroom and a *Starry Night* poster as her backdrop. "I'm listening," she called.

"We are," Demi laughed. "We walked out across a causeway. We're technically on the island of Kranai."

"It's so cute," Sophie said. "It has a little white chapel, and there's a lighthouse and a tower at the end of it. I'll send you some pictures."

"I didn't know there was an island near Gytheio," Marina said, returning with a glass of water and her hair combed loosely into a bun.

"Neither did we until Mihalis told us about it," Demi explained. "He said that *kranos* means 'helmet.' Legend has it that Paris left his helmet in the tower here, where he spent the night with Helen before leaving for Troy." She paused. "Although I'm not sure why they'd name an island after someone who started a war. Even if it is mythical, and I'm guessing he probably wouldn't have left his helmet behind."

"Unless he was so in love, he was distracted," Sophie suggested.

"You mean Helen of Troy? Are you talking about the Trojan War?" Marina asked.

"You know your mythology," Demi observed.

"Well, I am Greek," Marina said.

"Half," Demi teased.

"I'm guessing you didn't call me to discuss Greek mythology," Marina said. "What's going on there?"

Demi handed the phone to Sophie. "You can go first."

Sophie relayed her adventures in Kardamyli and Monemvasia, then returned the phone to Demi. "Wait," Marina said. "I need a cup of coffee for this. I'll be right back." Rays of sunshine now reflected off the Van Gogh poster. Demi could picture Marina opening the blinds and padding into their small kitchen barefoot to fix a quick cup of coffee in the Keurig. The call-waiting notification appeared on her phone. Stavros. An initial thrill went through her as she stared at the notification until she remembered that she was annoyed at him.

Sophie peered over her shoulder. “Aren't you going to answer?” she asked.

“He can wait,” Demi said. With each pulse of the notification, her resolve lessened. As the phone stopped vibrating, her heart started to pound. *Shit,* she thought. *Should I call him back*?

“Demi,” Sophie said. “You know you want to see him. Don't ruin your last night in Greece. Call him.”

Demi stared at the Van Gogh painting on the screen. “Okay, I'm back,” Marina said, obscuring the poster. “Where were we?” The phone buzzed again.

“Marina, I have to go,” Demi said. “I'll see you soon. Love you.” She waited a few seconds, took a deep breath, and answered. “Hello?”

“Dimitra,” Stavros began. “I am sorry . . .”

CHAPTER 14

Loud music reverberated from the large speakers on either side of the band. Five musicians occupied a section of the street in front of the restaurants: a clarinet player, a bouzouki player, a guitarist, a keyboard player, and a drummer. White plastic tables and chairs adorned the entire plateia, except for the spot where the band played. "Wow!" Demi shouted over the music and noisy chatter. "This is some serious festival!" The restaurants were closed, but the smell of pork and chicken roasting on outdoor grills filled the plateia.

Georgia and Zoe scanned the tables for empty chairs. Demi scanned the plateia for Stavros and Sophie scanned the plateia for Dinos. "There!" shouted Zoe over the din. Four chairs sat empty at a long table occupied on either end by two older couples. They wove through the tables, and Demi and Sophie sat beside each other, leaving seats for Zoe and Georgia across from them. "Why don't you girls save the seats, and we'll go get some food?" Zoe said.

"What?" said Sophie. Zoe pointed to the chairs and mouthed, "Save these."

Georgia and Zoe headed to the opposite side of the plateia, where a throng of people waited in front of two long tables. Behind the tables, men and women were heaping large servings of meat and potatoes onto sturdy aluminum trays. Among them was Kiria Stavropoulou. "Where is the end of the line?" Zoe asked.

"I don't think there is a line," Georgia replied. "I think we just have to wedge our way in." An older man pushed past Georgia and stood in front of her. "Excuse me!" Georgia said, then "*Signomi*!" when he didn't react, but he continued to ignore her as he pushed his way to the front. "That's it," she said. She stood on her toes and called, "Kiria Eleni. *Yeia sou*!"

Kiria Stavropoulou looked up at the sound of her name and saw Georgia waving at her. She nodded and grabbed four paper plates from the pile in front of her. Then she ladled large chunks of pork, several pieces of roasted chicken, and a large scoopful of lemon-roasted potatoes onto an aluminum tray. She placed a scoop of tomato salad on another tray with kalamata olives, savory onions, feta cheese, and fresh oregano. Next to this, she placed a loaf of freshly baked crusty bread. She nodded to Georgia and motioned to the side of the table. "*Efharisto,* Kiria Georgia," Georgia said. "Thank you so much."

"*Tipota, Kiria.* You pay over there," she pointed to the next table. "I talk to you later," she added, "when not so busy."

"I'll go get some wine," Zoe said, pointing to another table where carafes of red and white were jammed into large metal tubs filled with ice. A few minutes later, she returned holding four plastic cups of white wine by their rims and joined Georgia in line to pay.

Georgia and Zoe carried the food and drink back to the table. Two young men stood behind their seats across the table from Demi and Sophie. One pointed to the empty chair. "May I?"

"Sorry," Demi said. "My mom's sitting there."

"I do not see anyone sitting here," he said. "Perhaps she is invisible?" He winked and pulled out the chair.

"Oh, thank you," said Zoe and reached past him to set down the cups of wine.

The man drew his hand back in surprise. "*Signomi, Kiria*, I did not see you there."

"Perhaps because she is invisible," Demi said sarcastically.

The second man patted his friend on the back and laughed. "*Kalispera, koritsia*," he said to the girls, and they walked off.

"Girls, you are like magnets," Georgia laughed. She set down the tray of meat.

"That's okay," Sophie said. "Demi is the anti-magnet. She compels the magnets."

Demi rolled her eyes. "*Re*pels?"

Georgia set down the trays of food. "Oh, my goodness, that looks amazing!" said Sophie. She grabbed a set of plastic utensils from the tray and unrolled the napkin. As they ate, the music seemed to get louder. "I feel like they could hear this in the next village!" Sophie shouted.

"I think that's the idea," Demi said. She looked around the plateia and caught a glimpse of Nadia and her friends, but there was no sign of Stavros. "Sophia!" they heard. They looked up to see Dinos winding his way through the tables and chairs. He stopped at the end of the table, as there did not appear to be a clear path to Sophie. "*Kalispera*," he called.

"Hi, Dino!"

"You want to come to my friends?" he asked.

"Sure!" she answered. She turned to her mother. "Do you mind?"

"Of course not, Sophie. Have fun."

Sophie pulled out her chair. "Come on, Demi."

"That's okay. I'll stay here and digest," she said and added, "I'm not done with my wine."

"Bring it with you!" Sophie said.

Demi shook her head. "I'll see you in a little bit."

Sophie sidestepped her way to Dinos between the tables. His smile grew as she approached, wearing the colorful scarf and earrings that Georgia had bought her. Dinos leaned over to talk into her ear. "You look beautiful!" he said. His face flushed, and Sophie smiled. "Your cousin, she is not coming?" Dinos asked.

Sophie shrugged. "Maybe later."

A large area in front of the band had been cleared for dancing, but for now, it was empty, except for the people who cut across it. "Why is no one dancing?" Demi asked. Georgia and Zoe turned around and looked at the empty dance area. Georgia recognized the familiar 7/8 beat of the popular *kalamatiano* music.

"You want to dance, Demi? Let's go!" She pushed her chair back and stood up. "Come on, Zoe."

"Now?" Zoe said. She looked again at the dance area. "But no one is dancing."

"Let's go," Georgia insisted. "Someone has to start it." Demi, Zoe, and Georgia snaked through the tables and chairs and arrived at the dance floor at the same time as two of the village women took the floor. The women smiled, and one of the villagers took the lead as they formed a chain, taking each other's hands and holding them up at shoulder height. The dancers picked up the beat of the amplified music, moving eight energetic steps forward in a counterclockwise motion and four backward. The small line circled the dance floor a few times, and soon, other dancers joined in, cutting in between the ladies or tagging on to the end of the line. Within minutes, the line of dancers had steadily grown into two layers of the same chain.

Demi felt a tap on her shoulder and looked to her left to see Nadia breaking into the line. She smiled as they continued to move in a joyful circle. The tempo increased, and the dancers found themselves stepping more quickly. The song morphed into another song and then another as some left the line and others joined. The sun had set, and the evening air helped to cool the sweat from Demi's body. For a moment, there was only the fragrant air, the steady movement, and the upbeat music, and Demi was content. She felt someone prying her hand from Nadia's as Maria broke in. She took Nadia's hand in her left hand and Demi's in her right as they circled the dance floor in a steady rhythm. Then, Demi felt her let go. Maria raised her right hand, shouted "*Opa*," and led the long line of dancers away, leaving Demi at the end of a short line. Demi clenched her jaw as she continued to dance. *She seriously just highjacked the line?* She thought. *I am not going to let that bitch ruin my night.* She placed her left hand behind her back and danced with an extra jump in her step.

"Did you see that?" Sophie said to Dinos and his friends. Dinos nodded. "Let's go," she said, grabbing Dinos by the hand. She tapped Demi on the shoulder and took her left hand as Dinos brought up the end of the line, his clumsy steps almost in time with the music. Still moving forward as Sophie stepped backward, he stepped on the back of her right ankle. "Sorry!" he said.

"That's okay," she said. "This is fun." She squeezed his hand and kept dancing, stretching out her left arm to keep Dinos just a little farther away. They continued to dance as one song faded into the next and eventually came to a stop. Demi followed Sophie and Dinos over to his group of friends. She recognized one of them. "I thought you said you would be dancing tonight," Demi said.

Kostas smiled. "You will see," he said. "I am waiting for a special dance."

"Let's get some water," Sophie said. She and Demi turned to go to the drink table.

"Dimitra." She heard a voice in the crowd and looked behind her. Stavros looked tentatively at her, his eyebrows arched slightly, his mouth in a half smile. "You are still angry with me?"

"It's my last night in Greece," she said. "I'm not going to spend it being angry with you."

"But you are going to spend it with me?" he asked.

She crossed her arms. "That depends."

"On what?"

"On whether you dance with me or not." They stared at each other's eyes—his hazel eyes focused on her grey-blue ones—and her heart melted. His had melted the moment he saw Demi in her black sleeveless dress and long silver earrings.

"Yes, of course," Stavros said. The slow clarinet strains of the *tsamikos* three-quarter beat filled the plateia. Stavros held his finger up. "But first, I must do something." He ran to join a group of four other men on the dance floor. Kostas took the lead, followed by a short, middle-aged man, Stavros, and two other young men. They clasped hands, elbows bent, and formed a line. Demi observed the simple steps of the dance, much slower than the *kalamatiano*. Suddenly, Kostas kicked his right leg into the air, followed by his left leg in a high scissor-like motion, slapping his left foot while it was still in the air. More jumps and acrobatic twists followed until he broke off and moved to the end of the line to loud applause and whistles, and the next man took the limelight. Surprisingly limber, the short man repeated Kostas' moves at an even faster speed to the delight of the crowd, but after a minute, he relinquished his spot. Stavros wasted no time. After leaping into the air, he bent at the knees into a deep backbend, balancing with a tight hold onto the man to his left, who gripped his hand tightly to hold him up. Stavros kicked his leg up and hoisted himself again into a standing position. Demi grinned and clapped, joining the crowd yelling, "*Opa,* and *bravo, Stavro!*" The two others took their turns, and the dance ended to raucous applause. Stavros came back to Demi and Sophie.

"That was amazing!" Sophie said.

"You like it?" Stavros asked Demi.

"It's beautiful," Demi said. "What is it?"

"It is a *tsamikos*. It is the warrior's dance."

As Kostas passed the group, he stopped and addressed Demi. "*This*, you see, is dancing." He continued past her to his friends.

Stavros's eyes narrowed. "How do you know Kostas?" he asked.

Sophie jumped in. "Because of Dinos. Come on, let's go get some water." She grabbed Demi's arm, and the men followed.

The full August moon had risen above the buildings surrounding the square, a bright yellow sphere against the indigo sky. Its glow fused with the festive lights strung around the plateia, illuminating the dancers.

"Look," Sophie pointed at the dance floor. Georgia and Zoe were dancing with two other ladies. Georgia had tied her shawl around her hips, which she twisted to the beat of the spirited *tsifteteli*. Georgia and Zoe smiled at each other and shimmied their shoulders. Georgia threw her head back and laughed.

Demi smiled. *They are so happy*. She looked at Stavros, and her heart skipped. *I just want to capture this feeling in a bottle.* She closed her eyes and breathed in the night.

"You are having a good time, Dimitra?" Stavros asked.

Demi opened her eyes. "I am."

Stavros bent down and kissed Demi, then pulled away. "*Ela*, I promised you a dance." He took her hand and led her to the dance floor, winding through other dancers until they were close to Georgia and Zoe. They danced, arms held out at shoulder level, thumbs and middle fingers together as if they were going to click their fingers. They circled each other, stepping to the downbeats of the bouzouki. The song continued for several minutes, then morphed into another, before changing rhythm. Georgia and Zoe danced over to the couple to form a larger circle, and Sophie ran over to join the group. Stavros leaned over to speak into Demi's ear. "You dance," he said. "I will be over there." He pointed towards the wine table and walked over.

"So," Stavros heard and turned to see Elias. "Your flower is here." Stavros ignored him. "And she has the rest of her bouquet with her," he laughed.

"You are an idiot," Stavros said.

"I like this dark-haired flower," he said, nodding towards Sophie.

"She is with Dinos tonight," Stavros said.

"Dinos? That fool? She will not be with Dinos after she meets me."

"*Vre, Malaka*, go find your own *loulouthi*. I'm sure you can have your pick." Stavros waved towards the tables. Many of the older patrons had gone, and some of the tables were now occupied by young men wearing jeans and tee shirts and women attired in short tight skirts and high heels, more reminiscent of a nightclub than a street festival.

"Yes, perhaps," Elias replied. "But I prefer this one." He raised his eyebrows in Sophie's direction as she and Demi approached them. "*Kalispera, koritsia*," Elias greeted them.

"Dimitra, this is Elias," Stavros said. "And this is Sophia."

"Hello!" Sophie said. "Nice to meet you."

"The pleasure is mine," Elias replied. He picked up Sophie's hand and kissed the top of it.

"Oh!" Sophie said. She giggled and drew her hand back.

"How do you like Greece?" Elias asked.

"I love it," Sophie replied.

Elias turned to Demi. "And you, Dimitra? You are enjoying your time in Greece?"

"Yes, of course," she said.

"Good," Elias said. "I am sure Stavros is an excellent guide." He followed this up with a wink.

Stavros shook his head at Elias and took Demi's hand. "Come, Dimitra, let us find a place to talk that is not so crowded. Sophia, you are coming?"

"Oh, no, thank you, Stavro, I'm going to find Dinos."

"I think he is over there," Stavros said, pointing to a corner of the plateia where several other young men and women had gathered.

"Dinos?" Elias said. "No, you are too beautiful to be with that buffoon. You must stay here with me tonight. I will show you a good time."

"Oh, no, thank you," Sophie said politely. "I'm already having a good time." She spotted Dinos across the plateia and caught his eye. She returned his wave and left to join him.

"Well," said Demi, "Obviously, she's not only beautiful but smart."

Stavros burst out laughing. "Who is the buffoon now, eh, Louie?"

Elias shrugged. "Eh, it is a big garden." He headed towards the group at the tables.

"What is he talking about?" Demi asked.

"*Tipota, agape mou*, nothing. Let's go sit."

* * *

"Don't these guys ever take a break?" Zoe asked, out of breath.

"I don't think so," Georgia said. "I feel like one song just morphs into the next." The band had been playing continuously with no sign of fatigue and no sign of a break. "Shall we sit for a few minutes?"

"Definitely," Zoe agreed. "Let's grab some water." The line for refreshments was shorter now, and the volunteers at the food tables were cleaning up the last of the dinners. In their place were plates of sweet *baklava* and nutty fried *diples*. "Shall we?" asked Zoe.

"We shall!" They stopped at the food table, where Kiria Stavropoulou was taking off her apron. "Kiria Eleni," Georgia asked. "Will you join us?" She nodded to an empty table.

"*Nai, duo lepta*, two seconds," she said.

"I'll get the sweets," Zoe said. "You get the water."

They sat down at a table on the edge of the plateia. The night air cooled the sweat from their arms and faces. Zoe looked up at the full moon. A halo of soft light surrounded it. "What a wonderful night," she said.

Georgia nodded. *I wish Jimmy were here*, she thought, happy to be missing him rather than feeling annoyed at him. *We really need to work on the bickering.*

"Look who's here," Zoe said, nodding at a nearby table. Georgia recognized the head of bright red hair. Yiorgos and Gloria sat next to each other, leaning their heads together. His lips brushed her ear, and she giggled.

Georgia shook her head and laughed. "That didn't take him long! I guess we'll need to call a different taxi tonight." She broke a piece of the *diples* and took a bite, savoring the nutty honey taste of the pastry.

"*Yeia sas, kiries,*" Kiria Stavropoulou said. She pulled out a chair and dropped into it.

"You must be exhausted," Zoe said.

"Yes, it is much work, but it is for the church," she replied. "No dance for me tonight." She turned to Georgia. "Dimitra, she bring me your book. *Efharisto*." She reached into her purse and pulled out a small square item wrapped in blue tissue paper. "*Orieste*," she said, holding the box out to Georgia. "Is for you."

"Oh," said Georgia. "You didn't need to . . ."

"Tsst," Kiria Stavropoulou raised her chin. She pushed the package towards Georgia.

Georgia brushed the crumbs from her hand and took the gift. She carefully ran her index finger under the tape and unwrapped it. "Oh, Kiria Eleni, this is beautiful!" Georgia held up a small square painting of the church at the plateia, the sky in the background a bright cerulean blue. Tiny red geraniums dotted the small pots on either side of the entrance. "Thank you so much. Did you paint this?"

Kiria Stavropoulou nodded. "For you to remember Xirokambi. And me," she added with a smile. "I don't forget you," she said to Zoe, handing her a small package in identical blue tissue paper. Inside was a glass *mati* on a long cord. "You wear here," she said, patting her chest. "To stay away the bad."

Zoe bent her head down and placed the necklace around her neck. "Thank you," she said. "That is so nice of you."

The music stopped, and the dancers dwindled from the dance floor. "Is it over?" Zoe asked. Kiria Stavropoulou lifted her chin. The bouzouki player leaned into his microphone and made an announcement in Greek. A tall brunette woman in a form-fitting sleeveless silver dress took the stage. Her bright red lips neared the microphone as she said *Efharisto* in a breathy voice and nodded to the musicians. The keyboardist played a brief introduction of simple notes, and the singer joined in, her voice clear and expressive. The chatter in the plateia quieted, and her voice rang through the night.

Demi looked up from her conversation with Stavros to watch the singer. Her mouth fell open as she listened to the passion in her voice. "What is this song?" she whispered to Stavros. "It's beautiful."

"It is *Avgoustos*," he said. "August."

"I don't understand the lyrics, but you can tell it's a sad song," Demi said.

"Ah, it is a love song," Stavros said. "They are all sad."

The singer's voice quivered with emotion as she began the chorus, and any chatter that remained stopped as she poured her soul into the song. "What is she saying?" Demi asked.

"She say, 'the road we have taken is impossible. Have faith, you will tell me.'" He paused as the song continued. "She say, 'how I can forget her loose hair, the sand, washing down . . . like a waterfall." He looked into Demi's eyes and ran his fingers through her hair, pulling her face to his.

Demi understood the next words: *I'll go, even if it turns out wrong.* She raised her mouth to meet his.

From across the plateia, Kiria Stavropoulou shook her head. "This is not good," she said, nodding towards Stavros and Demi. "*Tha tis rayisei tin kardia*."

"She might also break *his* heart," Georgia replied. "But they are young and romantic. They will be alright," she said, with more conviction than she felt.

* * *

Several taxis lined up at the corner of the plateia as the crowd at the festival dispersed. "It seems strange not to have Yiorgos taking us," Sophie said.

"Don't worry, you'll see him tomorrow," Georgia said. "He agreed to take us to the airport."

"Oh, good!" Sophie said. "Will we see Charles tomorrow before we leave?" She interrupted herself. "Oh, wait a minute — Why wasn't he at the festival?"

"Peter was able to make it to Greece after all," Georgia said. "Charles went to pick him up in Kalamata. Hopefully, we'll get to say goodbye in the morning before we leave."

They walked towards the first taxi in line, and Zoe grabbed Georgia's arm. "Georgia! Where's Demi?"

"Demi's staying with Stavros."

"What do you mean, staying with Stavros? As in, she's not coming back to the hotel tonight?"

"Yes."

"But we're leaving for the airport in the morning!"

"Yes, we are."

"What if she's not back?"

"She'll be back."

"But what if she isn't."

"Then she isn't, and we leave without her. But she will be." Georgia opened the front door of the taxi and greeted the taxi driver.

"*Pou pate*?" he asked.

"Gytheio. Aktaion City Hotel."

"*Elate*."

They got into the car, and Zoe leaned over the headrest. "Georgia, aren't you worried about her?"

"In what regard, Zoe? Worried that she won't make the flight? No. Worried that she'll stay in Greece? No. Worried that she's going to have her heart broken? Yes. But it will heal."

"If she stays in Greece, Jimmy will kill you."

Sophie touched her mother's arm. "Mom, I think you're being a little dramatic."

"I'm not being dramatic, Sophie," Zoe said. "I'm just worried about the welfare of my niece and my sister."

Georgia sighed. "Zoe, please stop worrying about my impending death and my daughter's demise."

"Yeah, Mom. Everything will be alright in the end. If it's not alright, then it's not the end."

"Hmph," Zoe snorted. "Well, look how well that worked out for John Lennon." She leaned back in her seat.

"Zoe, seriously. Stop. Demi is a smart woman who can make and live with her choices. It's been a wonderful night. Let's savor it. Tomorrow is going to be a long day." *And a tough one for Demi,* Georgia thought.

CHAPTER 15

"You are early this morning, Dino," Mihalis remarked as Dinos quickly entered the lobby. "You are anxious to begin the day?" Dinos nodded at Mihalis, then peered into the breakfast room. Mihalis chuckled. "She is outside, Dino. You did not see her? Go." He waved him towards the door.

Dinos pushed open the hotel door, letting in the morning sunshine. He glanced towards the left and right, his heart pounding in anticipation. He spotted Sophie at one of the neighboring restaurant tables, her tea and pastry from the breakfast room in front of her. "Sophia!" he called.

"*Kalimera*, Dino," she said. "I saw you go by, but you looked like you were in a hurry. I thought maybe you were late for work."

"No, no. I . . ." he paused for a second, his attempt to be suave evaporating rapidly. "I want to see you before you go."

"Oh," Sophie said. "That's so nice of you." She looked out at the reflection of the sun sparkling off the dark blue waters of the gulf. "What a beautiful morning. I hate to leave."

Dinos pulled out a chair and sat down across the table from Sophie. "Sophia," he said. "You must write me. Maybe give to me your Facebook? Maybe we talk sometime?" His face blushed a soft red as he held his phone out to her.

"Of course, Dino. I would love that." She took the phone and entered her information, then handed it back. "I had so much fun with you and your friends. I'll always remember this summer."

"Maybe sometime you come back?" he asked. His eyebrows raised in a question.

"You never know," Sophie replied. She sipped the last of her tea and set her cup down. "I better go finish packing." She stood up. "I'm sure I'll see you on the way out."

Dinos stood up and faced Sophie. He found that his arms were frozen at his sides. He opened his mouth to speak, but his voice was equally frozen. Sophie hugged him. His arms regained their movement, and he hugged her back, then kissed her on each cheek. "*Yeia sou,* Sophia. *Kalo taksidi.* Have a good trip."

She smiled, picked up her empty cup, waved, and turned towards the hotel. Dinos breathed in deeply and let out a long sigh, already feeling nostalgic.

Sophie walked into the hotel to find Georgia and Zoe heading to the breakfast room. "Hi, Honey, are you done packing?" Zoe asked.

"Just going up to finish," Sophie replied. "I just said goodbye to Dinos," she added.

"I bet that was tough for him," Georgia said. "I think he was pretty smitten with you."

"Smitten?" Sophie asked.

Georgia smiled. "It's an old-fashioned term. He has a crush on you."

"Oh!" Sophie said. She paused and cocked her head. "I guess maybe he does!" She smiled, nodded, and left.

"She is so freaking cute," Georgia said.

Zoe rolled her eyes, but she smiled. "I know." They walked towards the breakfast bar, which held fresh meats, cheeses, and today, *tiropitakia*, the delicious baked phyllo dough triangles filled with cheese. "Yes!" said Zoe. She lifted the lid to smell the buttery baked goods and set two crisp cheese pies on her plate.

Georgia poured coffees from a silver carafe and carried the cups to a table by the window. She looked out beyond the street to the pedestrian walkway, where a young couple jogged in unison past the hotel. Two small white fishing boats anchored at the sea wall barely drifted in the stillness of the morning. "I'm going to miss this view," Georgia said. "But I think I'm ready to go home."

"Any word from Demi?" Zoe asked.

"No," Georgia said. "She said she'd be here by ten." She glanced at her wrist out of habit, still not used to her decision to forego her watch for the summer.

Zoe took her phone out of her pocket. "It's only eight-thirty," she said.

"Oh, thank heavens, I was afraid I'd miss you!" They looked up to see Charles bounding into the room. His hair was unkempt, and he wore round wire-rimmed glasses, a rumpled grey tee shirt, and plaid pajama bottoms. A couple at the next table raised their eyebrows and covered their mouths to hide their laughter.

Zoe's mouth dropped open, and Georgia started to laugh, taking in his uncharacteristic disheveled appearance. "Charles! What in the world. . . . I didn't know you wore glasses?"

"Yes, contacts, actually, for the most part. We got back late last night from Kalamata. Peter is still sleeping, of course, but I woke up and thought, crikey! I hope they're still here! I didn't want you to leave without saying goodbye." He looked down at his pajama bottoms as if he'd just realized he was wearing them and then down at the untouched breakfast plates. "I guess I would have had time to comb my hair and put on a decent pair of pants."

"You look fine, Charles. Although, I may always remember you this way," Georgia said.

"Yes, well, perhaps I'll send you my professional headshot to erase that image."

"Hmmm, I don't know, Charles. Some things just can't be unseen," Georgia teased. "Why don't you sit down? There's fresh coffee over there." Charles wrinkled up his nose, and Georgia laughed. "Oops, right. There's also a selection of tea."

"No, thank you. I'd better wait for Peter. He should be up any hour now." Charles turned to Zoe. "I hear you have an interesting opportunity," he said with an impish smile.

"Did you have something to do with it, Charles?" Zoe asked.

"I may have indulged in a spot of light meddling on your behalf," he said. "But your sister got the ball rolling."

"There's a lot to think about," Zoe said. "It's a big decision."

"Don't overthink it, Zoe. Sometimes, you just have to take that leap. Whatever you decide, I wish you well. Do whatever is best for you in the long run. I hope you do what gives you joy."

"We should all follow that advice, Charles," Zoe said, looking at Georgia.

"What's that supposed to mean?" Georgia asked.

"Georgia," Zoe began. "You're a wonderful teacher. No one would dispute that. But is that where your heart is now? Don't you want to make writing your full-time job?"

"There are a lot of writers who write part-time."

"Name one."

"I can't just name one off the top of my head," Georgia said. "Zoe, not everyone has the luxury of forgetting everything else and writing every day."

"Right. But you do. Jimmy's successful. Your house is paid for. Demi's an adult. And you've already shown you can write." She spread her arms out to encompass the room. "If you want to stay connected, teach a college night class, but focus on your writing. I have faith in you."

"As do I," Charles added. "But now, I must get back upstairs before Peter wakes and thinks I've left him for Apollo or some other handsome Greek godlike creature."

The sisters stood up to hug Charles. "It was such a pleasure meeting you and getting to know you, Charles," Georgia said.

"The pleasure is all mine. Please give my regards to Sophie and Demi. Absolutely delightful young ladies."

"Charles, thank you for . . ." Zoe paused. *Counseling me? Listening to me? Driving us around? Giving me confidence?* ". . . everything."

"Hope to see you in London," he replied. He motioned a salute and waved his hand. "Cheerio, Ladies . . . 'til we meet again!"

* * *

Demi sensed the daylight streaming in through a gap in the blue curtains. She opened one eye, then the other, turning her head to face an empty pillow. "Stavro?" she said. The implication of the morning struck her with the force of a punch, and she sighed deeply.

"Dimitra." Her name sounded forced, choked out. Stavros took a deep breath. "You are awake."

She looked toward the voice in the bedroom doorway where Stavros stood in shadow. "What time is it?" she asked. She reached the bedside table for her phone, and her heart rate quickened. "Oh, shit," she said, "my battery is dead!" Stavros approached the bed and held his hand out for the phone. She gave it to him, and he plugged it into the charger on his desk.

They had spent the night wrapped in each other's arms, alternating between the desperate, ardent lovemaking of two people who knew they would soon be parting and the sporadic, fitful sleep of emotional turmoil. Demi trembled as she recalled Stavros's mouth exploring her breasts, her stomach, and the warmth between her legs. Her pleasure waned as she recalled their sorrowful midnight whispers, his voice imploring her to stay through tearful *I love yous*. She felt both vital and drained, eager to hold on to the passion of the previous night but aware that their clock was ticking. "Stavro," she repeated. "What time is it?"

He glanced at her charging phone. "It is only eight thirty. Don't worry."

In the light of morning, Demi noticed the matching desk, dresser, and nightstand, all made of light blonde wood. Two landscape paintings decorated the white walls of the bedroom. She tried to fight the constriction in her throat with conversation. "Did your grandmother paint those?" she asked. Stavros nodded. "She's amazing."

"She don't paint no more. Ever since she have the *karkinos*, she stop. She say she is too tired, but I think she is afraid."

"Afraid of what?"

Stavros shrugged. "Maybe she forget how to paint."

Demi sat up and pulled the sheet around her. She looked around for her dress, spotting it on the chair in the corner of the room. "I have to go," she said. She picked up her clothes and walked down the hall of the apartment to the bathroom.

Stavros sat down at the desk, holding his head in his hands. He heard the muted spray of the shower for what seemed an eternity as he waited for Demi to return. His eyes were tinged with red when he looked up at her. Her wet hair hung in ringlets, and a few drops of water dripped onto her black dress. "Dimitra. Demi. Please don't go. Stay here with me." His eyes held hers.

"We've been over that, Stavro. I would love to stay. I can't." She spoke with a certainty she did not feel.

"Why you don't stay another week?"

"Why? We'll be in the same situation a week from now."

"Yes, this is the idea." He gave her a hopeful half-smile. "Maybe you will change your mind. Maybe you will stay with me. What I will do without you, Dimitra?"

"Whatever you did before me." Demi felt tears welling in her eyes. "I'm sure there are women waiting for me to leave so they can have you for themselves." She thought of Maria, and her throat tightened.

Stavros stood up. "No! *Sou to orkizomai*. I swear to you. There is no one." He grabbed her shoulders. "Dimitra, *s'agapo*. I love you."

"This is crazy. I haven't even known you a week."

"This is all that is necessary to fall in love when you have found your *adelfi psihi*."

Is he my soul mate? Demi wondered. "I'll come back to visit. I'll come back next summer and stay longer."

"You say this now, but you will go back to your home and your job and your friends, and you will forget me."

"No, I won't." Demi looked into his eyes and felt her resolve melt. She closed her eyes and took a deep breath. She looked back at Stavros. "Stavro, I love you. This week was amazing. You are amazing. I will never forget you. But let's call this what it is—a summer romance."

He dropped his hands and stared at her. "No. This is not *kalokairini agape*. You don't believe this. You say this, but you don't mean it."

She sat, silent with her thoughts. *I don't mean it. I am in love with you. I want to stay with you*. But these feelings were quickly replaced by the recollection of abandonment and heartache. She could not leave her heart open to that pain again.

Stavros sensed an opening. "You must stay with me."

"I can't," Demi said. "I've been down that road before."

"But this road is in Greece. It is not the same. I would never leave you." He pulled her into his chest and wrapped his arms around her as if his fervent embrace might keep her from going away. He let go of her and took her head in his hands, kissing her deeply and passionately, and she melted into his caress. She felt a strong urge to stay, to call her mother and say, "Sorry, Mom. I can't leave." To call work and say, "I won't be back for a while—or maybe ever." But in the back of her mind, her thoughts festered. *I can't get burned again. I can't give my heart so easily.* She ran her hands through his hair, pulling his head away from hers, and looked at him directly. "Stavro. I have to go." She slid away from his grasp and bent down for her sandals. She sat on the bed and buckled them.

"You are leaving me?" he asked. She did not look up, and his hope evaporated. "*Endaksi*. I will take you back to your hotel."

Demi stood up. "No. Please call a taxi for me. I don't want to repeat this at the hotel. It is hard enough to leave you here."

"Ah, if it is so hard to leave me, why you are going?"

She pressed her lips together and blinked to hold back her tears.

"So, you will go," he said. "And I will never see you again."

"Why not?" A bolt of panic shot through her at the finality of his words. "I told you I would come back. We can write and talk . . ."

"For what, Dimitra? If this is just a summer romance, as you say, we must leave it at that."

"You don't want to stay in touch with me?"

He lifted his chin. "What is the point? You have made your decision. I will call your taxi. Goodbye, *koritsi mou*."

PART II

CHAPTER 16

Georgia sat at her laptop, arms leaning on the desk, fingers poised over the keys. She wasn't writing, however—she was staring out the window in front of her. From her nook in the dormer of their guest room, she watched a bright red male and a soft brown female cardinal sharing the bird feeder, which had space for four birds on the perches around the seed cylinder. A house sparrow attempted to land on one of the perches, but the crimson male flapped his wings at her and scared her off.

"Hey honey," Jimmy interrupted her reverie. "Are you busy?"

Georgia swiveled in her chair to see her husband at the door. Small bits of sawdust decorated his white tee shirt and floated on the dark hair of his forearms. "I was just watching Fred and Lucille," she said. She leaned back in her chair, clasped her hands, and stretched them above her head. "I'm glad they're still here. Thanks for filling the feeder."

"No problem," he said, offering her the frappe he was holding. "I figured you might miss these."

Georgia accepted the glass with rich dark coffee in the bottom, a milky liquid in the middle, and foamy caramel-colored froth on the top. "Thank you," she said and took a sip. "That's delicious." She nodded towards the ladderback chair upon which sat the cat, curled up on a pile of folded sweaters. "Have a seat," she said. "Just throw those on the bed."

Jimmy lifted the pile, cat and all. Gus opened an eye but remained firmly embedded in the sweaters. Jimmy laughed and set the bundle on the bed. "Didn't want to interrupt the writer at work."

"I'm afraid my muse is hiding today." Georgia frowned. "She's been hiding from me since I came back from Greece."

"It's only been a week, honey. She'll come back."

"I hope so," Georgia said. "What did you want?" Jimmy nodded at the frappe, but Georgia shook her head. "I know you well enough to recognize your 'I want to talk to you' face."

Jimmy sat down and took a deep breath. "Okay. I didn't like the way things were between us when you were in Greece." Georgia sat up, folded her arms, and opened her mouth, ready to launch on the defensive, but Jimmy raised his hand. "Hold on, Georgia. Let me talk." She leaned back in her chair but kept her arms folded. Jimmy continued. "I want to apologize. I'm not sure what was wrong with me. I think I was jealous," he paused and shook his head, "No, jealous isn't the word. Envious. I wanted to be there with you, and since work kept me from going, I was resentful that you were there. And no, Demi didn't tell me to say that. I realized it myself when I saw how happy you were about the conference and everything you told me about. I just needed to mull it over and work up the courage to talk to you about it."

Georgia's breath caught. "Why would you ever need courage to talk to me, Jimmy?"

Jimmy gave her a half-smile. "It takes courage to admit you've been a complete *malakas*."

Georgia smiled. "I wouldn't say you were a *complete malakas*. I could work on not letting myself bristle every time I interpret something you say as a criticism. And, no, I did not come up with that one myself—Demi pointed it out to me. And she's right." Georgia looked at the frappe on her desk, and a glow came over her. "Let's both try not to bicker. There's too much love here to waste time on petty arguments. I love you, Jimmy."

"I love you too, *Agapi mou*. And look," he added. "I want you to write. I get that this is more than a hobby. I'm sorry that I ever treated it as anything else. I'm glad that you're so devoted to something. I guess I felt like your spending time here," he nodded at the computer, "was time that you weren't spending with me."

"Jimmy," Georgia said. "I love spending time with you. Let's just make sure that we communicate. It's not like I can't take a break from writing. But you also need to understand that when I'm in the middle of a scene, I need to focus."

"How 'bout I make you a "do not disturb" sign for the door?" Jimmy joked.

Georgia smiled. "That's actually not a bad idea."

Gus stood up, stretched with all four legs straight, and his back arched like the proverbial Halloween cat. He surveyed Georgia and Jimmy and rearranged himself, curling back upon the pile of sweaters and shutting his eyes. "That's not a bad idea," Georgia said. "A nap might be what I need to bring back my muse. Care to join me?" she asked Jimmy.

"I would," Jimmy said, with a grin and a raise of his eyebrows. "I'm not sure how much sleeping we'll do, though."

* * *

Demi surveyed the ballroom. The black tablecloths, a last-minute decision by the bride, gave an air of sophistication to the large room, where each table was adorned with a spray of miniature white roses in a short glass vase. Outside the large windows of the ballroom, the sky was already a dusky blue. Demi pushed up the sleeve of her white shirt to check her Fitbit, a gift from her mother. Its pink band contrasted with the severity of her black dress pants and her hairstyle, a low ponytail. Five forty-five. Out of habit, she glanced below the time and saw that she'd already made her goal of 10,000 steps for the day and wondered how many more there were to come once the guests began to arrive and the festivities were underway. She wanted to make sure things ran smoothly, especially if she hoped to be promoted. She'd worked her way up from Events Coordinator to Assistant Banquet Manager, but after three years and over a hundred events, she was ready for the responsibility and challenge of a higher position. More importantly, she craved daylight hours. A rumor was floating through the club that the head banquet manager was leaving to open a restaurant, and Demi was hoping to talk to the General Manager about her prospects.

"Demi!" a shrill voice preceded Lisa, one of the waitstaff, into the room.

"What's the matter?" Demi asked.

"Kim just called in sick. She has the flu. She said she tried to sleep it off, but when she woke up, she . . ."

"Okay," Demi said, turning on her heel towards the door. "Call Brandon and see if he can fill in. I'll see if we can snag Sydney from the Tennis Banquet. They should be finishing up. Maybe she'll want the extra hours."

"I doubt it," mumbled Lisa under her breath as she took out her phone.

Demi strode past the bar, where a lone bartender arranged champagne flutes on a tray. "Where's your partner?" she asked.

"She's running late," he replied. "Got a flat tire on the parkway. Some dude is fixing it for her. Don't worry, she'll be here soon."

Demi paused to rub her temples. *Not a good start to the evening*, she thought. "Let me know if you need any help," she said. "And let me know when your partner gets here." Before he could answer, her phone beeped. 'Brandon's a go,' the message read. *Disaster averted*, she thought, *for now*.

The country club's restaurant was lively that evening, with patrons from a golf outing that afternoon and the usual Saturday night members. Demi noticed two couples waiting at the hostess stand, and no hostess was in sight. "May I help you?" she asked.

"Miss . . ." One of the women peered closely at Demi's name tag, ". . . Karras. Yes, we've been waiting to be seated."

Demi walked around to the other side of the podium, checked their names on the reservation list, picked up four menus, and ushered them to their tables. "Someone will be here to take your drink orders shortly," she said. She approached the nearest waiter and asked him to take care of the couples. When she returned to the door, she saw the hostess chatting with the woman at the coat check room across the hall. "What are you doing?" Demi asked. "There are people waiting to be seated."

The hostess narrowed her eyes at Demi. "None of your business," she said. "Last I looked, you weren't my boss."

Demi let out a long, slow breath. "You're right," she said. "If I were, you'd be out of a job."

* * *

"What are you doing with these books?" Georgia asked. The dining room table was strewn with books, and an array of knickknacks from small glass animal figurines to a Willow Tree® figurine of two young girls holding hands.

Zoe appeared not to have heard Georgia as she picked up the figurine and smiled. "It's *Sisters by Heart,*" she said. "You got it for me for my birthday a few years ago."

"I know," Georgia said. "I couldn't resist. It reminds me of us growing up." She pointed at the books on the table. "What about these?"

Zoe wrapped the figurine in newspaper and laid it in the bottom of a large box. "I was going to donate them. Why?"

Georgia picked up a copy of William Zinsser's *On Writing Well* and leafed through the pages. "I had this one a long time ago. It's one of the better ones. Do you mind if I take it?"

"Help yourself," Zoe said. "It's probably yours anyway. But don't you have enough books?" she chided.

"Zoe," Georgia answered, "You can never have enough books." She stopped at a page and began to read, becoming absorbed by Chapter 6 on *Words*.

"Georgia. Georgia!" Zoe's voice penetrated Zinsser's astute writing advice. "Time for that later. Please help me get these things in a box."

Georgia picked up a glass elephant and began to wrap it. "Where in the world are you going to put all this stuff, Zoe? You're trying to move a mansion worth of stuff into a patio home."

"I'd hardly say a mansion," Zoe said. She looked at the space around her, emptier by the day as she packed furniture, dishware, and the accumulations of almost thirty years. "I am going to miss this kitchen, though." She looked fondly at the large kitchen with oversized maple cabinets, granite countertops, and massive cook's stove.

"Why?" Georgia asked. "It's not like you did a lot of cooking, Zo."

"I know. But we had great parties here."

"*We,* Zoe. That was years ago. When was the last time *you* threw a party here?"

"I know. I think I'm holding on to what once was, or maybe what could have been, instead of what is."

"It's a new chapter, Zoe. I'm so proud of you. This is a brave thing you're doing." Georgia smiled at her sister. "I'm really excited for you."

"Thanks, Georgia. That means a lot." She wiped her eye with her sleeve and picked up another figurine, this one a glass swan. "Speaking of chapters, where are you on that rewrite?"

"Almost done, Zoe. I would have finished this morning, but . . ." She put out her arms to encompass the room."

"Hey, don't blame me for your procrastination," she said. "I just can't wait to get your book to the printers. And I want to finalize the book launch and promotion."

"Good thing you rented office space," Georgia said. "I can't see anything getting done in the midst of this."

"I checked into a few places for the launch. What do you think about having it at Café Notte? I wanted to have it at Kostas, but I think it's too small."

"Do you really think it's too small? I don't know how many people will actually come to this. And I really would like Greek food, especially since the setting is Greece."

"Jerry can make Greek food. And you will definitely need the space. Anyway, Kostas said he's closing down for a couple of weeks while he takes a break and works on a new menu. His mother is finally retiring, and he needs to train a new cook staff."

"His mother has to be close to a hundred!" Georgia remembered what she and Zoe thought when Kiria Stavropoulou told them about her cousin Kostas that summer. "Well, I do love Café Notte. If you don't think we'll be rattling around in there . . ."

"We won't be. And once the band is set up . . ."

"The band? What band?"

"I asked Sotiris if he was available. I thought it would be fun to sort of turn this into a Greek party. You know—music and dancing."

"Are you crazy, Zoe? Where is the money for this coming from?"

"Your future book sales," Zoe smiled.

"What if there are no future book sales?" Georgia asked.

"Well then, I guess we're just throwing one heck of a party!"

* * *

The front door of Georgia and Jimmy's house was propped open to let the fresh air pass through the screen door. September had begun much the same as August, with hot, humid days and warm evenings, but true to Pittsburgh's fickle weather patterns, a spate of cooler, drier days and chilly nights had intervened—good "sleeping weather," as Jimmy would say. Demi rapped twice on the aluminum screen door before entering the living room. "Mom? Dad?"

Jimmy had remodeled the older brick house to open the floor plan, erasing the border between the living room and the kitchen. The door to the backyard was also open, and a cool cross breeze flowed through the house. Jimmy leaned over the large farm table, the sleeves on his denim shirt rolled up, a half-finished mug of coffee within his reach. He looked up from his blueprints and smiled when he saw Demi. "Hi honey! What brings you here?"

"Hey, Dad, where's Mom?"

"Your mother went to help Aunt Zoe pack some boxes."

Demi hung her purse onto the back of a sturdy chair and bent down to kiss her father on the cheek. "I can't believe she's really moving. She's been in that house for so long. I remember playing on the swing set with Sophie and Marina when we were little." She opened the cupboard and took out a white ceramic mug. She pointed at the French press on the counter. "Is this still hot?" Jimmy nodded, and she poured a cup of coffee, adding a splash of milk from the refrigerator. "I'm gonna miss that pool, too. Although I didn't use it much this summer." She pulled out one of the heavy chairs and sat down.

"That pool is a hassle for Zoe," Jimmy replied, "and it's not easy for one person to take care of a house that big. It's about time she got out of there. Sometimes I think we should do the same thing. I get tired of raking leaves and cutting the lawn."

"You love this house, Dad. I can't see you ever leaving it." She looked around at the familiar kitchen with its hand-painted Italian ceramic backsplash tiles and sturdy oak cabinets. "I miss living here. I love this kitchen. And I miss my room. It's so much quieter than my apartment."

"You know you can always come back here."

"Dad. I'm 29. I don't need to be living with my parents."

"Think of the money you would save," Jimmy said. He raised his eyebrows and nodded as if in agreement with himself.

"I'm saving money already. And you and Mom don't need another person in this house." Demi furrowed her eyebrows and peered closely at Jimmy. "Does it still bother you that I moved into an apartment?"

He waved his hand as if pushing away the thought. "No, honey, I've gotten over that. It *would* bother me if you moved away. I'm sorry things didn't work out with Andrew, but I'm glad you didn't take the job in Philly."

"Philly is only five hours away. Sometimes, you have to go where the job opportunities are."

"There are plenty of opportunities in Pittsburgh."

"It's a limited market, Dad. I can't stay on an evening shift forever."

"Keeps you out of trouble, doesn't it?" Jimmy took his empty cup to the sink, rinsed it, and placed it in the basin. "What did you need your mother for?"

"I just wanted to talk to her about something. No problem, it can wait."

"Anything you want to talk to me about?"

"No, but thanks, Dad. Just girl stuff." Demi got up from the table. "I need to get a few things out of my closet. I think I left my boots there from last fall."

"You wouldn't have to worry about closet space if you lived . . ."

"Dad."

He put his hands up in surrender. "Alright, no more. I'll be here if you need me."

Demi walked up the wooden stairway, recognizing the familiar creaks on the third and seventh steps. The door to her room stood open, and sunlight streamed through the sheer white curtains. A cozy white comforter covered the double bed, and "Bearly," a relic from childhood, still guarded the pillows. Although her room was now used as a guest room, she maintained a section in the closet and two of the dresser drawers for items that didn't fit in the tiny closet in her apartment. Demi opened the door and found a pair of brown leather booties in the back of the closet on the floor. She surveyed the shelves and selected a pair of grey jeans and two sweaters for the fall weather that had descended upon Pittsburgh.

Juggling the clothes, she reached the top shelf and grabbed a folded shopping bag. As she closed the closet door, she spotted two hoodies hanging on a hook inside the heavy wood door. With a jolt, she thought about Stavros, and the memory of the beach came rushing back. A twinge of longing hit her, and her heartbeat quickened. She took a deep breath, put the clothes into the shopping bag, then sat down on the bed and looked out the window at the backyard.

Her mother's garden was overgrown, as late fall gardens tend to be when the enthusiasm for watering and weeding wanes as summer comes to an end. The parsley had gone to seed, and the herbs grew wildly. A few zucchinis were scattered randomly against the last of the tomatoes, which threatened never to ripen. Jimmy had gone out to the detached garage and was measuring something on a plank of wood he had laid on a couple of sawhorses in the driveway. From her berth above the yard, Demi noticed a slight bald spot on the back of her father's otherwise thick, curly head of greying hair. *When did that happen*? She wondered. Jimmy bent down to pick up the piece of wood he had sawed off the plank, and she noticed his slow movement to retrieve it. A pang of uncertainty struck her. Did her parents need her there? Was her father right—should she keep waiting for an opportunity in Pittsburgh? But for how long? Her career was already off track.

Demi picked up the bag and went downstairs. She opened the kitchen door and called out to Jimmy over the whirring of the circular saw. "Dad!" Jimmy stopped the saw and looked up as Demi approached him. "What are you working on?"

"I'm making some bookshelves for your mother. Her books don't fit on the ones she has. I told her to get rid of some of them, but that didn't go so well!"

Demi laughed. "I'm sure it didn't! Tell her I stopped by. I'll talk to her later." She hugged Jimmy and kissed him on the cheek. "I love you, Dad."

"Same, *Dimitraki*."

Demi smiled at the nickname her dad had given her in childhood—"little Dimitra" or, actually, "little Jimmy." But her smile faded as she thought about the possibility of moving away.

CHAPTER 17

The banquet room at Café Notte had a festive air. Although it was early October, small white Christmas lights were strung around the windowsills. The room was alive with chatter and background jazz coming through the speakers in the ceiling. The girls clustered around a high-top table by the windows. Demi, her hair loose and wavy, wore an olive-green knit dress that complemented the remnants of her summer tan. Sophie had splurged for an orange and purple dress from Anthropologie, and Marina opted for a black sweater and leopard print pants.

The ladies had dressed to the nines for the occasion—Georgia in an off-the-shoulder teal cocktail dress with the blue earrings from Santorini and Zoe in a rust-colored two-piece suit and black pumps.

"This is unbelievable!" Georgia said. "Is that the reviewer from the *Post-Gazette*?" she asked Zoe.

"It is," Zoe replied.

"But how . . ."

"It's amazing what you can do when you have a little support. Go ahead—go talk to her."

"I need a drink first," Georgia said. She flagged down the waitress, who was circling with a tray of *tiropitakia*. "Could I get a gin and tonic, please?"

The waitress pointed across the room where red cone lights hung suspended over a marble bar top. A hockey game played soundlessly on the television mounted on the wall behind the bar. "Over there," she said. "Would you like a cheese pie?"

Georgia snagged a *tiropitaki* and napkin. "Wish me luck," she said to Zoe and walked to the bar.

Zoe's eyes roamed the room. Some of Georgia's former co-workers stood around high tops, intermingled with family friends and a few distant relatives. Zoe was pleased to see people picking up and looking at the books lining the windowsills, interspersed with photos of Greece. She caught a glimpse of a man in the doorway. The backlighting cast his body in shadow, but she recognized his frame immediately. Apparently, so did Demi. Zoe watched from across the room as Demi's mouth dropped open, and she froze momentarily. She pressed her lips together, swallowed, and strode to the doorway. Andrew stood before her, his blond hair freshly cut in a close crop. He wore a blue shirt and tie, which, of course, complemented his eyes, and a grey sports jacket. He held out a cold bottle of Moet & Chandon. "Hi Demi, good to see you."

Her words came out in staccato notes. "*What* . . . are *you* doing here?"

"Your father invited me."

"*What*?"

"I ran into your dad at the hardware store. He invited me to come."

"Unbelievable." She shook her head. "Why would he do that to me?"

"Everything's not about you, Demi. I'm here to celebrate your mother's book. I remember when she was writing it."

"Are you kidding me?"

"Hello, Andrew," Demi heard Zoe's voice behind her. "Nice to see you." She nodded at the champagne bottle. "Thank you—you can take that over to the bar. Demi, I need your help over here." She grabbed Demi's elbow and led her over to the dessert table, laden with plates of artfully arranged *baklava* and *melomakarona*. "What is *he* doing here?" Zoe asked.

"Apparently, Dad invited him?" Demi answered.

"Are you kidding me?" Zoe said.

"Right?"

They both turned to glower at Jimmy, but he was heading down the passageway towards the men's room, unaware of the impending wrath he would soon face.

Georgia stepped onto the platform in the corner of the room and picked up the microphone. She tapped it gently for the reverberation to signal that it was on. "Hello!" She waited for the conversations to pause. "Thank you all so much for being here to celebrate the relaunch of *My Heart's Path*. As some of you know, the book won the Melinda Handler Emerging Writers First Book Prize last year, and with that came an initial printing of 500 books. I'm so pleased to tell you that with the help of Laurel PR and Press, we've been able to relaunch the book, giving it new life and extended distribution both in the states and internationally . . ."

"Dad." Demi intercepted Jimmy as he came back into the room. "What in the world were you thinking?"

"About what, honey?"

"Inviting Andrew?" She put her arms out, palms up, and waved them for emphasis.

"I thought you might enjoy seeing him." Jimmy grinned at his daughter.

Demi squared herself and put her hands on her hips. "What in the world makes you think I'd enjoy seeing him after what he did to me?"

Jimmy shrugged. "Time heals all wounds, Demi. The course of true love never did run smooth." He winked.

"Oh, okay, Lysander," she said sarcastically. "But I am not in love with Andrew. That is over."

"Well, then," Jimmy reasoned, "it shouldn't bother you to see him."

". . . I couldn't have done this without the help of my sister, Zoe, who has always pushed me to find my voice as a writer, my amazing daughter, Demi, whose close reading and sage advice has made my writing shine, and my husband Jimmy, who encouraged me to take this book to new heights." Georgia clapped in the direction of Jimmy and Demi, who stood at odds, face to face.

The applause broke through their showdown, and they slowly turned to face the attendees clapping in their direction. Demi recovered first. She clapped, then blew a kiss to her mother and put her hand on her heart. Jimmy raised his glass and shouted, "To Georgia!" He turned to Demi and put his arm around her. "I'm so proud of your mother, Sweetheart."

Demi looked at Georgia on the platform, beaming. Her heart melted. "Me too, Daddy."

* * *

Sophie grabbed Marina by the elbow and pulled her off to the side. "The Eagle has landed," she whispered.

"What?"

"The *Eagle* has landed," she repeated.

Marina narrowed her eyes and peered at Sophie. "What the heck are you talking about?"

Sophie leaned closer to Marina. "The *Greek* Eagle," she emphasized, "has landed."

"Oh!" Marina nodded and giggled. "Roger, Tranquility. I copy you." Sophie scrunched her face in confusion. "Never mind," Marina said. "Where, exactly, has it landed?"

"In the kitchen. He's talking with the chef. I told him to wait there."

Demi approached the girls. "What are you guys up to?"

"Nothing," they said in unison.

Demi cocked her head. "If you say so." She turned to walk past the entrance to the kitchen.

"Wait! Where are you going?" Sophie asked.

"The ladies' room."

"You can't!"

"Excuse me?" Demi stared at her cousin.

"You can't go!" Sophie said as she positioned herself between Demi and the hallway.

"Why not?"

"Because *I* have to go. It's an emergency!"

"Okay, we'll both go."

"You don't want to do that!"

"Why not?"

"It's going to get ugly in there!" Sophie turned and ran to the ladies' room.

Demi looked at Marina and rolled her eyes. "I think there's another bathroom in the lounge. I'll be back."

Marina heaved a sigh of relief. "Whew!" *However, what was the plan, exactly? she* thought. *We haven't really thought it through.*

Sophie returned. "Where's Demi?"

"The other restroom."

"Good, okay, so I was thinking we would just start to reminisce about Greece and talk about how nice it would be to see everyone from there again, and then we could . . ."

"*Koritsia mou*!"

"Hi, *Thia* Pitsa! Hello, *Thie* Antoni!" The sisters greeted Jimmy's brother and his wife as if they were their aunt and uncle, exchanging hugs and kisses. Pitsa's short hair was dyed jet black, and her lips were painted bright red, as evidenced by the prints she left on Sophie and Marina's cheeks. Marina discreetly rubbed her cheeks with the backs of her hands. Sophie's smile froze on her face, unsure of what to do until Demi returned a minute later, and Sophie took advantage of the distraction. She grabbed a napkin and rubbed quickly as she watched Pitsa, her lipstick only slightly faded, leave a light imprint on Demi's cheek.

"How was the trip to Greece?" Pitsa asked. "Tell me everything." At this, Antonis nodded to the girls and headed over to the men at the bar.

The girls filled Pitsa in on the highlights. *A perfect segue,* Sophie thought and started to speak. "We met so many nice people . . ."

Pitsa interrupted her. "Who is that young man?" she asked, pointing across the room. Their heads turned to follow her gaze. No one answered her. "Is it Lexi's boy home from college?" Pitsa leaned in and whispered. "I don't remember him being so handsome."

Demi swallowed his name before it could escape, cracked and raw. It settled in her chest, pushing her heart to beat faster and harder. She found her voice. "*What* is *he* doing here?" she asked for the second time that night.

Oblivious to her niece's turmoil, *Thia* Pitsa asked, "Oh, you know him?"

Sophie cheerfully replied. "Yes, we met him in Greece this past summer." She turned to Demi. "He's helping his grandmother's cousin at his restaurant."

"Noohhh. I mean *here*," Demi said, pointing to the floor of the restaurant.

"Oh. I..um . . . I invited him."

"What? When? You've been talking to him?"

"Well, not exactly. I talked to Dinos, and he . . ."

Demi turned to Marina. "Did *you* know about this?"

"I . . . um . . ."

"Seriously? What is going on with my life?" Demi peered suspiciously to the left and the right. "Is Tommy here, too?"

"Tommy?" the sisters asked.

"Tommy Katsafanas. My Greek school crush in eighth grade. Is this *This is Your Life* former boyfriends episode?"

A chuckle escaped from Marina before she could suppress it. "I'm sorry, Demi. We thought you'd be happy to see him."

"Happy. You thought I'd be *happy* to see him? The man who broke my heart last summer. Oh, and right after seeing the man who broke my heart last spring."

"That's not fair, Demi," Marina replied. "We didn't know Andrew would be here."

Demi strode to the chair and grabbed her jacket and purse from the seat back.

"Where are you going?" Sophie asked.

"I have to get out of here." She forced her arms into the denim jacket and slung her purse onto her shoulder.

"You can't leave," Marina said. "This is your mom's night."

"She'll understand."

"That's not the point."

"Oh? Is there a point?" She looked at their blank faces. "Right." She took a step towards the hallway.

"I'm sorry, Demi," Sophie called after her. "I just thought . . ."

Demi whirled around. "There was no *thought* involved here."

"Demi," Marina said. "She was just trying to help."

"Help what?"

Sophie and Marina exchanged glances. The bright spots that bloomed on Sophie's cheeks matched the red flush on Demi's face.

"What?" Demi insisted.

Marina sighed. "Demi. You have been miserable since you came back from Greece. I can't remember the last time I saw you having fun. You sigh more often than the trees in the wind."

"I just thought you'd be excited to see Stavros," Sophie explained.

Marina looked across the room at Stavros, who had left the cover of the kitchen and was now talking with Sotiris. His white shirt sleeves were rolled up, revealing darkly tanned arms and hands moving animatedly as he chatted with the musician. She raised her eyebrow suggestively. "I know *I'm* excited to see him."

Demi laughed despite herself. She shook her head, sighed, and paused before speaking. "I'm sorry for overreacting, Sophie." The girls relaxed as the tension evaporated. "I was just caught off guard. Please, no more surprises." She pointed at Marina. "And, *you* should know better. What in the world would make you think that I would appreciate this surprise?" Marina shrugged as Demi took another step towards the door.

"Where are you going?" Sophie asked.

"Don't worry. I'm not leaving. I just need some air." Demi pushed open the glass door and inhaled the cool night air. She plopped her purse on one of the wrought iron tables and sat down. As the adrenaline boost subsided, she realized that her hands were shaking. *Where is Nadia with a cigarette when I could use one?*

* * *

Strains of bouzouki music and laughter escaped the restaurant when Stavros opened the door to the patio. He spotted Demi leaning back in a chair, her elbows on the armrests, at one of the black metal tables. An open umbrella shadowed her face while the large lamplight on the restaurant's brick façade illuminated his. He approached her.

"Dimitra." Demi turned her head to look at Stavros but did not shift her position in the chair. The dripping of a fountain behind her filled the momentary silence, along with the woosh of passing cars beyond the hedge that separated the patio from the boulevard, "You are not happy to see me?"

Happy, outraged, confused, ecstatic, astonished. Demi's emotions took her heart on a perilous ride. She looked up, incredulous, but his face was backlit against the glow of the lamplight. "Did you think I would run into your arms?"

Stavros bent down to peer more closely at Demi under the umbrella. He raised his eyebrows and shrugged, his actions barely masking the nerves threatening to expose themselves. "Well, yes, of course."

She shook her head. "Life isn't a Hallmark movie, Stavro." She observed his familiar shrug. From the speaker mounted on the restaurant façade, Darius Rucker's rich baritone penetrated the night. *Don't think I don't think about it. Don't think I don't have regrets. I know what I felt, and I know what I said, but don't think . . .* Demi glared at Stavros. "Why haven't you called me? You talk to Sophie, but you don't talk to me?"

"Dimitra, we agreed . . ."

Anger rose to the top of her emotional heap, and her voice rose. "*We* didn't agree on anything. *You* decided we should never see each other again. *You* decided not to talk with me. *You* turned your back on *me*."

"This is not fair, Dimitra. You tell me we were *kalokairini agape*. How I was to know I would see you again? How I was to know you were not gone forever?"

"Because I told you that we would meet again."

Stavros pulled out the chair next to her and sat down. "Yes, so I am wrong. This is a good thing." He gave Demi a tentative smile, but she ignored it.

"Why are you here?" Her words were terse.

"Because Sophie tell me to come."

"No, why are you *here*?" Demi waved her arms to encompass the world beyond her. "In Pittsburgh?"

"Ah, you remember my Yiayia's cousin have a restaurant here?"

She cut him off. "No, I get why they *asked* you to come. I just don't understand why you came."

"What do you mean?"

"You told me you were happy in Greece. That you didn't want to leave Sparta. Why would you agree to come here? Are you telling me they couldn't find anyone else to cook for them?"

"Dimitra. This is family."

"Your family is in Greece."

"But *you* are here."

Demi leaned back in her chair as the anger drained from her body. She looked closely at Stavros now. She noticed that he'd cut a few inches from his hair and grown a neat goatee, and she saw an earnestness in his eyes. She spoke softly. "Why didn't you call me to tell me you were coming?"

"Because I am afraid you tell me not to come."

"Why would I tell you not to come?"

"Because you are angry with me."

Demi rubbed her temples with her fingers. She sat for a moment, elbows on the table, eyes closed, head in her hands. John Fogarty's raspy voice singing *Who'll Stop the Rain* intruded upon their silence from the single speaker. Demi heard the scratch of metal on concrete as Stavros slid his chair next to hers.

"Dimitra," he whispered. He brushed her hair back from her face, and she felt her teeth unclench and her body relax. "I am sorry you did not like this surprise." She dropped her hands from her face and looked at him. "But I have never stopped thinking about you."

I haven't stopped thinking about you either, she thought, but the words did not come out. She was still too stunned to think clearly. "So, now what?" she asked. "What happens now?"

"Now?" Stavros asked, letting out the breath he seemed to have been holding for five minutes. He wanted to take her into his arms and kiss her, but something told him to move slowly. "Now, I think we go inside to celebrate *Kiria* Georgia."

* * *

Marina stood in the hallway, her heart nudging her out the door to check on Demi, but her head advising her to leave her cousin alone. She chose the latter and returned to the high-top table where Sophie was explaining the situation to *Thia* Pitsa. Their aunt listened, nodding her head, pursing her lips, and raising her eyebrows while the girls finished their story. She paused before she spoke. "Well," she said. "I wouldn't worry too much about it. Demi can handle herself. You girls didn't do anything wrong. I'm sure everything will turn out just fine." She looked around the room. "Now, where did Antonis disappear to?" She hugged the girls and left to find her husband.

Sophie turned to Marina and sighed. "I think we messed up."

Marina glanced at the doorway and smiled. "I'm not so sure about that." She nodded towards the entrance. Sophie beamed, and Marina held her hand up to Sophie for a high-five.

"Yes!" said Sophie, swinging her arm up to make contact. She failed to make a direct hit, and the high-five was more of a slight swish than a resounding smack. "Oops," she giggled.

Marina rolled her eyes. "Again," she said, raising her hand a little higher to reach Sophie's height. The hearty slap left both their hands stinging, and they shook them as they saw Andrew approach.

"Who's that with Demi?" Andrew asked.

"Hello to you, too," Marina said.

"Hi Marina, long time no see."

"That's your fault," she retorted.

"I'm not here to argue, Marina," Andrew replied.

"Then why are you here?" Sophie asked.

"I'm here because Mr. Karras invited me."

"Seriously?" Marina said. "Why did you accept? You knew Demi would be upset. Why would you spoil her night?"

"I knew no such thing," Andrew said. "And . . ." He hesitated. "I wanted to see her." They all looked over at Demi standing with Stavros by the bar. "Anyway . . . who is that with her?"

"That," Marina answered, "is Stavros. And if you'll excuse me," she added, "I'm going to go say hello. Coming, Sophie?"

As they departed, they heard Andrew mutter, "Who the hell is Stavros?"

* * *

"Dad," Demi said. Jimmy turned away from the small group of men who had gathered at the bar. "This is Stavros."

"Hello, Stavros," Jimmy said. He looked questioningly at Demi.

"*Hairome pou sas gnorizo, Kirie,*" Stavros said, shaking Jimmy's hand.

"*To ithio kai etho,*" Jimmy replied. "You're Greek?" he said. "Are you . . ." He looked around, unsure as to what he was going to ask.

"Dad," Demi said. "This is Stavros. From Greece."

"Yes, I know he's from Greece," Jimmy replied, wondering why Demi would point that out as if his greeting hadn't given it away.

"Stavros," she emphasized. "From Sparta."

"Oh-h-h-h." Jimmy nodded in understanding, but he was unsure how to react. This was the man who had broken his daughter's heart. Yet, she seemed composed . . . almost happy? He was rescued from a reaction as Georgia approached them.

"Stavro! What in the world are you doing here? How nice to see you!" She glanced sideways at Demi to gauge her emotions before proceeding. "Jimmy, this is Stavros—my knight in shining armor who made sure we got to Gytheio in time for the presentation."

"We've met," said Jimmy, still tentative.

The music slowed, and Sotiris spoke. "This would not be a proper celebration without some Greek dancing. *Elate paidia, opa*!" With that, the bouzouki, keyboard, and guitar combined to start a *kalamatiano.* "Excuse me," said Georgia as Jimmy led her onto the dance floor. One by one, Greek and American guests joined hands and began forming a line. They danced —some expertly, some following the steps of the leader or the person in front of them — as they circled the small dance floor. Stavros took Demi's hand, and along with Marina, they joined the growing line of dancers as he clasped hands with Sophie at the end of the line. Andrew watched from the bar, reacquainting himself with the step pattern. *Right, left-back, right, left-front, right, left. . . .* He shook his head. *Might as well just jump in*, he decided. He waited for the line to circle the floor until the end was in front of him. Rather than tag on at the end of the line, he broke in between Marina and Demi. Their rhythm was thrown off as Andrew tried to match his steps to the music's beat by watching the other dancers' feet.

Demi looked past Andrew at Marina. "It's okay," Marina mouthed to her over the music. "No, it's not," Demi mouthed back. She backed out of the line, taking Andrew's hand and Stavros' hand and joining them together. The men eyed each other suspiciously, realizing they must be rivals, but they held hands and continued to dance.

Suddenly, Stavros dropped Andrew's hand and said, "*Ela*, Sophia!" She let go of the person in front of her, and they moved to the middle of the floor. "*Ela,* Marina!" Stavros called, and she let go of Andrew's hand and joined the line of three. They formed a small circle within the large circle, and Stavros guided them around the floor, throwing in acrobatic hops and squats.

Andrew crossed his arms and glared from the edge of the floor where a few other people stood watching. A woman leaned towards him and said, "He's good, isn't he? I wonder who he is?"

* * *

Demi found her mother chatting with a group of ladies. "Mom!" she yelled to be heard over the music.

"Hi, Sweetie!" Georgia smiled. She looked closely at her daughter. Demi's face was pallid, but her eyes were bright. "Are you okay?"

"I'm okay. I feel a migraine coming on. Would you please tell Marina that I took an Uber home?"

"Oh, honey. I'm sorry." Georgia hugged her daughter and looked past her at the scene on the dance floor. She pulled away, held Demi by the shoulders, and looked into her eyes. "This has been quite a night for you, hasn't it?"

"It's your night, Mom. Don't worry about me. I'll be fine—I just need to get out of here. It's a little too much right now. Have fun, and don't worry about me, okay? I love you."

Georgia hugged Demi again and kissed her on the cheek. "I love you too, sweetheart. I'll talk to you in the morning. Text me when you get home, okay?"

"I will, Mom. Goodnight." Demi grabbed her jacket and purse from the back of her chair once again and went outside to wait for the Uber driver. The night was cooler now, and she threw her jacket over her shoulders.

"Demi." Andrew stood in the open doorway. "Where are you going?"

"Home. I have a migraine."

"Oh. I was hoping we'd get a chance to talk."

"We have nothing to talk about."

"Let me take you home."

"I have an Uber on the way."

"Cancel it." Andrew directed with false confidence. He read the negative response in Demi's eyes and changed his tone. "Look, I need to apologize. It's just that . . ."

"Not now, Andrew. Please. Not now."

"Then when? I have so much I want to say to you."

"That's funny. I have nothing to say to you."

"Demi. Just give me a chance to explain." The Uber driver pulled up, interrupting Andrew's plea, and he sighed. "Alright, I'll call you tomorrow."

"Please don't."

Demi checked the license plate and got into the back of the red Mazda. She looked to see that the driver's likeness matched the photo of a dark-haired middle-aged man and shut the car door. The driver glanced over his shoulder at Demi. "How's your evening going?"

"I've had better."

The driver nodded knowingly. "Fighting with your boyfriend, eh?"

Demi clenched her jaw. "Excuse me? Why would you say that?"

"I just thought . . . sorry, Miss. I spoke out of turn."

"It's fine," Demi said.

The driver pulled out of the parking lot and turned left onto the four-lane highway. The road, a main thoroughfare during the day, had few cars on it at this time of night, and a quiet darkness enveloped the car as they headed towards Demi's house in Mount Washington. Demi laid her head back on the headrest and closed her eyes. Despite the dull throbbing behind her eyes, she was happy for the momentary peace and isolation of the Uber. After a few minutes, she took a deep breath and opened her eyes. The driver was watching her in the rear-view mirror. "Are you okay, Miss?"

She closed her eyes again for a moment, replaying the unexpected events of the night. She was surprised to find that what rose to the surface was not anger, frustration, annoyance, or shock. It was a giddy joy that came with processing that Stavros was in Pittsburgh. Whatever uncertainty accompanied that—whatever chaos it brought—she would deal with. "I am," she replied to the driver, "thank you." She nodded to herself. *Yes, I'm okay.*

CHAPTER 18

Georgia wrapped her plush white robe around herself and padded downstairs in fuzzy slippers. The aroma of coffee mingled with the smell of toast. Jimmy looked up from the counter, where he buttered a piece of whole-grain toast. "I thought I heard you moving around up there," he said. "Good morning."

She came over to him and kissed him lightly on the mouth. "Good morning, handsome," she said.

"How are you feeling?"

"A little foggy," Georgia said. "But considering the late night . . ."

". . . and the gin and tonics," Jimmy said.

". . . and the champagne," Georgia added, "pretty good overall. Nothing that a cup of coffee won't fix."

"Eggs?" he asked.

"Just one. I think I'm still full from all the *mezethes* I ate last night."

"We brought enough home for a meal or two," Jimmy said. He reached into the drawer under the counter and took out a small frying pan. Georgia poured herself a cup of coffee from the carafe as Jimmy drizzled some olive oil into the pan. She walked over to the refrigerator. "Sit down, honey. I'll get the eggs."

Something soft brushed against Georgia's leg as she sat. "Oh, Gus!" she said. She bent down to scratch the head of the small black cat, who let out a little 'eek.' "Did you feed him?" she asked.

Jimmy cocked his head. "What do you think?" The cat wove around Georgia's legs, then strutted to Jimmy and did the same. "Does he always have to be in my way?" he complained, shuffling his feet. Gus eeked again and sauntered into the living room, finding the spot where the sun streamed through the window onto the couch and began kneading the cushion.

Georgia blew on the hot coffee and took a sip. She watched as Jimmy cracked the eggs into the pan. His hair was disheveled, and his flannel plaid pajama pants were rumpled. She felt a shiver of joy. *Amazing that after all these years, I still get butterflies,* she mused.

"Here you go," Jimmy said, offering a plate of two fried eggs, a piece of toast, and a slice of tomato drizzled with olive oil and a pinch of oregano.

"I only asked for . . ." Georgia began, then stopped. "Thanks, Jimmy. That looks delicious." Jimmy sat down with only his cup of coffee.

"Aren't you having any?" Georgia asked.

"I've been up since seven thirty," he said. "I already had some cereal. I want to save my appetite for this afternoon."

"This afternoon?"

"The Steeler game?" Jimmy replied in disbelief at the question. "It's Sunday . . ."

"I know what day it is. I just wasn't thinking beyond last night. Are we supposed to go to your brother's today?" Jimmy nodded. "Do you mind if I don't go? I could use a little time to myself."

"I don't mind, but Pitsa might. Something tells me she might want to hear more about Greece—especially after the drama last night."

"Speaking of the drama, Jimmy," Georgia set her fork down and looked directly at her husband. "What were you thinking, inviting Andrew to the book launch?"

Jimmy took a deep breath and huffed it out quickly. "Look, Georgia. I ran into him at the hardware store. I've always liked him. I guess I just wanted to, I don't know, help Demi."

"How would that possibly help Demi?"

"She's been so sad ever since she returned from Greece. I can see it in her eyes and the way she carries herself. I just thought maybe Andrew . . ."

Georgia reached for Jimmy's hand across the table. "Your heart was in the right place, honey. But Andrew is not the answer."

"Then, what is? I just hate seeing our little girl sad."

"Well, for one thing, you need to realize that she's not our little girl anymore and that she'll have to solve her own problems. And I don't think Andrew or any man is a quick fix. She has a lot going on with work, and her heart is still hurting from this summer. What was it you said when she started dating Andrew? 'When it comes to matters of the heart, you shouldn't interfere'?"

"I know," he said reluctantly. "My father said that to me years ago." He paused and sighed, remembering his father, who had succumbed to Alzheimer's the previous fall. Georgia reached across the table and squeezed his hand. He looked down for a moment and then back up as something occurred to him. "About that. What was that guy—Stavros—doing there last night? *Who* invited *him*?" Jimmy sought vindication.

Georgia laughed. "It seems that everyone is trying to help Demi shake off the doldrums, but she's going to have to do it herself." She glanced up at the clock. "I better get a shower. I need to make something for you to take to Antonis and Pitsa."

"Don't worry about it. I'll just take some of the leftover appetizers from last night."

"Okay, just leave me some *tiropitakia*," she said. The cheese pies and a cup of coffee would make a good afternoon meal. And if she wasn't going to Antonis and Pitsa's, she might just stay in her pajamas and robe all day.

* * *

A soft tapping teased Demi from her sleep. She raised her heavy eyelids and squinted at the light filtering in between the slats in the blinds. Her eyes rested on the lavender walls and the framed poster of Frida Kahlo, which revealed that she wasn't in Greece, where her dreams had taken her. They were fading already, but she recalled walking on the side of the road towards the plateia in Xirokambi. In the darkness, she could hear music and laughter from the plateia, but as she tried to reach it, her legs moved as if they were trudging through a quagmire. The more she tried to run, the heavier they felt.

The tapping continued.

"Demi?" The door opened, and Marina entered, holding a blue ceramic mug. "Good morning, Sunshine."

"Shh," Demi said, closing her eyes, "why are you so cheerful?" She rubbed her eyelids with the base of her palms, yawned, and stretched her body the full length of the double bed.

"You look like Bella when she wakes up," Marina said, although the cat remained in a curled ball of brown and caramel-colored fur at the foot of Demi's bed.

Demi pushed herself up and scooched back against the headboard, tucking her feather pillow behind her. She held her hand out for the coffee mug. Bella stirred, stood, and arched her back. She sidled up to Demi and rubbed against the mug. "Easy, Bella. Don't spill my coffee," Demi said, bringing the mug to her lips for a sip. "Thanks, Marina. You're the best."

"Careful, it's hot," Marina said. She sat down at the foot of the bed. "How's your headache?"

"Better, I think."

"Good," Marina nodded. "Soooo?"

Demi shook her head. "Coffee first." She blew on the coffee and took another sip. "What happened after I left?"

"Let's see. Well, your mom got a little tipsy. I'm pretty sure she was feeling no pain. I don't know about this morning, though," she said, raising her eyebrows. "Andrew cornered Sophie and cross-examined her about Stavros. And Aunt Pitsa cornered Stavros and gave him the third degree."

"What did she find out?"

"Stavros is here on a ninety-day tourist visa to help his Yiayia's cousin keep the restaurant together until he can hire and train a new cook. He's staying with him in Dormont. He's been here a few days."

Ninety days, Demi thought. *And then what?*

"Stop it, Demi," Marina said. "I can see those wheels turning. A lot can happen in ninety days."

A lot can happen in five days, Demi thought. She took another drink of coffee. "And where were you during all of this?"

"Talking with Sotiris."

"Talking?" Demi raised an eyebrow. "Or flirting?"

Marina pressed her lips together, but they curved into a smile.

"Isn't he a little old for you?" Demi teased.

"Papou was twenty years older than Yiayia," Marina retorted.

"That was an arranged marriage."

"Hmmm," Marina smiled. "I could arrange a marriage . . ."

"Marina!"

"Just kidding, Demi. It's not like there was a plethora of single men at that party," she paused to reflect, "or any besides Andrew and Stavros, and they were both taken."

"Shut up," Demi laughed. "What else?"

"That's about it. We have to go back to get the rest of your mom's stuff. But they're closed Sunday and Monday."

"I don't think it's anything she needs right away." Demi set her coffee mug on the nightstand. "Thanks, Marina. I needed this." She looked down at her lap. "How did she get here?" Bella lay in her lap, purring softly.

"She's a Ninja," Marina laughed. "Oh, are you going to Aunt Pitsa's today?"

"Probably not. I'm not in the mood for an inquisition. And I'm definitely not in the mood for rowdy football fans."

* * *

"You're still in your pajamas?" Demi entered the house to find her mother still in her plaid flannel pj's and fuzzy slippers as she searched the refrigerator. "Must have been some party last night," she teased.

"Mmm hmm," Georgia nodded, taking a Styrofoam carton out of the frig, "and I plan to stay that way."

"So, you're not going to Pitsa's either?"

"I just needed some peace and quiet after all the excitement."

"I get that," Demi said. "It was a really nice event, but I'm sure it was exhausting. I won't be long. I forgot to get my winter jacket when I came over the other day. I think I'm going to need it." She opened the hall closet and pushed aside the coats until she located her jacket.

"That's okay," Georgia said. "You can stay if you want to. I was just heating up some leftovers, and I was going to watch a movie."

Demi's eyes widened in surprise. "You're not watching the Steeler game?"

"Not today. Enjoying a little me time."

"In that case . . ." Demi said. She unzipped and removed her leather boots, leaving them strewn in the hallway. "What movie are you going to watch?"

"Do you have one in mind?"

They both smiled mischievous smiles. "Never gets old," Demi said.

Georgia popped their favorite movie into the DVD player. She retrieved a paper plate of warmed leftovers from the microwave and set it on the mosaic TV tray beside the sofa. Demi sank into the cushions of the plush leather sofa. Georgia plopped down next to her, and they nibbled leftover *tiropitakia* and stuffed grape leaves. *Love You Till the End* played in the background as Hilary Swank stomped away from an exasperated Gerard Butler down the dark New York streets. "Perfect," Demi said. She lay on her mother's lap, and Georgia absentmindedly stroked her daughter's hair. As the lush green fields of Ireland burst onto the screen, the piano riff ringtone of Demi's phone interrupted them. She sat up and took it out of the side pocket of her leggings. When she saw Andrew's name, she silenced the phone and set it on the TV tray.

"Do you need to get that?" Georgia asked.

"No, it's not important," Demi said, settling back into her mother's lap. They were absorbed once again by the charms of Gerard Butler when the doorbell rang.

Georgia paused the video and moved to rise.

"Ignore it," Demi said. "It's probably someone with a political flyer. Or someone taking a survey." The doorbell rang again. Demi sighed and lifted her head as Georgia slid off the couch. *I hope that's not Andrew*, Demi thought. *It would be just like him to show up if I don't answer the phone.*

Georgia peeked through the small window in the door and smiled. "*Kalimera*!" she called through the screen door as she pulled open the main door.

Definitely not Andrew, Demi thought. *But who?*

"Stavro, how nice to see you! How did you find us?" Georgia's greeting jolted Demi from her reclining position on the couch. She squinted to hear the reply.

"My cousin tell me where you live. I have this for you," Stavros said, launching Demi into action.

Georgia pushed open the screen door, and Stavros came in carrying the box of books and photographs they had left at the restaurant. "How nice of you to bring them over," she said. Would you like to come in?"

Stavros peered around the room and then looked at Georgia. "I think you are not ready for company today."

She looked down at her flannel pj's and laughed. "I can make an exception for a handsome young man who came all the way over to deliver this box." She watched Stavros as he peered behind her into the kitchen. "That *is* why you came over?"

Stavros broke into a sheepish grin. "Marina tell Sophie that Demi is here."

". . . and Sophie told you."

Stavros nodded. He spotted the boots in the hallway. "She is not?"

Georgia laughed, looking around herself. "She was a minute ago. Come in, let me make you some coffee."

"Efharisto, *Kiria* Georgia." He followed her into the kitchen and sat down at the large butcher block table as she made coffee.

"*Kalimera*," he heard behind him. He looked over his shoulder at Demi, who had smoothed her hair and applied lip gloss and mascara. She no longer wore her oversized sweatshirt but had changed into Georgia's grey sweater.

"Dimitra!" Stavros stood up, knocking into the table. "I didn't know you were here!" He shot Georgia a stealthy glance, and she turned towards the sink to hide her smile.

"What are you doing here?" Demi asked.

"He was nice enough to bring over my things from last night," Georgia said. Demi and Stavros remained standing. Georgia handed each of them a mug of coffee. "It's nice out. Why don't you two go sit on the porch swing and catch up? I'm going to watch my movie." She put a hand on each of their backs and urged them towards the front door.

"Actually, I've had enough coffee today," Demi said. She turned to Stavros. "Do you want to go for a walk?"

"Yes, of course," Stavros said. He took Demi's cup and set them both on the table. "Thank you, *Kiria* Georgia. Sorry," he nodded at the cups.

Demi zipped up her boots and put on her jacket. Stavros opened the door and followed her out. He grabbed her arm before she went down the steps. "Wait."

She turned to him. "What?"

"This cannot wait," he said. She met his eyes, and his lips met hers in a long, slow kiss. The tension of the previous night evaporated, and when she pulled away, she was smiling.

Georgia saw them from behind the open blinds and sighed. *Here we go again*, she thought.

* * *

Marina sat at the kitchen table, which was barely visible under a heap of books, a notebook, assorted Post-It notes, and her laptop. Her dark hair was pulled into a messy bun on top of her head, and she twirled wayward strands around her finger as she stared at the computer screen, her eyes strained. She looked up at the rattle of the key in the door lock. Demi entered, her face flushed and her eyes bright, contrasting with Marina's tired, red eyes.

"Hey!" Demi said. "I didn't think you'd be home. I thought you were going to Aunt Pitsa's."

"I was," Marina said. "But you weren't going, and I figured I'd get some work done on my paper while the house was quiet."

"Am I that noisy?" Demi teased.

"No, no, I just . . ."

"I'm kidding, Marina." Demi looked at the array of pencils, pens, and paper Marina had strewn in front of her. "Can you take a break?"

Marina looked out the window, surprised at the dusky sky. "What time is it?" she asked, patting the papers on the table in search of her phone.

"It's almost six."

"I've done enough work today." She pushed back from the table, interlaced her hands, and stretched them towards the ceiling.

Demi sat down at the table and pressed her lips together, but it wasn't enough to keep the smile from her face.

Marina raised her eyebrows. "Hmm," she said. "something's up." Demi released her lips, letting the smile take over. "I know that smile," Marina said. "You talked to him?"

"Better," Demi replied.

"You *saw* him?" Demi nodded. Marina folded her hands on the table and leaned in towards Demi. "So . . . ?"

Demi relayed the events of the afternoon, uninterrupted except for an occasional interjection by Marina, who gazed at her thoughtfully. "Demi," she began. "Is this a good idea? I mean, you seem really happy right now. Happier than I've seen you since you came back from Greece. But . . ." she trailed off, uncertain how to put her concerns into words.

"You don't think I should see him."

"It's not that. I'm just not sure what good can come of it."

"I know, Marina. I was up most of last night trying to make sense of it. But he's *here*." Demi shook her head at the wonder of it. "He is actually in Pittsburgh!" She sighed, hesitating before speaking again. "I let my guard down in Greece, and I fell in love. I need to see where this leads."

"Even if it leads to a broken heart . . . or two?"

"I've weathered a broken heart before. I can do it again if I have to. Right now, I'm going to make the most out of the time we have. I owe that to myself."

CHAPTER 19

The late afternoon sun spilled into the casement window of Sophie's office. She pulled on her yellow wool jacket—a recent splurge. Since returning from Greece, her Aunt Georgia's words had become a sort of mantra: *Wear what makes you happy. Do what makes you happy. Dance, run, sing—and don't worry about what anyone else thinks. You don't have to conform to anyone's notion of beauty.* "Bye-bye, Anna," she called to her coworker. "Have a nice weekend."

"Wait, Sophie!" Anna called. "Do you want to grab a drink before you go home?"

"I can't tonight—I'm hanging out with my sister and my cousin. Raincheck?"

"Sure."

Sophie tied the orange and yellow scarf from Greece around her neck and pushed the door open. The late afternoon sun was bright in the clear autumn sky, and she reached into her purse for her oversized sunglasses. The crisp air gave a spring to her step, and she walked lightly despite her brown suede high-heeled boots. As she neared the bakery, the aroma of freshly baked bread and sweets teased her nostrils. *I should get some thumbprint cookies*, she thought. The promise of sweet chocolate icing dabbed in the middle of melt-in-your-mouth peanut butter cookie dough made her mouth water. She stopped suddenly and was promptly run into by someone behind her. She wobbled on her heels as a firm arm grasped her elbow and steadied her. She turned around, ready to chastise her assailant.

"Excuse me! I shouldn't have been tailgating." A tall, dark-haired man about her age grinned as he released her elbow.

Sophie's mouth dropped open, but no words escaped.

"I shouldn't have been staring at my phone. Bad habit." The man looked closely at the seemingly incoherent Sophie. "Are you okay?"

She squinted through her sunglasses and peered into his blue eyes. "Mark?"

The man cocked his head to the side, still grinning. "I'm sorry, do I . . . ?"

"You went to Pitt, right? You were on the men's tennis team."

"Well, yes, but . . ."

"I was on the club team. I used to watch you practice." *Darn it*, she thought. *Not cool.*

"Wait." His grin broadened. "You're *her*. The girl with the long legs and the long ponytail!" He looked down at her short skirt and tall boots as if making sure. "I remember you! You used to sit in the bleachers with a couple other girls after your practice. You always wore a navy-blue tee shirt."

He remembers me! Color rose to Sophie's cheeks. "Yep, that was me," she said. "I can't believe you remembered me."

"Why wouldn't I remember a pretty girl in the stands?" He looked at her closely. "I almost didn't recognize you—you look so . . . stylish. Well, not that you weren't before. I mean, I don't know if you were before—I only saw you in a tee shirt." It was Mark's turn to blush, but he quickly recovered. "Hey, you obviously wanted to get something from the bakery. They serve coffee, too. I'll buy you a cup—it's the least I can do for crashing into you."

* * *

"Wait. You told him you *don't drink coffee*?" Marina asked in disbelief as she poured a glass of red sangria for herself and Sophie from the pitcher on the table. The electric heaters above their table emitted just enough warmth to let them enjoy sitting outside on the restaurant patio, although they all kept their jackets on.

"It makes me jittery," Sophie clarified.

Marina sighed and shook her head. "What were you thinking?"

"I wasn't thinking. I was an idiot."

"No, you weren't," Demi said. She took a sip of her margarita, savoring the salt on the rim of the glass.

"Thanks, Demi."

"No, I mean you weren't thinking. You *are* an idiot," Demi laughed. "So, then what happened?"

"I bought some cookies." She reached down next to her purse and held up a small cardboard bakery box tied with striped string.

"Sophie!" Marina and Demi both said, exasperated. "What happened with Mark?"

"Oh, well, nothing really. He said it was nice seeing me and told me to be careful the next time I walk past a bakery."

"Did he ask for your number?"

"No." Sophie shook her head and stuck out her lower lip in an exaggerated frown. Demi and Marina sighed.

"Did you ask for his?"

"No, of course not."

Marina glared at her sister. "What do mean, of course not? It's not 1960, Sophie. Women can take the lead, you know." She waved a tortilla chip at Sophie before dipping it into a bowl of salsa.

"You had Dinos following you around like a puppy in Greece," Demi said.

"That was different."

"How was that different?"

"I don't know," Sophie shrugged. "It just was."

"Wait!" Demi said. "Do you know his last name?"

"Mark's?"

"No, Dino's," Demi smirked. "Yes, Mark's."

"No," Sophie frowned.

"That's okay," Marina said. "You can find him on social media. Just search 'Mark' and 'Pitt tennis.'" The girls slid their chairs over to Sophie's and looked over her shoulders while she searched.

"Try University of Pittsburgh," Demi said.

"Maybe he's on LinkedIn," Marina added.

"Try . . ."

"That's him!" Sophie said, showing them a photo of a smiling blue-eyed man sitting next to a smiling blue-eyed husky dog.

"Cute," Marina said.

"Scroll down," Demi commanded. "Aha!" She sat back, crossed her arms, and smiled.

"What?"

"He's single."

"Give me your phone," Marina said, already reaching for Sophie's phone.

"Why?"

"Because it's not 1960."

Reluctantly, Sophie handed her phone to her sister. Marina began to type. "Wait!" Sophie's eyes widened. "What are you doing?"

"Nothing," Marina said. She handed the phone back to Sophie. "All you have to do is press send."

Sophie looked down at the phone. Marina had written a message: "I do like tea, though."

"What do you have to lose?" Demi asked, raising her eyebrows.

Sophie looked at Demi, then at Marina, and then back at Demi. She took a deep breath and pressed the send button.

* * *

Stavros looked at the long line of cars ahead of him and sighed. "I don't understand this *emmoni me tis kolokithes*."

Demi laughed as they waited in the Starbucks' drive-thru line. "What are you saying about pumpkins?" She pulled up her grey SUV as the car in front of her moved.

"This . . . this . . ." Stavros shrugged, unable to find the word. "They are everywhere. You see them for decorations, you bake the bread, you eat the pie, and now you are drinking them. What is so special about this 'poompkeen'?"

Demi laughed out loud. "I don't know—it's a fall thing. It means fall is here."

"You don't need *kolokithia* to tell you that fall is here." He pointed out the open car window at the bright red leaves on the maple tree across the street. "The weather he tell you that fall is here." He began to drum his fingers on the car door. "Why no one is moving, eh?" he said, waving his hand towards the line in front of them. "All these people, they want the poompkeen?"

"I don't know, it's like fall gives everyone a fresh start. Summer is officially over; kids go back to school; the weather changes. It's like a new lease on life." She looked over at Stavros, who was clenching his jaw. "And pumpkin-spiced lattes mean that fall is officially here."

"*Vlakies*," Stavros said. "So, we wait for a half hour just to make sure it is fall?"

Demi laughed. "Stavro, it's been ten minutes." She inched up another car length. "Do you want one or not?" she asked.

"*Vevaios*," Stavros said. "Why not?"

She shook her head and pulled up to the speaker. The static buzzed, and the speaker relayed a garbled, "Welcome to Starbucks; how may I help you?"

"Two grande pumpkin spiced lattes," Demi ordered.

"Anything else?"

Demi smiled to herself. "Yes, two pieces of pumpkin bread."

* * *

CHAPTER 20

"How can I help you, Demi?" the General Manager asked. He sat at a large wooden desk in a windowless office behind the reception area of the country club. Papers cluttered the top of the desk, and Post-it notes and business cards were stuck in the corners of the blotter directly in front of him. A worn coffee ring stained the smooth dark wood next to the blotter. Although he had invited his employees to call him Richard, something about his countenance was intimidating enough that they all addressed him as Mr. Murray, at least to his face. To each other, they referred to him as "Dickie." Richard looked at his watch and then up at Demi. He did not invite her to sit down.

She took the cue. "I'll get right to the point, Mr. Murray. I understand that Michael is planning to leave at the end of the month. I've been here for three years, and I think I've proven myself with my work ethic and dependability. I'm hoping that you'll consider me for the Banquet Manager position."

Richard leaned back in his chair and tapped his fingers on his desk. "I see." He paused and cleared his throat. "I'm afraid that position has already been filled."

Demi drew her eyebrows together. "Filled? But it hasn't even been posted."

"This isn't the Marriott, Demi. Hiring and promotion are at my discretion."

"But who?" Demi's mind spun in circles. *I have more experience than anyone here.*

"I'm bringing in someone from the outside who has extensive banquet management experience."

Demi worked to keep the anger out of her voice. "But *I* have extensive experience *here*. I know our operations, I know our clientele, and I've worked my as . . . my butt off for three years." She took a deep breath and let it out. "Shouldn't I have at least gotten a chance to interview for this position?"

"You're a hard worker, Demi, but I need someone here for the long run. You're a pretty girl. It's only a matter of time before Prince Charming comes and sweeps you off your feet. My hire just bought a house in Sewickley, and his daughter is starting kindergarten next year. I know that I can count on him to be here for the duration."

Demi stared at Richard. "That's discrimination."

"Hardly," he replied, looking unphased. "That's being realistic. Frankly, if I were you, I wouldn't go throwing terms like that around so easily. I do have some reservations about your interactions with our clientele." Richard leaned forward and looked directly at Demi. "I've been told that you've spoken rather sharply to some of them."

Demi's mouth dropped open. "Excuse me? I have never spoken sharply to any of our patrons!"

"Not according to my niece."

"Your niece?"

"Miranda has witnessed the way you speak to our members. She didn't want to get you into trouble, but she did want me to be aware."

"Miranda," Demi recalled the hostess that she'd recently reprimanded. She shook her head. "You must be kidding." She took a deep breath and let it out slowly. *Hold your tongue, Demi, before you say something you regret.*

"Is there anything else?" Richard asked, looking directly at Demi.

"No. Thank you, Richard. That's all I needed to know." She turned and opened the door, resisting the desire to slam it. She was aware of her heart pounding in her chest as her ears echoed the beat.

* * *

Demi stepped out into the night, wishing she had worn her jacket. This time of year, it was easy to forget that when the sun went down, the temperature dropped quickly. Her thin white blouse was doing little to protect her from the chill in the air. She crossed her arms and tucked her fingers under her armpits to keep her hands warm as she walked across the country club parking lot.

"Demi!" she heard. Although the path was well-lit, the voice seemed to emanate from the darkness. She reached into her pocket for her keys and held them with a key sticking out between her fingers, ready to strike.

Andrew stepped out from the shadows.

"What the hell are you doing here?" she said. "You scared the shit out of me."

"Sorry," he said. "It's your fault, though. You won't answer my calls."

"That's because I don't want to talk to you." Demi resumed the walk to her car, but Andrew grabbed her by the arm. She shook him off and continued walking.

"Come on, Demi. Just give me a chance to explain."

She stopped and turned to face him. "Andrew, it's cold out. Today was not a good day at work. I'm tired, and I want to go home."

Andrew's eyes pleaded. "Just five minutes. Come on—just come sit in my car. I'll turn the heat on. Please?"

Demi sighed. "Alright. Five minutes." She turned and followed him to his car. He pointed proudly at the BMW X3, its black paint gleaming under the overhead streetlight. "What do you think?" he said.

"I think if you don't unlock the door, I'm turning around and leaving. I'm freezing." She glanced at Andrew who wore a suede jacket over his wool sweater. "Can you at least let me use your jacket?"

"Well, then we'd both be cold," Andrew chided. He pressed the fob and unlocked the doors, and Demi slid into the leather passenger seat, greeted by the "new car smell" of the SUV. "It'll warm up soon enough."

Demi grit her teeth. "What did you want to talk about?"

"I just think we left things poorly." Andrew turned on the ignition and the heat.

"*We* left things poorly?"

"Okay, *I* left things poorly."

Demi rubbed her hands together and warmed them in front of the vent.

"Heat's up quickly, doesn't it?" Andrew said.

"I don't want to talk about your car. Tell me what you wanted to tell me."

Andrew launched into why he had pleaded with her to decline the job in Philadelphia and stay with him, with the promise of a ring, only to dump her six months later. "I was afraid to commit, Demi. I mean, I was only thirty—I had the rest of my life in front of me, and I wasn't ready to settle down. I mean, I am now. I realize what I lost." He tried to meet her eyes, but she was in profile, her eyes gazing beyond the windshield.

"So, now that you're all of thirty-one, you've had an epiphany?"

"Come on, Demi. Aren't you being a little harsh?"

"Harsh?" Demi turned to glare at Andrew. "What about me? I gave up a great opportunity and stayed in job that is going nowhere because you asked me to—because you said we had a future together."

"We still do—I mean, we still can. Give me another chance, Demi. You won't be sorry." He leaned across the console towards her and put his hand behind her neck to draw her towards him, but she ducked under his arm and pushed it away.

"We're done talking, Andrew. I hope that you find someone now that you're ready to commit." She opened the car door and slid out. Before closing it, she leaned in and looked at him. "And, by the way . . . you lost any chance you might have had when you didn't let me use your jacket."

CHAPTER 21

Stavros hung his apron on a hook and walked through the kitchen into the main dining room of the restaurant. Kostas leaned over the counter, the glow from an overhead fluorescent light reflecting off the top of his balding head. His eyes looked tired behind thick glasses as he tallied the day's receipts with paper and pencil. Behind him, on the shelves, a plastic container held bunches of forks, knives, and spoons. An industrial coffee maker stood next to this, with white ceramic cups lined up on their saucers, ready to be filled. On the shelves above the counter, small white demitasse cups were piled high for those patrons who might prefer the thick Greek coffee. Handmade baskets, a bottle wrapped in jute, and bronze plates, along with photographs and vases from Greece, adorned the top shelf.

"*Ela, Stavro, katse.*" Kostas nodded toward the closest table. He put the papers in a drawer under the register and opened a door in the cupboard underneath the drawer, from which he retrieved a bottle of ouzo. He reached into the cupboard behind him, took out two small glasses, and poured a shot of ouzo into each. He dropped an ice cube into each glass, releasing the pleasant anise scent of the liquor, and the clear liquid turned a cloudy white. He brought the glasses to the table and handed one to Stavros. "*Ti kaneis, agori mou*, how you are doing?"

"*Kala*, Kosta," Stavros said. "I am okay." He took a sip of the ouzo and looked around the long, narrow room. The walls were painted a golden yellow that had lost its brightness over the years. Dark brown wood paneling ran across one of the walls. Blue plastic tablecloths covered the tables that were surrounded by drab brown cane chairs. A glass case held a variety of knickknacks, including faded black and white photographs of distant relatives, ceramic vases, mosaic plates, and an old bouzouki leaning on its side. A lone plastic Doric column stood on the floor next to the far wall, which featured bright blue street signs with names in white Greek capital letters. Overhead, the suspended lighting lent a glow of warmth to the room. "Kosta," Stavros began, "you ever think about making some changes to the restaurant?"

"What kind of changes?"

"I know these things are all important to you." Stavros waved his hand to encompass the room full of memorabilia. "They cannot be replaced, I know." He hesitated. "But I think maybe you are losing business. Your customers are getting older, and they don't come downtown so much. Maybe you can attract more young people if you make some changes."

"What kind of changes, Stavro? I don't have so much money to put into an old restaurant."

"Ah, but that is the point. This does not have to be an old restaurant, and it does not have to be expensive. So, maybe you get rid of the paneling and put a fresh coat of paint on the walls—maybe white. This will make the space feel bigger."

"What I'm supposed to do with all of this?" Kosta raised both hands towards the walls and pivoted on his chair to encompass his collection.

"Maybe you put a shelf high up, going all around the restaurant. On here you put the vases, dishes, maybe some baskets."

"And the photos?"

"Kosta, nobody look at the photos. There is too much clutter here. You want your restaurant to feel open."

"No, *you* want it to feel open." Kostas slammed down his ouzo glass.

"Kosta . . ." Stavros said. He noticed tears threatening to spill out from the old man's eyes.

Kostas waved his hand at Stavros. "I know this place is old. I am only one man. There is only so much I can do. I need help."

"I am not helping you?" Stavros clenched his teeth. "I leave Greece to come to cook for you and help you with the restaurant and you say you need help?" He began to rise.

"Sit down, *vre Malaka*. Of course, you are helping. But this is temporary. And I am not the only reason you leave Greece. I think this woman has your heart. This is not so?"

Stavros relaxed and nodded. "Dimitra," he said. He took a deep breath and exhaled slowly.

"What you have told me," Kostas said, "about the restaurant. I know this. You are not the first person to notice how it has aged. How I have aged."

"No, Kosta . . ."

Kosta put up his hand to stop him. "It is true. I think maybe I have a solution for this and for you."

Stavros raised his eyebrows.

"I know you leave next month. But what if you come back?" Kostas leaned in toward Stavros. "We can get you a work visa if you have a business here. You can work as my partner, and eventually, you will take over the business—it will be your restaurant, and you can do whatever you want with it."

Stavros looked intently at Kosta. His eyes roamed the room, his imagination already redecorating the walls, the tables, and the kitchen. His lips parted slightly, but he spoke no words, although his thoughts raced. *Move to America? Stay with Demi? Leave my friends, my family, my country . . . my life? Have my own restaurant?*

"This is a lot to think about," Kostas said. "Take your time, *agori mou.* It is a big decision." He hesitated, then added. "If you don't do this, I will work another year, maybe two, and then I will sell the restaurant," he paused, ". . . or close it." Kostas sighed deeply, and his shoulders seemed to collapse. He glanced at the clock on the wall. "I'm sure you will have questions. We can talk about this when it is not so late."

Stavros picked up the empty ouzo glasses and took them to the kitchen.

"Leave them in the sink, Stavro. Let's go." Stavros came back into the dining room, and Kostas patted him on the shoulder. "You will make the right decision. Of this, I am sure."

* * *

"Are you sure this is what you want?" Georgia asked. The chain on her porch swing creaked as Demi and Georgia pushed it back and forth in a slow, steady rhythm. Although it was chilly enough for sweaters, the sun warmed their faces.

"Mom, I'm stuck."

"I get that, honey. I do. But there must be other jobs in Pittsburgh that you'd be qualified for. Better jobs with better hours and more pay."

Demi shrugged. "Maybe there are, maybe there aren't. It's not like I haven't looked. And it's not just the job. I need a change."

"That's a pretty big change."

"Mom," Demi sighed, "I've never lived anywhere else. I went to college two hours from here. Going to Greece made me realize how limited my life has been."

"I'd hardly call it limited," Georgia said.

"You know what I mean. I really haven't seen much beyond the tri-state area."

"So, travel, Demi. Make it a priority."

"Mom, I know. But I can't travel on the salary I'm making. Not the way I want to. I couldn't have gone to Greece if you hadn't taken me. This job pays almost twice as much. And I feel like I need a fresh start. I'm almost thirty. It's time to grow up and take charge."

Georgia nodded but said nothing. She looked across the street where her neighbor was wrapping a rope around ornamental seagrass.

Demi continued. "And Marina is graduating soon. She could end up anywhere. I can't afford to live without a roommate. And I'm not moving back home."

"But, why Chicago?"

"Why not Chicago? The job is perfect. The Oasis is a boutique hotel with an awesome banquet room and restaurant. And as Events Manager, I'd be working mostly days. I've researched the city. It's only an eight-hour drive." She saw the grimace on Georgia's face. "I know, I know. You hate driving more than five hours. It's like an hour plane ride. I know I'll miss you guys, but Aunt Toula and Uncle Angelo are there. I can hang out with Anna and Niko. I'll be fine."

But will Jimmy be fine? Georgia thought. "Have you accepted the offer yet?"

"No. Not yet. They're going to fly me up next Thursday to meet the staff and see the hotel in person."

"I don't know why she's cutting that sea grass," Georgia said. She nodded across the street, where her neighbor was now chopping the stalks of seagrass she had tied. "It looks so pretty when it dries out in the winter." She looked at the butterfly bushes and ornamental grass that she and Jimmy had planted in front of their house.

"Mom, you're not listening to me."

"I am, Demi." She sighed. "You're going up next Thursday to meet the staff."

"Do you want to come with me? We can stay overnight and go to the art museum."

Georgia dragged the balls of her feet to stop the gentle rocking of the porch swing. "I do love the art museum there." She leaned back in the swing and folded her arms as she pondered Demi's invitation. "There's a great Greektown in Chicago." Demi nodded, and Georgia continued. "Maybe I can visit with Toula or do some shopping downtown while you're interviewing."

Demi grinned. "See why I'm excited?" Her smile faded. "Although . . ." She sighed. "I don't want to be the one to tell Dad. Could you?"

"Hmmm. That's a 'no.' As you said, it's time to grow up. Consider this step one. And you better say something by tomorrow, or he's going to wonder why we're jetting off to Chicago randomly."

"Can't you tell him there's an author thing up there or something?"

"Demi."

"I know. Okay, I'll call him tonight."

"Call him?"

"Fine, I'll come over tonight."

"Demi," Georgia's tone softened. "What about Stavros?"

Demi looked out beyond the rooftops across the street. "What about him?"

"Come on. You've been spending a lot of time with him."

"Right. And he's going back to Greece in a month. So, what difference does it make where I'm living?"

"I just see how happy he makes you, Honey. What if he were able to come back to Pittsburgh? Maybe his uncle would sponsor him?"

"Why would he want to do that, Mom?" Demi shook her head.

"Because he loves you?"

"I love him too, Mom. That doesn't mean he's going to upheave his whole life for me." She sighed. "Even if that was possible, I'm pretty sure Stavros doesn't want to leave Greece or his grandmother. He might say he does, but what are the chances that he would return once he goes back to his family and friends? Am I going to sit here and wait for him on the chance that he comes back? I'm not going to put my career on hold again."

* * *

"Vre, Malaka!" Elias shouted over the phone.

"Quiet, *vre Malaka*. Just because I am across the ocean does not mean I cannot hear you." Stavros caught Kostas' eye and pointed to his phone. He left the kitchen and moved to the front of the empty restaurant. Outside the window, the late afternoon sun shone on the vacant patio. The leaves and stems of the leftover summer flowers were brown and dry in the large ceramic pots that adorned the corners of the small city patio, and the cushions on the wrought iron chairs showed wear. *We need to empty those pots, maybe get some artificial flowers. I need to talk with Kostas about buying new cushions.* He glanced at the time on his phone; in a half hour, they would be opening, and he hoped that the weather would encourage people to come to town for dinner or stay for a bite after work.

Elias continued with exuberance. "How are you? You are seeing the American girl?"

"Yes, of course," Stavros answered.

"Eh, something to do while you are in *Peeetsborg*." He elongated the word with a hint of distaste.

"Pittsburgh is not so bad," Stavros said.

"No? Does it have the sea? You have been fishing there? What you do at night? You have a plateia? Friends?"

"Aide 're, Louie. Come on. I am here to help Kosta."

"Yes, yes, I understand. But your friends miss you. Here, listen . . ." A chorus of voices, male and female, sang through the phone: *yeia sou, Stavro, eh Malaka, ela piso*—come back, Stavro—we miss you, *s'agapame 're file, filakia.* "You see? You have friends in Pittsburgh or only this girl?"

"*Vre, Malaka.* When I have time for friends when I work at the restaurant? Why I need friends if I am coming home soon?

"*Ela, Louie, pame,*" Stavros heard in the background as Elias spoke. "Okay, we are going to Lefki now." Stavros conjured the image of the plateia in Sparta surrounded with high-top tables and chairs, alive at night with music—traditional Greek and American pop competing with the sounds of laughter and conversation. He felt a pang of . . .*what*? It couldn't be nostalgia—he had only been gone for two months. But it felt like something lost. Was he seriously considering making Pittsburgh his home? Was he already missing his life in Sparta? "*Ta leme,*" he said to Elias, but he had already hung up.

CHAPTER 22

Fan-shaped yellow ginkgo leaves lay scattered among soggy brown oak leaves, blending with footprints on the snow-dusted sidewalk to form an autumn collage. A few stubborn leaves clung to the almost bare branches whose dark limbs stretched into a winter-white sky. Heavy, wet snowflakes coated Demi's light blue beanie and the shoulders of her black coat. A snowflake landed on her eyelashes, and she took her hand out of her pocket to wipe it off. Her other hand was in Stavros's firm grasp. "I wasn't expecting this today," she said. "I don't think it was supposed to snow. I would have worn gloves." She shoved her free hand back into her coat pocket.

"*Chione* is playing with us," Stavros said. "I am not ready for this."

"*Chione*?"

"The goddess of snow. She is the daughter of *Boreas*."

"North?" Demi asked.

"He is the god of the North Wind. But I don't think they are angry because the wind he is not blowing."

"Well, thank goodness for that," Demi said. "It's hard to believe it was seventy degrees out yesterday. This weather is crazy."

"It is always so crazy?" Stavros asked. He shivered inside of his brown leather jacket.

"Don't you have a winter coat?" Demi asked.

"Why I would need a winter coat?" Stavros asked. "This is *fthinoporo.* This is not supposed to happen until January, yes?" Stavros brought his free hand to his face and blew on it, his breath creating a cloud of steam.

"Let's forget the walk," Demi said. "We can go into the museum." She nodded towards the formidable dark stone building, which also housed the library.

"We have many museums in Greece," Stavros said. "In Athens is the Acropolis Museum, the National Archaeological Museum, the Benaki . . . even in Sparta we have the Archaeological Museum."

"I know, I went there," Demi remembered the day she met Stavros after leaving the museum in Sparta. *Was it only three months ago? I could never have predicted we would be here, in Pittsburgh, together. What fate is this, wreaking havoc with my life?* She pondered the unexpected circumstances that had reunited them, then returned to the present. "You don't have this one," she said. Demi reversed course, pulling Stavros along by the hand. "Come on. I'll show you something you haven't seen before!"

They walked past gnarled trunks of old oak trees, the benches beneath their empty branches adorned with a light dusting of snow. On the corner bordered by still-green trimmed hedges towered a life-sized grey fiberglass statue of a diplodocus dinosaur. Half of his 84 feet in length was his very long neck, which stretched a few stories high, ending with a small head. Someone had dangled a large black and gold scarf around his neck and had somehow placed an oversized pair of glasses in front of his eyes. "Why they do this?" Stavros asked, pointing at the accessories.

"I guess he's a Steelers fan," Demi joked. "Look," she said and pointed across the street. The majestic steel-framed Cathedral of Learning rose 42 stories above the University of Pittsburgh campus. "Most of Pitt's classes are in that building," Demi said. "My favorite rooms are the Nationality Rooms. They're decorated to reflect the style and culture of different countries."

"There is a Greek one?" Stavros asked.

"Yes," Demi said. "Would you like to go see it?"

"I know what a Greek room looks like," Stavros said.

"Of *course* you do," Demi said.

They entered the museum through a massive set of double dark wooden doors. Demi approached a curly-haired, bearded young man sitting behind the welcome desk. "Hi there. Two, please. I'm a member."

"I will get this," Stavros said, taking his wallet from his back pocket.

"My turn," Demi said, and she handed her credit card to the man who gave her two paper wristbands. "Give me your hand," she said to Stavros. He was about to protest but closed his mouth, shoved the wallet back into his pocket, and offered her his wrist. She wrapped the wristband around his wrist and pressed the sticky ends together. "There," she said, patting his hand playfully.

They walked down a set of marble steps, the heels of Demi's boots echoing in the high ceilings of the spacious hallway. "In here," she said, motioning for Stavros to follow her into a room with displays of ancient fossils and colorful charts depicting dinosaur habitats and their history.

Stavros peered closely at one of the placards posted next to a display of bones embedded in a section of quarry rock. "Demi, what is so special about these bones? They find them in 1947. That is not so long ago. In Greece, we have artifacts over 3,000 years old."

"Right. They found them in 1947. But the bones themselves are at least 65 million years old."

Stavros raised an eyebrow. "How they know this?"

"They do radiocarbon dating where they look at how much carbon remains in the bones. I'm pretty sure they use a combination of methods. It's incredible, really." Children's voices echoed from the next room in oohs and aahs of wonder. "This isn't the good stuff, though. Come on." Demi motioned him to follow her around the display and through a doorway.

They were greeted by two massive dinosaur skeletons, each reaching dozens of feet high into the air, their necks and tails reinforced with poles to keep them from collapsing. The dark brown bones spanned the length of the sizeable room, towering high above the museum visitors, craning their necks to view the skeletons. Thick vertebrae extended into chunky rod-shaped tailbones that narrowed towards the end of the whiplike tails, which balanced the long, long necks of the dinosaur. Beneath them, bright green artificial ferns sprouted from a sandy loam. They were surrounded by larger-than-life painted murals of other dinosaurs in their natural environments. Demi and Stavros made their way around the room in awed silence. "I used to love coming here as a kid," Demi said. "You'd think it would get old, but it doesn't. The older I get, the more amazing I realize it is that we have these skeletons here."

Closer to the ground, a triceratops skeleton appeared to crawl in the sand, its enormous three-horned head supported by a metal pole. "This one looks like a Gorgon," Stavros said. "I would not want to be his dinner."

"You wouldn't be," Demi replied. "He's an herbivore."

"This is what?" Stavros asked.

"A vegetarian," she replied. "Ah, but this one . . ." She nodded across the room at the massive Tyrannosaurus Rex skeleton—a mammoth head with mammoth teeth in a mammoth jaw, disproportionate to the rib cage and narrowing tail section . . ." would finish you in one bite."

"Hmm, maybe. But he is not as scary as Medusa. She could turn you to stone with her eyes."

"Well, yeah, but there's a big difference."

"Yes?"

Demi scrunched up her face, stating the obvious. "The T-Rex was real."

Stavros stared at her. "What you are saying, Dimitra?"

"I'm saying Medusa was a myth. The dinosaurs are real."

"How you know they are real?"

"Stavro. Look around you. These are actual skeletons. Of real dinosaurs. Who existed millions of years ago."

"How you know this? Maybe they just tell you this to sell tickets to the museum."

Demi put her hands on her hips. "You don't believe these are real?"

"You don't believe *Medusa* is real?"

Demi's mouth dropped open, and she blinked. She shook her head, shrugged, and held her palms up, at a loss for words. Stavros turned away from her, the shaking in his back barely discernible. Demi narrowed her eyes. "Wait a minute . . ." She grabbed him by the arm and turned him around. His lips were pressed together, trying to hold back laughter. "Are you serious right now?" she said, punching him in the arm. He slid his arms around her, rendering her unable to punch him again, and smiled down at her. "There is only one thing I am serious about, Dimitra, and this is you."

* * *

Marina glanced at the message notification on her cell phone, then back to her laptop. *Nope, can't get distracted. I'll get it later.* She stared at the document on the screen, which listed possible sites for her internship. Choices were due, and she still had not decided. The chime of the telephone interrupted her. Marina saw "SOPHIE" on the screen and picked up the phone.

"Guess what!" Sophie's voice shrieked through the telephone.

Marina held the cell phone away from her ear. "What the heck, Sophie?"

"Well?"

"Well, what?"

"Guess!"

Marina rolled her eyes, although she couldn't help smiling at Sophie's enthusiasm. "Okay, what am I guessing?"

"Guess who messaged me?"

Marina's irritation at the interruption evaporated, given this interesting news. "He did not!"

"He did!"

"What did he say?"

"He said that he also prefers tea."

"And?"

"And what?"

"What did you say?" Marina tried to keep the impatience from her voice.

"I haven't said anything yet. I need to figure out what to say back."

"Sophie. You're 24. You're on your own. I have to get back to work. I'm following up on internships, and I have to get this done by tomorrow."

"Fine," she sighed, followed by a hopeful, "Where's Demi?"

"I think Demi's out with Stavros. And don't call Mom about this. Or Aunt Georgia. You don't want to start a relationship with other people's words."

"Umm . . . didn't I already do that?"

"That was just a follow-up to your 'meet cute.' We had to get you moving in the right direction. You have to take it from here."

"Wait. Did you say relationship?" Sophie's voice rose. "Do you think we could be in a relationship?"

"Not if you don't reply to him. Sophie, I have to go. You've got this."

"Okay, but . . ."

"Bye, Sis. Love you." Marina hung up the phone and smiled.

* * *

"Do you want to get something to eat?" Demi asked as they left the hall of the dinosaurs.

Stavros peered outside the large picture windows at the snow which continued to fall. "How far do we have to walk?"

"We don't," Demi said. "They have a nice cafe here. But first, you might enjoy this." To their left, mounted in front of a wide set of marble stairs, stood a larger-than-life white plaster statue of Sophocles, standing tall with one hand in front of his chest and the other on his hip, looking every bit the great orator.

"How this is here?" Stavros asked.

"It's a cast," Demi explained. "It's a copy of the original." She looked closely at the information card on the heavy marble base of the statue. "Actually, it's a copy of a copy. The Romans made a copy of the Greek original—it says here in 330 BCE. It's in the Vatican Museum. This one is a cast of that copy."

They walked up the marble stairs into the Hall of Architecture. Natural light poured in through skylights in the high ceilings, showcasing dozens of cast sculptures. Stavros pointed toward the wall where several statues stood sentry. "This one," he said. Demi looked up at the exquisite statue of Nike, headless, with her wings spread wide and her robes appearing to be swept by the wind.

"It's amazing," Demi said.

"Yes. But you know where this is? It is in the Louvre. With this one," he said, pointing at the famous armless statue of a female figure.

"The Venus de Milo," Demi said.

"This is what they call her," Stavros said. "But she is Aphrodite, goddess of beauty. She is a Greek one, but she was stolen by the French and now she lives at the Louvre, making money for the French. Many of our statues and pieces of the Acropolis have been stolen. Some by the Italians and French, and many by the British. During the Turkish invasion, many pieces were taken by Lord Elgin. He destroyed much of the Parthenon and took pieces of it to England." Stavros felt his breath quicken as his voice became louder. "They are in the British Museum, but they don't belong there—they belong in Greece. We have been trying to get them back for years, but the British government refuses."

Demi touched his shoulder. "I know this is a sensitive issue," she said. "I hope that someday the pieces are returned home. I've read where the Pope is getting involved and plans to return some of the marble from the Acropolis to Greece."

"This is a start," Stavros said. "But, Dimitra, why you have these copies in Pittsburgh? Why here?"

"That's a good question," Demi said. "I never really thought about it—I just enjoyed seeing them. When I was younger, I used to come here for art classes. We would sit and draw the statues." She paused in thought. *I haven't drawn for a long time. I used to love it.* A movement to her right caught her attention, where a uniformed guide wearing a lanyard watched over the great hall. "Actually, let's ask them." She turned to the guide. "Excuse me," she said and asked about the casts.

"My pleasure," the guide replied. "The museum was opened in the late 1800's. Andrew Carnegie had a vision for the Hall of Architecture. It's still much the same as it was then, although at one time, it had over 150 plaster casts and reproductions of sculpture. You can also see some bronze ones in the back of the hall."

"But why casts?" Demi asked.

"By using plaster casts, Carnegie was able to bring the world's masterpieces to Pittsburgh so people could study their form and detail in full scale. Some casts are used to help restore the originals. They're the last record of these pieces. In some cases, they're the only record." They pointed to a large, intricate cast of an archway decorated on either side with figurines of people, the peak of its arch almost reaching the high ceiling. "That one was used to help restore the original after it was partially destroyed during World War II. Without these casts, we'd have no record of some of these sculptures."

"Thank you," Demi said.

"No problem," the guide replied. "Let me know if you have any further questions."

"Stavro?" Demi asked.

"No," he said. He thought about the vulnerability of the Greek ruins through the many occupations of Greece and the raiding that had been done by so many countries. He waved to encompass the large hall. "I think maybe this is a good thing."

* * *

"Hey, you're home early," Georgia said, looking up from the sofa, where she sat with Gus curled up on her lap. She looked up from her book and tilted her face up to Jimmy, who bent down to kiss her.

"You're not writing?"

"Reading," Georgia smiled. "It's the next best thing."

Jimmy set his keys on the small entryway table next to a pile of unopened mail. He took off his jacket and hung it on the back of one of the kitchen chairs.

Georgia pursed her lips but refrained from asking him to hang up his jacket, remembering her vow to stop picking at little things. "How was the poker game last night? I didn't get to ask you this morning. I thought I'd see you at breakfast."

"I had an early meeting. The poker game was good." He smiled. "Good enough to take you out to dinner tonight if you don't feel like cooking."

Georgia looked out at the snow now coating the yard and the street. "Do you mind if I take a rain check?" she asked. "I made some veal patties earlier and I can cook up some rice pilaf. I think it would be nice to stay in this evening. And I don't feel like putting on makeup or getting dressed up."

"You don't need makeup, honey," Jimmy said. "But I don't mind. That sounds good."

"Who was there?" Georgia asked, referring to the poker game. She laid her book face-down on the table next to the sofa, careful not to disturb the sleeping cat.

"The usual suspects." Jimmy played every Thursday in the back of Mike's Barbershop with a group of men from the neighborhood, mostly Greek. "Kostas was there."

"Oh, good," Georgia said. "I know you said he hasn't been there for a few weeks. Is he feeling alright? He didn't seem himself the last time we saw him."

Jimmy sat down next to Georgia. "Yeah, he seems okay. A little down. He's worried about his restaurant. I know he misses his mother. She was there every day for so many years."

"Stavros is helping him, isn't he?"

Jimmy nodded. "Kostas told me he offered Stavros the chance to buy into the restaurant and become a partner."

Georgia sat up, and Gus scrambled from her lap. "Really? Demi didn't say anything about that. That's wonderful."

"I'm not sure Demi knows."

"Why wouldn't he tell Demi?"

"Maybe he's not sure if he wants to do it. Especially if Demi might not be here." Jimmy's body sagged, knowing that Demi was actively job hunting.

"Or maybe he doesn't want to influence Demi's career plans."

"Do you think that would influence her career plans?" Jimmy brightened. "Maybe we should tell her, Georgia. Doesn't she have a right to know? Shouldn't she make her decisions with all the available information?"

"Jimmy, this isn't a bid she's deciding on. If Stavros wanted her to know, he'd tell her."

"But *we* know. Are we right to keep this from her?"

Georgia watched the snowflakes cascading outside of their picture window. *Would it keep her daughter in Pittsburgh? Is that what was best for her*? She sighed and looked back at Jimmy. "This is between Demi and Stavros, and as much as you want to, I don't think we should intervene."

* * *

Demi and Stavros picked up red ceramic teacups from the bar top and carried them to a marble-topped table. Outside of the adjacent picture window stood a sizeable, rounded, dark granite statue, which may or may not have represented the human form. The snow had dwindled to flurries, but the sky remained grey.

"It looks like night outside," Demi remarked, glancing at her Fitbit, "but it's only a quarter to five." She dipped her tea bag a few times, then picked up the oversized cup with both hands and blew on the tea before taking a sip. Stavros leaned back in his chair, legs crossed, reading a message from Elias on his phone, the fingers of his right hand tapping the table.

"Stavro?" Demi asked. "Everything okay?"

"*Ti?*" He looked up, put the phone into his jacket pocket, and smiled a quick half-smile. "*Nai,* yes, everything is okay."

Demi took a deep breath and paused. "I have something I need to tell you."

Stavros stopped his tapping and raised his eyebrows at Demi. "So, tell me."

Here we go, thought Demi. "I'm going to Chicago on Thursday."

"You are visiting your aunt?"

"Well, yes, but there's more."

Stavros folded his arms, his eyes never leaving Demi's face as she told him about the job opportunity in Chicago. When she finished, he was silent. His eyes shifted, and he stared unfocused into the space behind her. Shrouded in an uneasy silence, they were oblivious to the laughter coming from the table beside them and the clinking of silverware and china from the bar where they had picked up their tea.

Stavros unfolded his arms, and his eyes found Demi's. "Why you want to leave Pittsburgh?"

Demi took a sip of tea, her hand unsteady as she set the cup back on the saucer. "What's here for me besides my family and a dead-end job? Working nights, I hardly see them. I have no life for myself. In Chicago, I'll have a day job and weekends off, and I'll be able to come home when I want to."

"You can't find another job here?"

"Not an opportunity like this one."

Stavros resumed drumming on the table with his fingers as he pondered something. He stopped tapping and spoke. "What if I was here?"

Demi shook her head. "But you're not."

Stavros leaned in towards Demi. "But what if I was? This would make a difference?"

Demi paused, thoughts spinning through her mind like a pinwheel in the wind. *Would it make a difference? Of course, it would.* Her mind began to picture a life with Stavros. She shook her head to dispel those thoughts. *Could I trust anyone enough to put my career on hold again? For someone who might change his mind? If I stayed and you left me . . . could I recover from that? Better to lose you now than to be abandoned.* She recalled how hurt, sad, foolish, rejected, and betrayed she had felt when Andrew broke up with her. Could she go through that again?

"Dimitra." The murmur of her name brought her back to the table, and she looked at Stavros. "Would it make a difference if I stayed?"

Demi felt her heartbeat quicken at the intensity of his stare. "I wish I could say that it would. But I can't answer a 'what if' question. I can only answer a question that's grounded in reality. And the reality is that you're going back to Greece in a month."

"But . . ." Stavros began, but he stopped. *Wasn't this the perfect time to tell her about the offer from Kostas?* He remained silent, questions racing through his mind. *Was it that he didn't want to influence her decision—or that he was afraid of her response? Or was he, himself, unsure about whether he wanted to stay? Was it fair to ask Demi to remain in Pittsburgh if he couldn't guarantee his return?*

For a moment, they sat quietly across the table from each other, looking at the snow, which had resumed in slow, wet drops, glistening against the grey backdrop of the buildings across the street. Demi placed her hand on Stavros', and he turned back to her. "Stavro," she said. "We have a month left together. I don't want to lose a minute of it. I've spent too much of my life worrying about tomorrow; I want to enjoy today. I haven't even made a decision yet—I just thought that you should know. But whatever happens, I want to enjoy the time that we have together. Can we do that?"

Stavros pulled his hand away, leaned back in his chair, and looked up towards the ceiling. *Where had not speaking to Demi gotten him after she left Greece*? He had been morose and moody, and his friends had chided him for letting the American girl get to him. He remembered how excited he had been at the prospect of seeing her again. Maybe his heart would break once more—or maybe Demi would turn down the job.

What would he gain by not seeing her? He felt his stubbornness crack like a boulder struck by lightning. His eyes found Demi's, and he took her hand. "*Nai, agape mou.*" he nodded. "This we can do."

* * *

Stavros opened his eyes to the empty pillow next to his head. He rolled over, picked up his phone, and checked the time. Eleven fifteen—he had slept longer than he'd planned. He'd had difficulty falling asleep and had slept fitfully. The whirr of the coffee grinder indicated that Demi was downstairs in her kitchen. He set the phone down and plodded to the bathroom, which was strewn with make-up, hair products, and toiletries. He retrieved his toothbrush from between a large can of hairspray and a tube of mascara, recalling with a touch of nostalgia how annoyed he had been with his mother and sister when they all shared a bathroom in Sparta. He calculated the time in Athens, returned to the bedroom, and grabbed the phone from the nightstand. The greeting at the other end of the line was an enthusiastic "Stavro!"

"*Yeia sou*, Mama."

"I'm happy to hear your voice! How are you? How is Pittsburgh? How is Kosta?"

"Siga siga, Mama!" Stavros laughed. "Pittsburgh is okay. *O Kostas megaloni*—he is getting old."

"And the *kopela*? Dimitra?" The phone line was quiet. "Stavro?" His mother's maternal instinct stirred. "What is it, *agori mou*?"

Stavros walked to the doorway and heard Demi talking to someone. *Marina*? *No, she'd gone away for a few days, making it possible for him to stay with Demi.* He heard Demi croon in a sing-song voice, "Hello, Miss Bella, how's my pretty kitty cat?" *Ah—the cat.* He was still amused that Demi and Georgia kept cats indoors. His experience with cats was limited to those who roamed the restaurants in Greece hoping for scraps. He heard his name over the phone, and with Demi safely engaged with the cat, he told his mother about her potential offer in Chicago and his offer from Kostas.

"Why you don't tell her about this, *Stavro mou*?"

"Den ksero, Mama. I don't know. I think maybe I belong in Sparta."

"*Agori mou*, no one belongs anywhere. You belong where the opportunities are. Why you think so many Greeks move to America and Australia? Why you think your father and I live in Athens? It is not because we love the traffic and the noise. It is because here we can work and have a nice apartment and a nice life."

Stavros bristled. "I have a nice life in Sparta."

"Yes, of course. Now. But you are young. You are going to be a cook in a village when you are forty? Maybe you marry a village girl? This is the life you want for yourself?"

"What are you saying?"

"You love this girl?"

"*Kai vevaia.*"

"You like working at the restaurant?"

"I think if I make some changes . . ."

"So, what's the problem?"

He glanced towards the bedroom door and spoke softly. "My life is in Sparta."

"Why you say this? Because of your friends? Because of *Yiayia? Yiayia* is okay now. She has friends and the church, and we are two hours away if she needs us. You know what? She has started to paint again! I know you feel responsible for her, *Stavro mou*. What you did for her when she was sick—she will never forget this, and neither will I. But it is time for you to live your life. What does your heart tell you, Stavro?"

"Mama, Dimitra might move to Chicago."

His mother contemplated this new information. "Because she thinks you will not return to Pittsburgh."

"I think it is more than this." He sat on the bed and told his mother what had happened with Demi and Andrew.

She paused. "Ah. This will be difficult."

"So, what do I do?"

"Stavro, I cannot tell you what to do. I can only tell you to listen to your heart. Whatever you decide, I support you."

CHAPTER 23

The aroma in Pitsa's kitchen was a savory blend of roasting turkey, sauteed onions, and freshly baked bread. Georgia and Jimmy had yet to arrive. Pitsa heard her sons, Alex and Manny, greet Marina and Demi from the living room, where they were watching football.

Manny waved from the couch. Alex got up and gave his cousins a hug. "Long time no see," he said.

"It's been a minute," Demi said. "Things have been pretty busy with work and, um . . ."

Alex looked over her shoulder. "Yeah, where is the new man?" he asked.

"He's dropping Kosta off at his cousin's house. He'll be here soon."

"Good. We've heard a lot about him."

Marina laughed. "From your mother, no doubt."

"Who else?"

"*Elate, koritsia*," Pitsa called from the kitchen.

"Coming, Aunt Pitsa." Demi and Marina hung their jackets in the hall closet and entered the large kitchen where Pitsa was bending over the oven rack, basting the turkey with a broth of orange and lemon juices, sage, sea salt, and ground pepper. Even with her apron on, she looked perfectly put together; her black hair was neatly coiffed, and her red lipstick was in place.

Demi noticed the stuffing surrounding the turkey. "You're making Greek stuffing!" That explained the sauteed onion smell. She loved the side dish of ground sausage and beef, onions, raisins, pine nuts, and whatever herbs Pitsa had on hand. Usually, Pitsa made traditional American stuffing to appease her boys.

"Fisika," Pitsa said. "We have a special guest coming." She winked at Demi, who felt her cheeks get warm.

"*Where is Thios Antonis*?" Marina asked. Pitsa nodded toward the kitchen window, and the girls peered outside. Antonis had loaded chopped wood from the back of the yard into a wheelbarrow and was bringing it to the front of the house. "I told him we don't need a fire today, but he insists."

"Are you fucking kidding me?" They heard shouting from the living room. "He couldn't score from the two-yard line? *I* could score from the two against this lousy defense."

"Manoli! What language is this? *Prosehe ti glossa sou*," Pitsa called.

"Sorry, Mama."

Marina squinted. "The Steelers aren't playing, are they? What's Manny so upset about?"

"I think maybe he put a little money on the game," Pitsa answered. "Come, help me to set the table."

* * *

Georgia sat in the passenger seat of Jimmy's Chevy Silverado, an unbaked macaroni casserole covered with aluminum foil in her lap. She flipped down the visor and checked her hair in the mirror, then flipped it back up and adjusted the baking dish on her legs. "I hope this is enough," she said.

"With all the food that Pitsa makes? It'll be fine, honey."

"Have you seen the way those boys eat? And we'll have one more mouth to feed today."

Jimmy pulled onto the highway and glanced at Georgia. "Has he said anything to Demi about the restaurant?"

"I don't think so. If he has, she hasn't said anything to me."

They rode in silence to the rhythmic hum of the truck's tires on the road. Jimmy broke the quiet. "Has Demi accepted the job?"

"Not yet, but I think she's going to." Georgia cracked the window open a few inches. She closed her eyes and took a deep breath, exhaling slowly. "It smells like spring out." The trees had shed their last leaves and now stood bare against the blue sky, but there was an unseasonable warmth to the air.

Jimmy cracked his window open an inch to relieve the pressure inside the cab and sighed. "I don't want her to leave."

"I know, sweetheart. I don't either . . . but remember, *we* left."

"What are you talking about, Georgia?"

"Are you forgetting that we lived in Minneapolis for three years?"

Jimmy took a quick look into the passenger mirror and pulled onto the exit lane, then stole a glance at Georgia. "That was different."

"How was that different?"

"Because I was supporting us while you went to grad school. I had to go where the jobs were."

"And how is this different?"

"Georgia, I was the breadwinner."

He did not just go there, Georgia thought. She blew out a gust of anger before speaking. "Really, Jimmy? And who is paying Demi's bills? You realize that she's been taking care of herself ever since she graduated? You keep telling her how proud of her you are."

"I *am* proud of her."

"Then let her go, Jimmy. Who knows, maybe she'll come back. We came back. Pittsburgh has her heart."

"She has *my* heart, Georgia."

Georgia's anger dissolved. "Oh, sweetheart." She placed her hand on Jimmy's. "I'll miss her, too. I love hanging out with our daughter. But she'll be fine, and so will we. We did pretty well as empty nesters when she went to college, didn't we?"

"Yeah, but she was only two hours away."

"Honey, she didn't come home at all her last semester. We survived."

"I know. But you talk to her on the phone all the time."

"Well, you'll just have to learn how to use Facetime, won't you?"

Jimmy grimaced. "You know I hate technology." He turned onto Pitsa's street and slowed down.

"Jimmy." Georgia's voice softened. "Let's enjoy Thanksgiving. No gloominess today. She's not gone yet."

Jimmy sighed. "Alright."

They pulled in front of the house, and Jimmy put the truck into park. Georgia turned his head to hers and kissed him. "I love you. She'll be fine. *We'll* be fine."

* * *

The doorbell rang, and Pitsa, who had been firmly ensconced in the kitchen, appeared from nowhere, no longer wearing her apron, to answer the door. "*Kalimera,*" she shouted, smiling broadly as she flung the door open. "Welcome to our home!"

"*Kalimera, Kiria* Pitsa," Stavros replied, searching over Pitsa's shoulder for Demi. Before he could spot her, Georgia materialized and greeted Stavros with the requisite kisses on each cheek. He handed her a box. "I bring the *poompkeen*!"

Alex was the next one to the door and shook Stavros's hand, introducing himself. "Nice to meet you. Come on in, Stavro." He led Stavros to the living room. Manny gave a wave and a nod, but his eyes remained on the television. Stavros searched the room with his eyes as if he might spot Demi behind a piece of furniture.

"I think the girls went upstairs," Alex said. "Mom wanted them to see her new comforter or something. They'll be down in a minute." On cue, Demi, Sophia, and Marina padded down the carpeted stairs in single file, Demi in the lead. Her heart somersaulted when she saw Stavros on the couch between Alex and Manny, looking as if he belonged there. He got up when he saw Demi. Despite an overwhelming desire to take her in his arms, with all eyes upon him, he greeted her with the standard two cheek kisses, followed by more kisses for Sophie and Marina.

Demi teased, "Did I hear you say you brought pumpkin pie? I thought you weren't a fan of the *poompkeen*."

"It's *kolokithopita*—Greek pumpkin pie with rice and pumpkin. I make it with phyllo, like baklava. Kostas, he show me how to make it."

"You made pumpkin pie?" Marina asked. "Nice!" She raised her eyebrows at Demi and nodded as if to say, *you've got a good one here*. Demi grinned.

"*Koritsia, elate*, help me to put out the food." The girls obeyed Aunt Pitsa's summons, and Stavros sat back down on the couch. Pitsa handed bowls of mashed potatoes, stuffing, and macaroni to the girls for the table.

Eleven chairs were crammed closely around the sturdy Mediterranean dining room table, which was extended out with leaves on either end. Pitsa had gotten out the "good china," large white plates with a gold Greek key border design set between gold knives and forks. She had a service for eight—her place, along with Manny's and Alex's, were set with plain white china plates and their everyday flatware.

"Come to eat; the dinner is ready," Pitsa called.

"Mama, *perimene*," Manny responded from the living room. "The Giants are on the one-yard line."

"The dinner is not going to wait. *Elate*. You can watch the football after."

The television volume rose as the commentator announced Saquon Barkley's run in from the one. "*Manoli!* We are not listening to football while we eat. Turn off the television. *Ela*."

Antonis sat at the end of the long table while everyone else wriggled into their seats, taking turns to pull out and push in chairs that were squeezed together. Pitsa brought in a large platter of turkey to a chorus of *ooohs* and *aaahs*, and the rapid passing of bread, stuffing, cranberries, and the accompanying dishes ensued. She took her seat opposite Antonis at the other end of the table. Manny doused his mashed potatoes with gravy and brought the fork up to his mouth. "*Perimene*!" Pitsa scolded. "First, we must all say something we are thankful for."

The table groaned collectively, and Pitsa glared at the occupants. "Mama," Alex said, placing his hand on hers. "Maybe there are too many of us here today, and your delicious food will get cold. Maybe if someone wants to, they can speak . . ."

Antonis held up his wine glass to Alex. "*Bravo, agori mou*. Good idea." Pitsa glared at him. Manny's forkful of mashed potatoes remained halfway between his mouth and his plate as he looked between his parents.

"I'll go," Zoe said. "I'm thankful for my supportive family and my friends, old and new. I'm thankful for my new job and for Charles and Georgia, who convinced me I could do this."

Pitsa nodded approvingly and raised her eyebrows. Clearly, one speaker was not going to appease her. She looked up and down both sides of the table. The reluctant diners were avoiding her gaze. Alex broke the silence. "I am thankful for this wonderful meal," he nodded to his mother, "and the football that is waiting for us after we eat."

A chorus of chuckles followed his remark before the room crept into an uncomfortable silence. Georgia spoke. "I'm thankful to be here among the people I love. I'm grateful that I was able to spend time in Greece with my family—for everything we learned there and for the people we met." She nodded and smiled at Stavros, then held up her glass. "Let's just toast to friends and family and to new opportunities and adventures. *Yeia mas*!"

"*Yeia mas*!" The room came to life as cousins caught up with cousins, and aunts and uncles talked across the table between forkfuls of turkey and stuffing. Snatches of conversation rose above the din.

"Stavro," Alex said. "You play football?"

"American football, no. European futbol, *nai*."

"That's cool," Manny said. "We play soccer in the church league. You should play with us sometime. The games are in the spring, but if the weather's good, we practice weekends at the park. Gimme your number, I'll call you."

"Marina, did you decide on your internship?" Pitsa leaned over Manny.

"I had to put down my top three choices and rank four more. I'm doing well in the program, so I think I have a good chance of getting one of the top three."

"*Brava sou, koritsi mou*. What did you choose?"

"Erie and Cleveland—they're not too far from home, and they have good hospital systems, which is a big component of the nutrition internship. I'm hoping to get one of those, but I'd also be happy with Chicago—that's my third choice." She stole a glance at Demi, who was chatting with Zoe, and continued. "I'm pretty sure I could stay with Aunt Toula for eight weeks. They have a huge house. Or maybe share an apartment with Demi if . . ."

Manny pushed his chair back and stood, diverting Pitsa's attention. "Manoli! Where are you going?"

"Oh, sorry, Mama." He picked up his plate to clear it.

"*Katse, Manoli.* We are not finished here. The football can wait. How often is the family together?"

Manny hesitated as he weighed his choices, then sat down with a thud.

Antonis reached for the gravy boat and poured some onto his remaining mashed potatoes. "Stavro, Kostas tells me he wants to make you a partner at the restaurant. *Bravo!* This is a good idea. He is an old man, and you are young."

Forks stopped in their tracks, and the scene froze into place like a still shot. Demi turned her head in slow motion to look at Stavros, who kept his eyes on his plate of food. She looked across the table at Sophie and Marina, who stared at her with their mouths open and eyebrows raised. Georgia dug her nails into Jimmy's leg under the table, and he patted her hand.

"Whaaat?" Antonis shrugged, palms up, as he looked around the dining room.

Pitsa picked up the bowl of stuffing and held it up. "More stuffing?" she asked. She passed the bowl to Alex, who loaded his plate, keeping his eye on the unfolding drama.

Zoe spoke. "Stavro, how exciting. That's quite a decision, isn't it."

He nodded, still quietly focused on his plate.

Demi picked up her napkin from her lap, folded it and placed it next to her plate of uneaten food. "Excuse me," she said. She pushed back her chair and left the room.

All eyes turned to Stavros. He slowly pushed back his chair. "*Me sihoreite*," he said, "excuse me," and nodded to Pitsa.

At his departure, Manny stood up again. "Well, I guess we're done here," he said, sprinting to the living room before his mother could stop him.

* * *

Demi sat on the top step of the front porch stairs. Despite the sun, she shivered in the chilly air and wished she had brought her jacket outside. She barely had time to process the new information before she heard the screen door slam, and Stavros appeared behind her.

"Dimitra . . ."

"Don't," Demi said. She didn't turn around. "Just don't."

Stavros sat down next to her on the step. Neither spoke for a moment. He leaned forward, his elbows on his knees. He peered at Demi. "I'm sorry."

"Why would you keep this from me? You know how much I care about you. Why wouldn't you tell me?"

Stavros sighed. "I was not sure . . ." He trailed off.

"Not sure about what? The job? Me? Us?"

"Dimitra, what difference it makes? You are going to Chicago. You tell me it will not make a difference if I stay."

"Is that what you heard?" She shook her head as if trying to shake loose the thoughts inside of it. "I told you I couldn't answer a what-if question."

Stavros breathed out, realizing that his heart was pumping rapidly. "So now, it is not a what-if question."

"What do you mean? You're coming back to Pittsburgh?"

Stavros hesitated. He put his head onto his hand. "It is a big decision."

She nodded in understanding. "Well," she said, with a false brightness. "It's not a problem. I've accepted the job in Chicago, so you don't have anything to worry about."

"You are leaving?"

"I'm not the only one, am I?"

Stavros softened his tone. "*Kopella mou.*" He took Demi's hand. "Why you are so angry with me? This is difficult for both of us, *etsi den enai*?"

Demi drew her hand away slowly. "I need some time to think. You should probably go. I'll tell everyone you said goodbye."

Stavros clenched his jaw. "This is what you want?" He stood up and looked down at Demi, but she refused to meet his glance. "Dimitra," he said. "Even if I tell you I am coming back, you will not stay. You don't believe me. I think your heart is frozen."

Demi looked up, but Stavros was already walking down the steps. She opened her mouth to call to him, then closed it.

* * *

"Hey."

Although Georgia spoke softly, Demi's shoulders flinched in surprise. "I didn't hear you come out."

"I came out quietly so we wouldn't have the whole table out here to see if you were alright."

"No, I'm not alright," Demi snapped and instantly regretted it. "I'm sorry, Mom. It's just that . . ." Her voice trailed off at the incomplete thought. Georgia sat down next to Demi and they both looked out across the street at the tall oaks, empty of leaves. Demi breathed in deeply and let out a long breath as her heart rate slowed. "I don't understand," she said. "Why didn't he tell me?"

Georgia cupped her chin in her hand, contemplating how to respond to Demi. She tried to look at the situation through both her daughter's and Stavros's eyes. What could she tell her daughter that could possibly make her feel better? She heard a soft *coo-coo-cooing* and looked up at the large oak tree in Pitsa's yard to see two mourning doves balancing on a low, thin branch that danced under their weight. One of the doves took off, causing the branch to bob slightly, and landed on the ground in front of her. The bird seemed to be looking directly at Georgia. Upon closer inspection, the dove was lovely—what had looked like pale gray was infused with soft brown. On the bird's body were black oval spots, and its tail was made up of layers of black and white feathers.

Demi's eyes followed Georgia's. "Did you know that mourning doves mate for life?"

"I've heard that," Georgia replied.

"They actually mourn when they lose their mate. I've read that they continue to visit the spot where their partner died."

"Yes, Demi, they do. And then they move on. And often find another mate."

"Are we talking about mourning doves, Mom?"

"*I'm* talking about mourning doves. What are you talking about?" Georgia pulled Demi towards her and kissed her cheek. "Sweetheart. I know your heart is hurting." They sat quietly for a moment before Georgia continued. "Do you know what else I've heard about mourning doves?" Demi glanced at her mother and raised her eyebrow. "I've read that they're a symbol of hope and renewal. According to numerology, their appearance is a sign of compassion during a time of transition."

Demi looked sideways at Georgia. "Since when do you believe in numerology?" She shook her head. "Anyway, doves represent love, not hope and renewal."

"Yes, the white ones do. But the grey ones represent the bridge between the old and the new." She pointed at the large dove, still squatting on the ground in front of them. "They show up in our lives when we're at a standstill, and they help us release ourselves from our self-imposed limitations."

"Mother," Demi chuckled. "You are just making that up."

Georgia crossed her heart and raised her palm. "I am not! Google it. Mourning doves encourage you to follow your purpose."

"If you say so." Demi noticed that the mourning dove was still looking at her. It turned and, with a thrust, took off and landed back on the branch with its partner.

"Still don't believe me?" Georgia asked. They watched the doves waddle on the branch until they were next to each other. "Demi. Forgive Stavros. Both of you are making decisions that will affect the rest of your lives. There is no right or wrong decision, but they are difficult choices. Once you make them, though, they're made, and you can't look back and wonder, 'What if I chose the other path?' Because you have absolutely no way of knowing where that path would have taken you. I love the quote by Somerset Maugham—"The most valuable thing I have learned from life is to regret nothing."

They heard a high-pitched whistle as first one, then the other mourning dove took off from the oak tree and flew across the street, their wings vibrating in flight. "Everything alright out here?" Jimmy stood in the doorway.

Demi looked up at her father and shrugged her shoulders. "I guess so."

"Aunt Pitsa is serving dessert. Are you guys coming in? Manny's being held hostage in the dining room—he's going to have a conniption if he can't watch football." Demi and Georgia both stretched out their legs and then stood up. "Don't worry, honey," Jimmy said. "You'll be okay. What is it they say? 'Everything will be alright in the end. If it's not alright, then it's not the end.'"

Demi and Georgia looked at each other and grinned. "Thanks, Dad. I've heard that somewhere." Demi hugged her mother and then her father.

CHAPTER 24

The city skyline was bathed in the sun's last rays as it set behind Mount Washington. Across the river, a bright orange glow reflected off the windows of the BNY Mellon building and the towers to the east of it, making it appear as if every office light was on. The shorter structures that lined the parkway next to the river were already in shadow, accentuating the contrast. Demi pointed to their right, beyond the skyscrapers. "There's the Cathedral of Learning, where we were a few weeks ago. See it?"

Stavros nodded. "I am surprised you can see it from here."

"The more you drive around Pittsburgh, the more you notice it from different vantage points. Sometimes, you're on a winding road, and all of a sudden, there it is way in front of you. There was a Spanish artist named Felix de la Concha who came to Pittsburgh for two years in the nineties and painted 365 views of the Cathedral from different perspectives all around Oakland—one for every day of the year. They're on display at the Alumni Hall at Pitt. Maybe someday we can go there." She stopped, realizing that their "somedays" were drawing to an end.

"Why he stay here two years if he paint one every day?"

"He didn't. I mean, he did stay two years, but he painted one *for* every day. The weather here doesn't always comply."

"Yes, I know this," Stavros said. The temperature had cooled as the sun sank close to the horizon. To the east, the land was cast in a blue-violet hue. Above it, the sky was a muted canvas of pale indigo, and above this, a soft magenta bled into a pastel yellow before blending with the light blue of the sky. Several ornate bridges spanned the curving river as it disappeared behind a bend.

Demi and Stavros held hands as they approached the overlook, which hung several feet out over the cliff. A few couples leaned on the sturdy wrought iron fence that surrounded the overlook, and a family of four took photos of each other with the cityscape in the background. A chorus of foreign languages mingled with the woosh of cars from the roadway far below them. Demi stepped onto the overlook, but Stavros dropped her hand and stopped on the sidewalk. Demi turned her head to look back at him and smiled. "Come on, it's safe, you won't fall!" He hesitated, then watched as a woman held her toddler up near the fence to see the view. Demi nodded toward the woman and shrugged her shoulders, daring Stavros to join her. "*Ela*!" she teased. He took a deep breath and edged towards the fence. Demi took out her phone and urged Stavros closer to her. She held out her arm to take a selfie. "Don't look so nervous," she said. "You're safe here."

"I am not nervous," Stavros said, looking apprehensive at the cliffside below. He took the phone from her. "My arm is longer." He held her close as he snapped a photo.

"Let me see!" Demi took the phone from him and shaded the screen with her hand to better see the photo. The sun lit their faces against the background of the city, and Demi's breath caught at how natural they looked together. "This is a really nice photo," she said. "I'll send it to you."

They turned around and watched a towboat with three barges laden with loads of coal slogging its way west through the muddy brown river. He pointed to the city which was surrounded on both sides by water. "It looks like an island. This is one river?"

"No, it's actually three." Demi pointed to the river below them flowing from the east. "This is the Monongahela."

"Mono . . . mo . . . monom . . ." He shrugged.

"Don't worry, some people from Pittsburgh can't pronounce it either. It's a Native American word—it means 'river with sliding banks.'" Demi pointed below to their left, where a triangle of land jutted between the rivers. "That's called the Point, where the rivers meet. That river is the

Allegheny—see where it meets the Monongahela to form the Ohio?" She paused and grinned. "You know, we have our own monsters here." Demi leaned towards Stavros and spoke surreptitiously. "Legend has it that there is a river monster who's lived in the Mon for over 200 years. They call him Ogua. He stays in the water during the day, but at night, he comes out to find deer." Stavros raised an eyebrow, but Demi continued. "Those who've seen him say he's reddish brown and he has very sharp teeth. They say his tail is fifteen feet long, and this is how he catches his prey—he drags the deer down to the water, drowns them, and then eats them. Some people say he has two heads."

"You believe this, Dimitra?"

Underneath the overlook, a truck engine rumbled, and Demi shouted over the din. "I didn't say that. But we have our myths too, even if they're only 200-year-old river monsters instead of 2,000-year-old Gorgons." Demi looked east as, one by one, the bridges began to light up, twinkling against the twilight sky. "I just love this view."

"In Greece, we have *Lykavittos*. It is the highest point in the city. From there you can see all of Athens. It is amazing."

"I'm sure it is," Demi said. "I'm sure it's much more beautiful than this. I just wanted to show you my favorite view. I forgot that everything is better in Greece."

"This is not what I am saying." The clang of a church bell echoed from the ancient cathedral behind them. Stavros waited while four more slow gongs defied the drone of a passing motorcycle. "Dimitra, if you love Pittsburgh so much, why you want to leave?"

Demi scanned the panorama of the city—the sports stadiums on the Northside, the congregation of glass skyscrapers and old brick office buildings in the Golden Triangle, as the business district was referred to, and the winding Monongahela to the east. "I do love Pittsburgh. It will always be my home. Chicago is the next step—it doesn't mean it's the final step. But the experience and pay I'll get at this level is a big career boost for me. It's not something I can say no to."

"You can, but you don't want to."

"You're right," Demi admitted. "I don't want to." She shivered and rubbed her hands together.

"You are too cold?" Stavros asked.

"No, I'm fine. Let's get a bite to eat. The Shiloh is only a ten-minute walk."

* * *

They turned down a one-way side street and walked up the steps to the Shiloh Grill, where several people stood just inside the rustic doorway. Formerly a Greek restaurant known for its piano bar, the Shiloh Inn had shed its dark, formal interior and heavy furniture for a more contemporary feel and menu. Demi nudged her way to the hostess stand, where a middle-aged brunette woman stood with a pen in her hand and asked, "How long a wait for two?"

The hostess surveyed a list on the podium in front of her. "About 30 minutes."

"Could we sit at the bar?" Demi asked.

"Of course," the hostess smiled and nodded to her left. "Right over there."

Demi looked back at Stavros and motioned towards the dimly lit bar. The room was cast in a cobalt blue light that gave it an aura of elegance. This stood in contrast to a large television above the bar playing a golf tournament and an incongruous mural of a single giant white spork on the wall next to it. The television was muted, and lively jazz music featuring an alto saxophone played through a speaker somewhere in the room.

They spotted two seats at the corner of the bar. At the other end, a bearded man sporting a backward baseball cap, jeans, and tennis shoes chatted with a woman dressed in an oversized Penguins hockey jersey and black leggings.

Stavros nudged Demi and nodded towards the couple. "Why they are wearing this?"

"Why they are wearing what?" Demi asked, hopping onto the barstool.

"Why he wears a hat to a restaurant? And this way," he said. He turned an imaginary hat around his head.

"I don't know," Demi laughed. "That trend went out a few years ago. But guys wear baseball caps all the time. And we *are* in a bar."

Stavros slid onto the stool around the corner from Demi, giving him a clear view of the other end of the bar. "Why she is wearing these clothes?"

Demi glanced over her shoulder. "It's a hockey jersey."

"She is not playing hockey. And these pants . . ."

"Leggings . . ."

"Yes, I know this. *Kolan*. In Greece they do not wear *kolan* to go out. You have seen how we dress in Greece. Not like this."

"Well, we're not in Greece. We're in Pittsburgh." Demi sighed. "Do you even like it here, Stavro?"

"What can I get you?" A pretty twenty-something bartender with a blonde ponytail smiled at Stavros.

"I'll have a Cab," Demi said.

The bartender kept her gaze on Stavros. "And you?" she smiled, cocking her head to the side. Stavros ordered a beer and turned back to Demi.

"That was a little obvious," she said.

Stavros looked over his right shoulder, then his left. "What was obvious?"

"Seriously?" Demi asked. "The bartender?"

"What about her?"

Demi folded her arms and looked sideways at Stavros. "Are you telling me you didn't notice her flirting with you?"

"You are jealous, Dimitra?" Stavros grinned.

"Nooo." *Dammit, was she jealous? Or was she feeling possessive? Either way . . .*

"And yes." Stavros picked up the trail of their conversation. "I like Pittsburgh. I don't like the weather. I think maybe it is much better in the summer. But I like the US. I think perhaps there is much to see here. Too much to see in three months."

Three months that have flown by, Demi thought. "I know," she said. "I feel like I only got a taste of what Greece is like. I want to see the islands and spend more time exploring."

"Yes, you should see the Cyclades. These are beautiful islands, each different from the other."

Demi's heart leapt and fell as she imagined touring the islands with Stavros and then thought about his leaving. *What are we doing*?

"Here you go," the bartender said, placing a Michelob on the smooth laminated wood bar top in front of Stavros. "You wanted Merlot, right?" she asked Demi, setting down a long-stemmed wine glass.

Demi blew air out slowly through her mouth. *Is it worth it? Should I complain or just drink the Merlot?* She opened her mouth to speak.

"No, she wanted a Cab," Stavros said, pushing the wine glass back. "Right, *koukla mou*?" He winked at Demi.

Demi rolled her eyes. *So effing charming*, she thought, shaking her head.

* * *

By the time they left the Shiloh, the air had cooled considerably, and the sky was dark and cloudless. Cars traveling across the bridges were now evident only by their headlights. Demi stopped as they approached the overlook. "The moon is almost full," she remarked. "The city looks so beautiful." The cityscape had lost its orange glow, and the buildings now stood black against a black sky, defined only by their lights, which cast long, wavy reflections of red, white, blue, and purple in the blackness of the river. A waxing gibbous moon hung above the Monongahela, lighting its path upstream until it disappeared around the bend.

"Yes," Stavros said. "This is beautiful. But I prefer when the only light is the moon. When you are on a beach at night, and the clouds are hiding the stars, and Selene comes out from behind the clouds to light the sea below her. Sometimes, when the moon is full, she is so close to the sea, you think that the sea will swallow her."

Demi remembered the reflection of the moon in the bay in Gytheio the night that she and Sophie were looking for her mother and aunt. "I get that," she said. "It's a kind of quiet beauty." They stood in silence, gazing over the cityscape before Demi spoke. "Stavro, why don't you come to Chicago? Visit me there before you go back to Greece. I'll have a few days before I start work, and we can explore the city."

Stavros kept his gaze on the city skyline. "Kostas needs me."

"You're making excuses. He's going to have to get on without you once you're gone. What difference does a few days make?"

Stavros turned to look at Demi. "Dimitra, why I want to come to Chicago? I'm not going to live there."

"You could . . . if . . ." She let her words trail into the night.

Stavros knotted his brows. "What I'm going to do there? I have no sponsor. I could not work in Chicago on a tourist visa."

"No. Not on a tourist visa." Demi hesitated. "There are other visas . . ."

Stavros raised his eyebrows in realization. "You are talking about a fiancé visa."

Demi nodded, holding her breath. The elephant in the room had been released. She watched Stavros for his reaction.

He seemed to freeze in place as his eyes held Demi's. *Ah, those eyes. They took his breath away. But marry her? Isn't that what he'd imagined when he contemplated moving to Pittsburgh? But that daydream was in the future, at some undetermined time far down the road.* "Dimitra. You want me to change my life after three months?"

Demi looked at Stavros with sudden clarity. She smiled ruefully. "And yet—you want me to believe that you'll come back to Pittsburgh if I stay."

Stavros searched for the right reply but found none. His shoulders sagged. "So, this is it?"

"Only if you say it is."

"I cannot have a long-distance relationship."

"I didn't ask you to."

"Then what?" Stavros shrugged. "You want to be *friends*?" The word came out in a sneer.

Demi frowned. "No, but . . ."

"Then what?" he repeated. "If we are not friends, and we are not together, what we are?"

What are we? Questions fluttered through Demi's mind like colorful scarves rapidly pulled from a magician's sleeve: *Was his unexpected appearance in my life a sign? A disruption? A confirmation? Is he here to make me realize that nothing will keep me from pursuing my career -or that some things are more important than a career? How can I make sense of the last three months? Were the Fates to blame—those mythical mischievous tricksters who wreaked havoc with humans? Now I'm thinking like Stavros!* Demi shook her head and smiled at the thought. She answered Stavros with tenderness. "We're two people who were lucky enough to cross paths not once but twice. I wasn't prepared to fall so hard, but I did. I love you, Stavro. Maybe fate played a role; maybe it's just a lucky coincidence. Whatever brought us together, I will always be thankful."

"Ah, Dimitra," Stavros sighed. "I do not want this to end."

"Neither do I," Demi said. "Life works in mysterious ways. Maybe this isn't the end. What if it's the beginning?"

Stavros pulled Demi to him and kissed her with passion. He felt her body yield to his. "*Ela,*" he said and took her hand. Their shadows walked ahead of them under the streetlights as they returned to her house.

CHAPTER 25

Demi stood next to the bed, upon which sat a laundry basket loaded with clothing, a curling iron, a hair straightener, a hair dryer, toiletries, and chargers. She surveyed her bedroom, the walls and dresser top now almost empty. A chilly December wind rattled the windowpane, and she picked up the woolly sweater on top of the basket, pulled it over her head, and pushed her arms through the sleeves. "I'm going to miss this place."

"I'm going to miss you," Marina said. "Although, I'm not too far behind you. January will be here before we know it."

"I'm glad Erie worked out for you. Can't believe you got your first choice! You must be smarter than I thought you were."

Marina picked up a blue throw pillow from the chair and threw it at Demi.

"Ouch," she said, although the pillow was soft. "JK, I know how smart you are. Although, I wish you'd gotten Chicago."

"I'll be looking for a full-time job when I finish. No reason not to look in Chicago."

"That would be awesome. Your mom would miss you, though."

"No more than Aunt Georgia will miss you. Anyway, Mom's got Sophie. She blabs enough for both of us. She won't have time to miss me."

"I don't know; Sophie might be a little busier than usual," Demi grinned. "She told me she has a date with the coffee/tea guy."

"All the more to blab to Mom about," Marina laughed.

Demi opened her dresser drawers and rifled through the remaining clothes. "I'll leave all my extra stuff in the bottom drawer in case we're able to sublease the room." Bella appeared from nowhere, jumped into the bottom drawer, and began to knead the clothes. *Where the heck did she come from?* Demi wondered. "Are you sure you don't mind watching Bella until I get settled? I'd smuggle her into my hotel room, but it's probably not a good idea since the Oasis is paying for it." She sat on the floor next to the open drawer and petted Bella, who rewarded her with a soft, rumbling purr.

"Watch Bella? She's not going to be hard to find. She'll be laying here on your bed waiting for you to come home."

Demi's heart sank.

"I'm sorry, Demi. I didn't mean to make you feel bad. She's a cat—she'll be fine. Speaking of feeling bad, though. What about Stavros? Is he okay? Are you okay?"

"Am I okay? Demi stopped petting the cat and wrapped her arms around her knees, clasping her hands. "Well, let's see. The man I love is going back across the Atlantic, and I may never see him again. He doesn't want to marry me. And, honestly, I'm not sure I want to marry him. I just wish we could give it a chance. But the only way for him to live in Chicago is if he does marry me. And the only way he would come back to Pittsburgh is if I don't take the Chicago job. But even if I don't, there's no guarantee that he'll come back to Pittsburgh. I don't think he really knows his heart. So, am I okay? Not really."

Marina studied Demi. "Are you having second thoughts?"

"About moving to Chicago?" She shook her head. "No."

"About opening your heart to Stavros."

Demi sat quietly before speaking. "I wouldn't have traded these last three months for anything. I've smiled more and loved harder than I ever thought possible. I know that I'll never settle for anyone who doesn't make me happy and make me feel loved and special. I wish it could be Stavros." She paused. "In my dream world, it is. But no, I have no regrets about that—only that it's coming to an end." Demi stood up and steadied herself on the dresser top. The *mati* from Kiria Stavropoulou lay on a small ceramic plate. She thought back to Kiria's paintings.

"Hang on," she said. She disappeared into the closet, and Marina heard her rummaging through the boxes on the floor. Demi dragged a box out of the closet, kneeled, and unfolded the cardboard flaps. Inside the box were old papers from college and a pile of tickets from concerts and sporting events. She peeked in the folder and pulled out a worn O.A.R. ticket from Stage AE and a faded ticket from a summer Warped Tour at the Amphitheater. She held them up to Marina. "Too bad everything is on your smartphone now. No one will have this type of memorabilia anymore." She set them back in the box. "I guess I'll look at them next time I'm home." *Home. Wasn't Chicago now her home?* She answered her question out loud. "I guess Pittsburgh will always be home." Underneath the papers, she found what she was looking for—a set of drawing pencils and a small drawing tablet.

"Something tells me you're not going to have much time to draw," Marina said. "With your new job, and apartment hunting, and Aunt Toula, and your mom and dad coming up for Christmas."

Demi got to her feet and set the pencils and paper on the dresser. She turned to her cousin. "I'm going to miss you, Marina."

"I know. I'll come up for a weekend as soon as you're settled. In the meantime, let's get this stuff loaded into your car. Tomorrow morning will be here before you know it. And you still have a few goodbyes to make."

"Why are goodbyes so difficult?"

"Because you never know if they're final."

"Geeze, Marina. Way to cheer me up." She threw the pillow back at Marina, who dodged it. It landed in the drawer next to Bella, who stood up, stretched, stared indignantly at Demi, hopped out of the drawer, and strode out of the bedroom.

Both girls laughed. "Well," Demi said, "I guess *she* has no trouble saying goodbye."

Marina walked over to Demi and hugged her tightly. "I love you, Cuz."

Demi felt tears well up in her eyes. *I hope I'm doing the right thing.*

Marina pulled back and looked at her cousin, reading her thoughts. "Fear of the unknown, Demi. It's a new beginning. You've got this."

CHAPTER 26

Stavros reached over his head to turn the air nozzle on full blast. The airplane was warm, and he twisted uncomfortably in the window seat, unable to maneuver to take off his leather jacket. A little girl with a curly blond ponytail sat in the seat next to him, her feet straight out in front of her, sporting pink tennis shoes to match her sparkly dress. "Excuse me," she said, pulling on Stavros' sleeve. "Are you okay?"

"Eh?" he replied, his answer coming out more gruffly than he intended, but the girl was unfazed.

"Are you okay? Is this your first flight? I used to be afraid of flying, but I'm not anymore. Do you want to hold Dolly?" She held out a cloth doll with painted-on blue eyes, embroidered eyelashes, and yellow yarn hair to Stavros.

He felt a pang in his heart as he remembered the girls in the caves the first time he knew he was falling for Demi. He also remembered how afraid the girls were of him and lightened his tone. "No, no, it's okay. Thank you."

"I'm Violet," the little girl said, offering her small hand to Stavros. "What's your name?"

He smiled and gently shook her hand. "Nice to meet you, Violet. I am Stavros."

"I've never met a Stavros," she said.

"I've never met a Violet," he replied. "I have only seen the flowers. *Hadn't he compared Dimitra to a violet when he spoke to Elias about her?*

At the time, he'd been mesmerized by her. Now it was no longer infatuation, but something more mature, stronger. He sensed the little girl looking up at him. "It's a very nice name."

A flight attendant in a navy blue short-sleeved dress and a red, white, and blue scarf pushed a cart through the narrow aisle. Her long brown braid fell across one shoulder as she leaned over the girl's sleeping mother. "Can I get you anything?" she asked Stavros.

He contemplated a drink and checked his phone—ten a.m.—too early for alcohol. But, he calculated, it was five o'clock in Athens. He remembered Demi at brunch once saying, "It's five o'clock somewhere," as she sipped a drink. "I'll have a Bloody Mary," he said.

The little girl sat up in her seat. "I'll have what he's having," she announced.

Stavros laughed, "In that case, bring me a tomato juice."

"Eww." Violet scrunched up her face.

"Do you still want what he's having?" The flight attendant asked.

"No," she pouted. "Can you bring me an apple juice?"

"Of course," the flight attendant smiled and winked at Stavros. "Would you like me to add anything to that tomato juice?"

* * *

Demi kicked off her heels under the desk and crossed her ankle over her knee. She kneaded the ball of her left foot, then switched to the right. She was going to have to get used to dress shoes again after wearing non-slip restaurant shoes for so long. Still, she loved getting dressed up for work now. How long had it been since she had worn a dress to work? She had packed her good dresses and a couple of blazers, but her wardrobe needed an overhaul. She would have to find time to shop, and the Chicago winter dictated that she might be filling her closet with pants; she was lucky that, for the time being, her commute was limited to taking the elevator or the stairs from the eighth floor.

She'd already fallen in love with the hotel's décor—the mosaic floors and marble ceilings reminded her of the Aktaion lobby, but her room at the Oasis was more upscale, from its crisp white sheets and downy comforter to the padded bench seat by the window overlooking Millennium

Park, and beyond that, Lake Michigan. Between training several hours each day and spending time in the evening with Toula's family, she hadn't had time to be lonely. Lunch times had been spent getting to know her co-workers who were happy to show her the city. She'd barely had time to look for an apartment, although she wasn't in a big hurry to do that given her complimentary accommodations, which she knew must come to an end eventually.

Demi looked up from her computer at the Monet print she'd bought at the Art Institute to bring some warmth to her cozy but windowless office. She heard her message alert and glanced eagerly at the cell phone. "Hi Sweetie. I know you're busy. Just thinking about you. Have a good day <3." She smiled at today's variation of the daily text from her mother. Still no word from Stavros. Their last night together in Pittsburgh had been fraught with sadness, passion, and a desperate need to cling to each other. *It was like our last night together in Sparta, only on steroids*, Demi thought, recalling the sleepless night with a rapid pounding of her heart. She wished he had come to Chicago before he left for Greece, but what good would that have done? Just another difficult goodbye. *And yet* . . . A week had gone by with little in the way of communication with Stavros. Their opposing work schedules didn't allow much opportunity for telephone calls, and their texts consisted primarily of *How are you, I miss you, and I love you*.

"Excuse me, Demi?" Her assistant tapped on the open door. "Your 11 o'clock is here. I'll show them to the conference room."

"Thank you. I'll be there in a minute." She slid her feet back into her pumps and pushed away from the desk. She didn't know if her stomach was fluttering from excitement or stress about her first formal client meeting or just the restlessness she experienced whenever she thought about Stavros. She took a deep, settling breath, held it, and blew it out slowly, then grabbed her laptop and went to meet her potential client.

* * *

Once the flight attendant had cleared away the drinks, Violet stuffed Dolly into a quilted bag and took out an iPad. She busied herself with an alphabet game, and Stavros leaned back on the headrest and felt himself drift off. He awoke to a slight bump, which precluded a loudspeaker announcement. "We are now beginning our approach. Please keep your seatbelts secured until we have landed, and the flight attendant says it is safe to unfasten them." Stavros opened his eyes and turned his head to gaze out the window. Far below him, the houses formed neat rows and squares. The clouds hung low over a body of water, and the air was foggy beneath them as they transformed from thin white clouds to wisps of blue-grey, blurring the landscape where the ground met the shore. Parting the clouds, sun rays glittered off the hoods in the parking lot beyond the runway, reminding him of the sun sparkling on the sea.

They landed with a quick thump, and the pilot taxied the airplane towards the terminal, past the bright yellow, red, and blue of the Southwest planes. Stavros watched several departing airplanes rise at a sharp angle and disappear into the blue until they were only a speck. He fidgeted in his seat, irritated at the long ride to the gate. The air in the plane felt warm again, and he smoothed his hair back from his face with his fingers and grabbed it into a ponytail to get it off his neck, but he had nothing to put it in.

"Here!" He looked to his left, where Violet was unwinding something from her tight blond curls. She held out a hair tie with a plastic "Hello Kitty" decoration.

"Oh, no thank you. Keep your *lastihaki, Koukla.*"

Violet smiled up at him. "It's fine. I have another."

"*Efharisto, Violeta,* thank you," Stavros said. He took the hair tie and wound it around his hair to form a low bun.

"Feel better?" She asked.

"Yes, much better."

A voice came through the intercom. "Welcome to Chicago's O'Hare Airport, where the local time is 11:39."

* * *

Demi shook hands with her clients—a middle-aged woman and her daughter who were looking at the hotel for the daughter's wedding. "Thank you for choosing the Oasis," Demi said. "I'll let you know when the ballroom is decorated so that you can come see it." She smiled and said goodbye, accompanied by a small, enthusiastic wave, and returned to the conference room for her computer. Her boss was waiting at the doorway.

"Demi, you nailed it! What a great beginning!" Her boss beamed at her and squeezed her shoulder.

"Thank you," Demi said, a huge sigh of relief threatening to escape from her throat.

"First client meeting, and you closed the contract! Come on, I'll take you to lunch. This deserves a celebration."

"Thanks, Jean. I'd love that. If you don't mind a quick one?"

"Of course," her boss replied. "We can go across the street to the deli if you like."

"Perfect! I just need to stop in my office for a minute." Demi walked into her office and sat down at her desk, letting out the breath that she hadn't realized she'd been holding. Her boss's words echoed in her head: *what a great beginning*. A smile spread across her face, and she felt a bubble of excitement in her chest. She picked up her phone and hit Aunt Toula's number, which rang straight to message. "Hi, Aunt Toula, it's Demi. I closed my first contract! I'll tell you about it when I see you. Listen, when you get a chance, could you text me the number of that woman who teaches the adult Greek lessons? I think I'd be interested. And don't tell Mom about the contract—I want to tell her myself! Love you . . ."

* * *

Stavros tapped his foot nervously as he waited for the passengers in front of him to deplane. He took his phone off airplane mode and waited for the screen notifications. Nothing from Demi, although he remembered that she had an important meeting that morning. Violet wiggled out of her seat and waved goodbye to him as her mother led her into the aisle.

The flight attendant with the brown braid stood at the front of the plane, thanking the passengers for their patronage and wishing them a good day. She smiled and winked at Stavros, but his thoughts were elsewhere. Once out of the jetway, he joined the procession of travelers in the concourse. A woman in bright orange tennis shoes and black leggings tugged a rollaway behind her, which was dangerously close to "too large to carry on." A large tote bag slipped down her right arm as she juggled a purse on her left shoulder.

Sun rays from a large glass dome on the ceiling sprayed a large American Airlines symbol on the rotunda, where a small child ran with teetering toddler steps as her father looked on absentmindedly. The loud whirr of an industrial blender and the strong smell of coffee drew Stavros to Starbucks; although he refused to admit that he liked American coffee, he joined the long Starbucks line. Over the intercom rang "Paging Jet Blue customers Adam Burke and Hannah Walter. Doors will be closing shortly. Please make your way to the gate." He studied the lengthy queue in front of him, thinking *they must be in this line.*

Several minutes later, pumpkin-spiced latte in hand, Stavros was back in the terminal hallway. Above him, large posters suspended from the high ceiling, beckoning passengers to visit a variety of destinations: San Francisco's magnificent Golden Gate Bridge, Rome—*So easy to go from country to country in the EU*, he mused. Philadelphia—*Damn Philadelphia. If the incident with Andrew had not happened, maybe Dimitra would see things differently*. The shrill beeping of the concierge cart behind him interrupted his reverie, and Stavros moved off to the side, where a string of empty white vinyl chairs offered a resting spot. He set his backpack down on the seat next to him and sipped his coffee. *Good,* he thought, *but not as good as his Yiayia's thick Greek coffee*. At the pub across from him, laughter rang out from the occupants of the barstools. The intercom crackled again. "American Airlines Flight 3963 to Athens will begin boarding at Gate 7. All passengers, please proceed to the gate."

Stavros took the last sip of coffee and shoved the cup and lid into the metal waste can next to the row of chairs. He took his phone out of his pocket in case the noise of the terminal had caused him to miss a text notification. The screensaver caught his eye, and he studied the photo of himself and Demi smiling together on Mount Washington. He put the phone back into his pocket, picked up the backpack, slung it over his shoulder, and joined the throng of people moving through the terminal.

ACKNOWLEDGMENTS

A rental car breaks down in a suburb of Wales, and the occupants are rescued by a kind, cheerful woman and her handsome and charming son, who happens to be a talented musician. She serves us tea and ginger cake in her lovely front room while we wait for a replacement car, and we chat for well over an hour as the afternoon sun streams in through her windows. As we drive away in the new rental car with a parting gift—the young man's music CD—my writer's mind starts to ruminate. What if? What if instead of the passengers being five middle-aged people on holiday, it was two women and their lovely adult daughters? What if a romance sparked between the young man and one of the daughters? I put the idea aside for the rest of the trip, but upon coming home and listening to the CD, my imagination churned. How would they meet again? Perhaps he is a musician on tour in the US? But what did I know about Wales or the music industry? Not enough. I did, however, know something about Greece. Thus, the setting was formed—my grandmother's village in the Peloponnese was the perfect location for the plot to unfold. My first thank you goes to Clare and Dan Bettridge, whose thoughtfulness has had ramifications far beyond, as Clare called it, "The Day the Americans Came."

I am so thankful for my wonderful readers: Daniela Buccilli, a dear friend and accomplished poet, who saw deep into my characters' motives and helped me understand the broader focus of the novel; my daughter, Alexandra, whose insight into my characters led to stronger relationships and more meaningful dialog; Brenna Wandel, whose suggestions aided me in expanding my scenes, and whose commentary in the margins made me smile, as I realized that the characters had become as real to her as they are to me. Many thanks to Toula Protopapa, my Greek teacher and friend, for ensuring my correct usage of Greek, and to Kelly Oalmann for her valuable commentary. A huge thank you goes out to my beta readers, Elizabeth Shannon and Terry Cheskey, who volunteered their time and provided meaningful, honest commentary as the novel neared completion.

Many thanks to Louis Vlahakis for taking the time to provide me with his perspective as a thirty-something Greek male in the Peloponnese—to him, I owe many of the details that belong to Stavros. Thank you to Markos Psarros who answered my random questions, often at odd hours, as I developed the settings in Gytheio and Xirokambi. I have many memories of the Peloponnese, but having "boots on the ground" was particularly helpful in developing descriptive scenes.

My sincere gratitude to the awesome team at Sunbury Press for their support in bringing this novel to life, with special appreciation to Katie Cressman and Kendall Taylor for their enthusiasm and encouragement.

Thank you to Sotiri Tsourekis, who gave me valuable input for the festival scene, to Nick Dupel, who provided insight into what a thirty-something male coming to Pittsburgh from Europe might find off-putting, and to Dimitrios Takos, who took the time to discuss his experiences emigrating and opening a restaurant. Thank you to my British friend, Chris Heath, who helped me with Charles's dialog, and made me laugh in the process, and to Brian Keller for helping me to learn about the hospitality industry.

Many thanks to my keen-eyed editor, Nick Wilson, whom the reader may thank for keeping me from verbosity.

I thoroughly enjoyed doing the Pittsburgh research for this novel. What a delight to visit the Carnegie Museum of Natural History to reacquaint myself with the dinosaurs and the antiquities and enjoy coffee in their café. My evening on Mount Washington rewarded me with a spectacular sunset (which I not only described in the book but painted) and a date night with my husband as we ended the evening at the Shiloh. Thank you also to Debbie and Jerry Santucci for letting me hang out at Café Notte, scribbling details into my notebook for the book launch scene.

A big thank you goes to my husband, John, for his patience when the writing muse struck suddenly. And, of course, thank you to my dog, Barkley, for keeping me company as I sat at my writing desk for hours, only interrupting me when his dinner was overdue. I especially want to thank my sister, Ellen Langas. She has been with me since day one, listening to my ideas and giving me feedback and encouragement. Ellen was my sounding board, counselor, and cheerleader; this book would not have been the same without her.

To everyone who was a part of this novel, *efharisto poli*—many thanks for your support and encouragement.

ABOUT THE AUTHOR

RITA WILSON is an award-winning artist, writer, and educator. Her work has been published in *Rune and Riverspeak Literary Magazines*, *Voices from the Attic*, *The 100 Lives Anthology*, and *Wisdom of the Crone*. "Nature's Bounty," her short story on the culling of wolf herds in the Northwest, was featured in wolfmatters.org, and her short story, "A Handful of Sand," was shortlisted for the Mani Litfest annual short story contest. Her first book, *Greek Lessons*, a biography and memoir, includes photos of her art, including Better Times, the painting of her mother and grandmother which graces the book's cover. Wilson's many travels to Greece inspired both Greek Lessons and her new novel When the Only Light is the Moon.

Wilson earned her MFA in Creative Nonfiction from Carlow University in Pittsburgh, Pennsylvania. A retired teacher, she has held creative writing workshops in the US and Europe and volunteered to teach professional writing for the US Coast Guard. Wilson is a fellow of the Western Pennsylvania Writing Project and has taught writing both to young adults and at the university level. She serves as Non-Fiction Editor for the *Northern Appalachia Review* and as a Director for the Writing Conference of Northern Appalachia.

Wilson enjoys painting and writing from her home in the Pittsburgh suburbs. When not indulging her creative side, she can be found on the tennis court, walking her husky, or chatting with friends or family over a cup of coffee.

www.ingramcontent.com/pod-product-compliance
Lightning Source LLC
LaVergne TN
LVHW041249110826
845146LV00005BA/1326